SO MANY HUNGERS!

SO MANY HUNGERS!

by

BHABANI BHATTACHARYA

LONDON
VICTOR GOLLANCZ LTD
1947

PRINTED IN GREAT BRITAIN BY RICHARD CLAY AND COMPANY, LTD.,
BUNGAY, SUFFOLK.

FOR

SALILA

WITH ALL MY LOVE

CHAPTER I

A MEEK, measured voice, wingless. A voice too bleak for passion, fire. History had yoked it to its purpose, though, with a sudden urge that made it dynamic. The Prime Minister, Rahoul knew, was a bitter-hearted prey of logical circumstance. Yet Rahoul, rapt, held in a spell, felt the far, flat voice cast across ether pound, as it were, on his ears. He felt a tingling through his nerves, down his spine, down to knee-pits. Tautness knit him. But he shook himself free and rushed to the door as a *sari*-clad figure passed slow-footed along the corridor.

"Mother!" And Rahoul moistened his lips. "What is it, Mother?"

She turned, saw his misery. Sentimental boy! Her glance lay warm on his face. Would he not fit himself into the hardness of life?

"Nothing yet." She moved her head faintly and said, quietly, "The moment is near. Not ten minutes between the pains."

The cool words hit him like a blow. He winced; he had to clutch the door-frame.

"Hard, heavy pains, as it should be. Another half-hour, Rahoul, and all will be well. You will hear the jewel of jewels screaming."

Another half-hour! Ages. But he pulled himself to calm, soothing inflamed thoughts with joyous vision.

"She will cry as soon as born?" His voice seemed to yearn. He could see her, his daughter, tiny fists clenched, legs drawn up in the one known posture, face crumpled with new-found screaming.

Mother smiled at the boyishness of her son. "He will, with the boom of his fist of a throat. But you won't hear him, Rahoul, unless you hush that chatter-machine."

His eyes flew back to the machine, and he listened for some moments, the clean-cut lines of his face absorbed.

"And she steps right into war! Mother, you have heard?" He turned, his voice shaking a little, the words tumbling out. "Great races that took centuries to grow will be caught in the blaze. Vast struggle and suffering. Worth while? Yes, worth while if it puts an end to the evil that has tried to strangle civilized living. And—oh!"—he gulped because of his excitement—"right into this she is about to be born."

Mother felt worry. "War? It has started, then? Why, we must buy rice and mustard oil, a half-year's supply, before the grocer has an inkling. Prices will touch the sky." She paused, dipping into memory. "Strange! You, too, came in war-time, Rahoul. The Great Killing was just on its way. It was——"

"Mother, I couldn't time it so well; I was born in mid-*aswin*," Rahoul interrupted. "Weeks late, Mother. Look at this one coming to-day!"

Mother smiled again, and went on: "Sugar, too. Clothing. I must get white English drill for the father and you two boys. And tinned butter, tinned fish. Strange tongues you children have. The rivers of Bengal choked with fish—every kind, large and small—still you fancy the year-old shapes packed in tins, both you and Kunal. The strong smell!"

The son, in his exalted mood, could not share Mother's worldly wisdom. His ears were back to the broadcast. His eyes behind the thick-rimmed glasses were keen and alight. Mother turned, passing down the corridor.

For the second time in a generation Great Britain is at war with Germany. . . .

Atmospherics made an instant explosive response, and Rahoul with absent hand turned the knob, across snatches of studio music, downpours of speech, off to Zeesen. A fascist voice, strident, bullying the world. Rahoul made a face of disgust. A great nation committed under gangster discipline to a programme of world disruption. War had become vital to its being, so it seemed to think, for defeatism was heavy on its chest, suffocating, and somewhere on the corpse-stiffened battle-fields of Europe it thought to find self-respect again. The delusion! Defeat—the only hope of German survival. Let England's reactionary forces destroy their Nazi kin. Then would Germany live again.

England, too. England, released from the spell of stupor cast upon her by diehard politicians; England, with new progressive leadership, kindling to moral grandeur. . . .

So Rahoul, in that hour of world crisis, mused in his heart.

A door slamming somewhere. With a violent start he choked off the machine. It was the street door. A voice greeted him—"Halt!"—as, nerves on edge, he rushed out to the corridor. Kunal, tall, slim, athletic in flannels, came striding with a tennis-racket in his hand. "Salute!" he ordered himself, and heels clicked, right arm shot up smartly.

"*Dada* [Elder Brother], allow me to introduce an officer of His Majesty's armed forces. Cavalry." His arm dropped, his voice lowered. "Maybe you have not heard the news? In your scholar's sanctum the petty affairs of this world——"

Rahoul grinned. "Haven't I? What's more, Kunal, to-day's *dramatis personæ*—I've seen them in the flesh. I have heard the Prime Minister address the House. Debate on India. In Berlin I had a glimpse of mankind's enemy number one——"

Kunal was waving a hand as though he had heard enough.

"There you beat me. Four—five years in Europe. Cricket at Lord's; Wimbledon; Olympics in Berlin. All the good things of life. What luck! Now it's my turn. Captain Basu leads his armoured spearhead against a strong point in the Siegfried Line, liquidates the enemy and gets mentioned in despatches——"

"I had an idea Lieutenant Basu belonged to the cavalry."

"Captain Basu, please. One gets promoted, after all, if one has the stuff in him. Captain Basu happens to belong to a mechanized unit. In the old days he would have been a horseman. To-day he rides a thirty-ton tank. *Dada*, I am dead serious. I'm going to see my O.C., Major Bird of our University Training Corps. I shall get a commission, I believe. I have had some training, haven't I? Under-officer and all that."

Rahoul was silent, brows knit in thought. Kunal, with his practical mind, had sprung into decision, untroubled by theories of right and wrong. The War would be a great adventure. The aims of war did not count. It was a matter of chance that Kunal would find himself in the armed forces of democracy. But he, Rahoul, holding inside him a weighing-machine for the finer values, felt the same swift urge to take an active part in democracy's war against fascist aggression—had he not, in the years past, longed for this struggle?

"I, too, might join up——" murmured Rahoul, his voice strangely like pleading.

"You?" Kunal stared. "Oh no. A great professor of Astrophysics. Cambridge D.Sc. One day you'll discover some unknown sunbeam, or is it starbeam?" Compassion softened the strong, statuesque lines of his face. He stepped closer. He was two inches taller than his elder brother. "You will be all right, *dada*. No, you can't join up. Anyhow, sister won't let you. As for me, I want action, enterprise, speed. To think I might have been doomed to a desk job! Father has been

3

pulling a hundred wires." He paused a moment, listening. "He will be home in a minute. I passed him at the street corner as I cycled up. I never saw him walk so fast. He, too, must have heard. I must rush off." He paused again, his eyes flying up the mosaic stairway, and his voice came low: "Give my love to the young chap when he turns up."

"The girl——" said Rahoul absently.

The War had receded. It was Monju again. She moaned, and tears dimmed her eyes. Earlier that day she had accused him, clutching his hand, gasping, "It's all your fault. If only you had told me not to have a baby!" But she had to have a baby. The urge of motherhood was insistent in her blood.

"The girl?" breathed Kunal, taken aback. Then his voice burst in an excited shout. "*Dada!*" He clutched his brother by the shoulders and shook him, crying. "Why didn't you tell me? The baby's come! It's great! I've been so worried. Poor sister——"

Rahoul loved his brother then. Whoever thought that Kunal would worry about such things! Rushing about all day, pursuing a thousand interests, he had no time for what was happening at home. How could one be concerned with petty household affairs when, down there in the *maidan*, Bannerji was making such a heroic innings?

"Not yet. Only I've been expecting it will be a girl." He smiled shamefacedly as he saw his brother's eyebrow lift. "Mother came down and said the moment was near." The smile sagged. "Monju will be all right. She is in good hands. Only, it's all so painful——"

"I hate pain," said Kunal, with sudden feeling—"pain in a woman. Let men suffer; they are strong. Not the women— the mothers and sisters and wives." Kunal stopped short, flurried by his outburst. "There comes Father, and he is sure to have some good advice for me!" His tennis-racket swung as he fled.

Father was near-fifty, thick-set, with shrewd eyes in a broad, heavy-jowled face under greying, close-cropped hair—a physical type that showed no kinship with his two sons. He wore ill-fitting English clothes, shiny black alpaca coat, black bow-tie and white drill trousers tight on his paunch, stopping short an inch above his ankles. A thick gold watch-chain gleamed on his chest.

"Then it is war?" He paced slowly up the corridor, turned round. "Rahoul, how long will it last, do you think?"

4

"Till the new epoch is born." Rahoul flung his answer as though he were thinking aloud. "The imperialist war will grow into a war of ideas, values. The diehards will have to use slogans they hate and release forces they fear most."

"Gold or Steels?" broke in Samarendra, his eyes narrowing. He, too, was thinking aloud.

Rahoul seemed perplexed.

"War material, both. War feeds on both——"

Samarendra shook his head with impatience.

"Don't you see? Gold bars or steel shares—which shall I buy?" His voice came low and earnest. "To-morrow there will be a storm in the share market. The bulls will carry all before them, the bears will be nowhere. Steels will rise steeply, so will gold—which to choose? The chance of a life-time."

Kunal was pleased with the War for one reason; so was Father, for another. "And you, too?" Rahoul asked himself in his heart. Kunal going to be a soldier, Father going to buy shares, and Mother rice and mustard oil. You?

The half-hour was almost gone—that one thought beat meanwhile through all else. The approaching moment on which lives hung, a great weight on a frail thread. If something happened to Monju. No! In these years together she had become part of his inmost being. Hard to imagine himself alive and she gone forever. Yet, had he not neglected her often? Sunk in his work, had he not denied her many little pleasures? Never again. She would have all she needed of him—all. If only she would live, happy in her motherhood, fulfilled.

A conch-shell startled him with its auspicious *oom oom !* At the bend of the stair stood Mother.

"Come, both of you. Stand by the door and have a good look at the newcomer—she has just been bathed. Big eyes, rose-and-milk complexion, the very image of her mother."

"If she has the face of her mother, she is lucky indeed," said Samarendra, beaming. "We shall not lose our sleep looking for a groom!" He laughed loud in his satisfaction. "Rahoul, you go first and see the pretty one. I am coming in a moment. Must ring up my stockbroker. Don't you see?" He squared his shoulders with the unspoken thought: Why, at a moment like this, with a great war on and a lovely grandchild born, you have to be a Napoleon of finance. Don't you see?

"Mother, Monju?"

She smiled a little. "You will see her in a while. She is tired, but happy. Let the lady doctor finish her work." And she went along to bring the child.

The scream! The thin, helpless, persistent scream of a new-born one! Rahoul stood rooted. The elation that made his heart swell! Two exciting things had happened to him this autumn day. The Prime Minister had declared war on the Swastika. Monju had given birth to a baby girl. Either event was a profound experience that made his emotions vibrate, as though he had achieved some personal fulfilment. It seemed symbolic somehow that his child should be born at the propitious moment when the reluctant voice of a politician, loving the old and decrepit world order, commanded that world order to dig its own grave.

Yes! In the blood-bath of war much else would be drowned besides the Swastika. A million youths would not die in vain.

CHAPTER II

THE NEW day, bright herald of the new epoch round the corner, broke in through the window-panes and touched his waking thoughts with wistful expectation.

He had slept well, freed from the strains of the night before. Monju twisting in agony; her wide eyes haunted by fear—and the evil omen of a cat moaning eerily in the dark street, close to the house-door, made the fear a certainty: that she would not live to see her child. Oh, she would hate to die so young—just over twenty—and possessing all that a woman could dream of. With advancing pain, clutching her husband's arm, pressing his arm hard against her bosom, she made her despair flow out into his nerves, till he felt in him the whispered echo of her premonition, and he edged close to her and took her head in the crook of his arm, enveloping her, shielding her from some mortal hurt. He saw the pupils of her eyes dilate, stained with deepening dread, as though Yama had tramped out of the night and stood at her bedside, in his hand the soul-holding tube into which he slipped life-sparks as he collected them, bits of phosphorescence.

The nightmare hours had dragged past. Monju a mother, baby the image of joy! All was well.

The Allied Powers were forced at last to make war on the

6

Swastika. Backed by the civilized conscience of the world, they would root out the scourge of the Reich and free its soul from a death-like strangle-hold. Fortresses would fall, and not in Germany alone. The idealism the Allied Powers would invoke against the enemy was a two-edged sword striking at the rot of one, striking back at the rot of the other. All would be well.

All would be well with India, too? Yes, India, too, hated the life-pattern of the hooked cross. India, too, would fight. It was her war.

Rahoul jumped out of bed. He could have shouted or sung for joy; but contented himself with whistling shrilly. World forces were dancing to his tune. Had he not often in his fancy mobilized an international army of freedom-seekers and declared war on the fascist plague? Rahoul washed, shaved. In his blood he felt the voice of India throb.

At the background of his thoughts was Monju, fretting to come to the fore. Rahoul hurried up the stair. Custom cast a new mother into isolation, so that she could not leave the room where her child was born for three weeks if it was a boy, for a month if it was a girl. Poor Monju! Her world would shrink painfully. Hindu taboos, odd-seeming and fast dying off, often revealed an inner purpose if you looked beneath the surface. Good for Monju, after all. She needed a long rest. Rest would hasten recovery.

He paused at the door, listening. The helpless scream! He had almost forgotten he had a child of his own, a little baby girl! Voices. . . . Mother urging, persuasive. Monju pleading it hurt her. And the child yelling—good lungs for her puny size! What could be hurting Monju? The yelling ceased all at once. Silence. Rahoul, curious, opened the door a crack, peering through. In an instant he drew back, lips pressed together, laughing in his silent inward way. The grace of a new mother! The wonder of a young girl turned mother!

Down the stair to his study. A servant brought tea and the papers. His eyes rushed over the columns. Then he sat back pondering, absently pouring out a cup of tea. The point of view was plain enough. Indian opinion was at one with progressive forces the world over. But how could a people step out into a war said to be waged for democratic freedom, so long as that very freedom was denied them? India in bondage asked to fight for world freedom!

But the bonds were breaking, breaking in that great hour, Rahoul saw, his eyes gazing and fixed in a dreamy smile.

7

Freedom went blowing across the frontiers of Europe from land to land and across the oceans to Asian lands. In the agonies of war the soul of humankind would be cleansed. Humankind after the War would not be the humankind of before.

The door opened and Mother stepped in slowly. Turning, Rahoul saw the woe in her face, and he cried in alarm, "Monju? No complication?"

Mother shook her head. "She is well. The child cried a little during the night, not much." Pause. "Your tea"—she felt the cup—"it's grown cold." She emptied the cup and refilled it from the teapot. "Drink your tea before it gets cold again." She sat down on a divan with a tired sigh.

"There's something on your mind, Mother. Tell me." He moved his chair closer.

She nodded. "Yes. It's Kunal." She mused for a time before she went on. "Kunal taps at the door of the lying-in room at night, and when I come out he breathes, 'She is well? And the little girl?' And then he says, 'Mother, I have something to tell you.' And his face is hot, as if he has done some wrong, and he takes me to his room and hands me a chair, and he sits down on the floor at my feet, his head on my lap, and he says, 'Mother, I am going to war. You mustn't say No.' I feel stunned. 'Kunal,' I tell him, 'when I am dead you can go anywhere; I shall not be here to forbid you. Wait till then.' He lifts his face; he says, 'Mother, you want to keep me stuffed up with cotton-wool? You will only break my heart.' I ask him, 'What have they done to you, the German people?' And he says, 'I have no high-sounding ideals to serve, Mother. I am going to war to serve myself, to find an outlet for my spirit, as it were.' And he springs to his feet and paces the room, restive, and his heart seems to shine on his face, and then I know I must not be in his way, I know I must not hurt him within, so I tell him, 'Kunal, do the right thing. You have my blessing, my son.' He stands still, as if dazed, and he sinks at my feet and drops his face on my lap, and his eyes are wet, and he says, 'Mother, I'll be all right. Do not fret yourself on my account.' And he lifts his face excitedly again and says, 'Why, at this very moment a million mothers the world over must be sending their sons to war'."

He was like that, Kunal, thought Rahoul, unhappy because of Mother's misery. Prompt in decision, that boy. No hesitation in his nature. That was his strength. His weakness, too;

8

even if he took a wrong track, he wouldn't turn back : he would press on, persistent, purposive.

And you? Rahoul asked himself for the tenth time. Research could wait. In the great drama that had burst upon the world he had his part to play. What the Press said was true. But the people of England were more than the politicians of England. The people meant what the politicians often lip-professed. The people were growing to value freedom as much for others as for themselves. They would now grow faster. Would they let the ideals they would be dying for be trampled on?

"Father wouldn't let the boy go, so he said. He has a post for him in an office. What good, if it will not make the boy happy?" She shook her head slowly to herself, sadly. "How could a mother break her son's spirit?"

She couldn't anyhow, Rahoul knew, and in her heart she would suffer terribly. Kunal was her favourite son, too—of them, Mother loved him more, Rahoul had always felt sure, even if she wouldn't admit as much. Kunal going to war. Brave Mother!

"Something queer has gripped Father. He had not a wink of sleep all night long. I looked in at dead of night when the police watchman on the streets went shouting his usual cry of warning against burglars—Father still at his desk, filling sheets of paper with calculations. Shares. Excited, as though something big is going to happen." Mother rose from the divan. "The daughter must have done with the feeding, Rahoul. You may go in. I shall get the hot water ready for baby's bath."

Mother walked off to the kitchen. Rahoul rushed up the stair to the lying-in room.

Over the drawn neck of her frilled white jacket Monju's full breast lay bare and upright, an ooze of milk on its shadowed tip. There was a new ripeness about her breast, like the ripeness of fruit. Her eyes, following his, bent to her bosom, her face flushed, her hand rose out of its languor to sheathe herself, but he intercepted, his hand took hers, holding tight. Her face flushed deeper, her eyes dropped close and she surrendered herself to his will. And in the instant of her yielding he, too, yielded ; he released her hand and gently, caressingly, he drew the jacket to the curved moulding of her throat. But the ooze of milk lingered long in his vision, stirring an emotion he could not suppress, for it was as though Monju was Monju no longer, the one he knew and loved, but something more and something less, remote, unattainable.

"It's a girl." He spoke softly. "I have said so, Monju, all these months, haven't I?" He sat down on the edge of the bed and bent over.

"Clever one! You have what you asked for. I wanted a boy."

"Disappointed, Monju?"

For answer she fumbled beside her till she felt softness and warmth, and she passed her hand all over the child, from the toes upward, and her face was withdrawn—a new, drugged face.

"She takes after you. Look. Your lips, your nose——"

"Eyes, too?" he grinned. His eyes were narrow under the glasses, amber, with straight brows that came together. "Then she must be a beauty!"

"Of course she is a beauty. Dare you mock her? Features! Complexion! Do you not feel proud? Won't you hold her?"

He stooped, slipping his arms under the mysterious stranger as she opened her eyes and blinked, lifting her clumsily; oh, so small! (Perilous job, holding the floppy head resting in the crook of your arm!) Then she screamed, and he quickly put her back on the bed, alarmed lest he had hurt some limb. And the tiny, pinkish face worked and puckered while the anxious mother drew her close, soothing her, '*Nah, nah*, here is mumma. O-oh, o-oh——" She gave her husband a sideways glance, and with a brilliant smile she wiped off his embarrassment. "This one does not know you yet. She knows only her mother." And she caressed the child, murmuring: "He is Papa, my sweet. Papa——"

Yet the odd feeling was heavy in him that Monju was Monju no longer, but something more and something less, remote, unknowable.

"Kunal is going to war as soon as he gets a chance."

She nodded. "Mother told me. Poor Mother! She had no sleep in her eyes all night long because of her worry." She turned to her child with an intense look in her face, pressing it close against herself. "I am glad this one is a girl. She will not go to war. Poor Mother!"

"You are choking her, Monju," Rahoul cried in alarm, looking down.

She laughed. Her teeth gleamed against her lips with the sheen as of pearls. "Mum-ma hurting her sweet jewel?" She leaned over, holding the child pressed against her bosom. "Don't I know how to handle a sweet jewel?" She kissed the tiny toes, the rounded belly. "Don't I, *hoon*?"

Just as well, then, that Monju had sunk herself in her creation, mused Rahoul. Her need of him was no longer intense. And he spoke:

"What if I also go?"

She looked up startled.

"You?" In an under-breath.

"Why not?"

"Go to war?" She opened her eyes wide.

He nodded, and suddenly he seemed far away. He might have been settling an old score with himself.

"Six months before I left England, fascist rebels were destroying the Government of Spain elected by the people. Madrid besieged, strangled. Then volunteers from many lands rushed to save freedom in Spain. I had an urge those days to join the army of liberation. Ralph Fox went. Many others I knew went. I kept back. I had an excuse: science. I could serve humanity better that way. And I came back to my homeland. Some sore in me throbs now and then. A greater war of liberation has started, the greatest ever. What am I to do this time?"

Her mouth opened a little and her alarmed eyes lay staring, not leaving his face, till she held his far glance, held fast, and then she saw the remote look roll off like a shadow and heard him murmur, "There's no hurry, Monju. No mobilization yet."

She reached out for his hand. Her fist nestled in his. She would not let him go. Never, never would she let him go. She would not be parted from him. Not for a day.

"All men are not made alike." She spoke with a joyous sigh because of her relief from shock. "Your true place is with your books, your mathematics, your strange instruments in the college room where you took me once. You have the stars. You belong to them. They belong to you. The stars and the unseen lights. You are not earthy." Her voice mellowed caressingly. "You are no more earthy than this little one we have."

He was dumb for a time, and then he said, dubious, "I must talk it over——"

"Yes, ask Father," the voice rushing and sweet; "he knows what you should do. Just ask Father."

Lips pursed, Rahoul shook his head. "Father? He has no understanding." Shamed by his irreverence, he hurried on: "Father only knows his own work. He does not care what

11

happens to the world. He belongs to a life, an age, that has fled."

Alarm rushed back to her eyes. Her slim fingers fretted in his fist. She knew with whom he was going to talk it over. Grandfather. An eccentric. He had odd ideas. Ever since he retired from his work as teacher at a city school he had lived by himself in a village not far from the sea; he lived like one of the peasant folk. Some years back, when Congress had launched civil disobedience against the Government, the aged one was deep in it: he formed a band of volunteers, peasants and fishers all, leading them to the Bay, making salt from sea-water in defiance of the law. Gone to prison. All over India a hundred thousand men—women, too—had gone to prison in a month. Rahoul was a student then. He, too, would have done something rash—yes, he had his face set towards prison—but Father kept his eyes glued to him and sent him off to England in the nick of time. So Father told Monju one day soon after her marriage; and how proud and happy he was that he could shield his son—impetuous one—from the flame-like unrest of those days! Father was wise, practical, unlike the aged one with queer ideas. Over seventy, and living a hard life all by himself, remote from his kin, with no one to hand him a glass of milk if he ever fell ill! With a great-grandchild born, why could he not come over and live in peace with his own kin, as became his advanced years, tended by all, reverenced?

And what would such a man say? What golden advice would he offer? Not one that would make sense—no! But Monju would fight for her husband. She would fight and never give way. She would not be parted from him. She could not bear to see him rush into danger. And why help the alien Government you so intensely disliked? Where was the logic of it, then?

"You men are sunk in self," she murmured, and her mouth pouted. "Never looking an inch beyond your own heart's desire. Here am I, relieved after nine months of agony; but no release for me yet, a prisoner within these four walls, alone save for my child, and you planning a trip to the village, if not to war. Oh yes, you are just fed up with me, I can see." Her eyelids flickered. "Of course it's all my fault."

His fist tightened round her fingers. "It's only for a day or two, Monju——" His voice was unhappy.

And she trailed on: "You feel for all humanity save for your near ones. You don't care for the child. You never wanted her, I know. She means nothing to you." Tears were welling to her eyes. Never, never would she let him go.

"Monju, I am not going just yet, anyhow. There's no hurry. Let's see how things take shape. Let's wait and see. Monju, listen."

. . . . .

Gold rush in Clive Street. A motley crowd surging by the Stock Exchange, the tall, massive, dark-brown door open only to privilege. On the road, on the concrete pavements shadowed from the angry sun by mammoth cement-grey structures, a big motley crowd surging, voices buzzing, brains pounding at full pressure. Inside, the brokers, the brokers' agents, sub-agents, booking orders from clients in the motley crowd, clients too excited to sit still at home or in office with telephone to mouth, pouring orders, buying, selling, buying again. Bees darting and buzzing for money-honey!

Pulses pounding. The blood beating in the ears. The crowd with cash in the banks, cash to play with. Hot activity in the street of Clive, who built Empire with a thousand muskets and a forgery.

Buy munitions of war—things that make guns, shells. Buy the materials of a battleship. Buy Steels. War eats steel. A ton of steel mangles a brigade. A hundred thousand tons mangle a city. A million tons mangle the earth. Buy Coals. Coal to keep the limbs of war warm. Man digging deeper than any animal, tearing the earth's bowels with iron claws. Buy aluminium—wings of planes need aluminium. Railways, buy Railways. Heavy traffic on wheels, traffic into cash. This is a war on wheels: steel wheels, rubber wheels. Buy Rubbers from Malaya. No rubber shares in this market? A telegram to Singapore does the trick. Send fast telegrams to Singapore. Shape up Singapore. Calcutta buying. Rubber for trucks, armoured cars, wheels, wheels. Buy Burma oils. War swims in a sea of oil.

High premium? Buy at a high premium. See it go higher, higher. Thirty per cent. Fifty per cent. Hundred per cent. dividend. Dividend to make death machine. Scrap-iron hurled from projectiles, a million tons a month. A million deaths a month. Death into dividend. Death into dividend.

SELL! Cash in your profits. This isn't like the last War. Going to be short. Only a blitz. Peace in a year. They don't want war. Pays better to share spoils. The Nazis to get East Africa. The Nazis have the Negroes to swallow—a bellyful.

Negroes grow like berries out in East Africa. Peace round the corner. Market crashing. Sell now for high premium. Sell Tata Steel. Can't compete with American steel. Slump round the corner. SELL!

BUY! Cotton for the Army. Troops to be sheathed in uniform. Ten million uniforms. Uniforms wasted on dead bodies. Boots. Woollens. Indian troops need to be warm overseas. Lalimli woollens.

What have you to buy with? Open your pass-books. Empty your accounts. Take a loan from friends. Mortgage your house. Sell, sell your gold, the gold on the body of your wife. See the funds doubling, the house reproducing itself, the gold growing for ten extra arms. Buy on the margin deposit system. You pay a quarter of the price, the broker puts down the balance at six per cent. Sell as the market rises. Take your profit and pay off the broker. See your capital doubled.

Sell on the margin system. You make a deposit. You sell a share you don't possess. The market falls. You buy at the cut rate and deliver the share you've sold. Take the balance of profit. See your capital doubled.

Buy Jutes. Jute bags to carry supplies; jute bags filled with sand to keep off bombs. Buy paper. Yes, yes, paper is a munition of war, paper.

Chance slipping by. Chance of twenty years. Not another war for twenty years. War, the most enriching industry. Prices mounting. Steels the favourite counter. The crowd surging. Bee voices buzzing for money-honey.

Shrewd eyes in a heavy-jowled face; shiny black alpaca coat, black bow-tie, trousers failing to touch ankles. Under the watch-chain the heart tapping a quick rhythm: Too late, too late; too late, too late.

Buy. It will be a ten years' war. The others won't sit with folded arms, watching. Japan. America. Buy to-day at a premium.

SELL, cash in your profit. Peace round the corner.

Buy and hold on. Seven years' war ahead.

CHAPTER III

STRIPPED OF midwinter harvest, bare and baked, the cracking earth of rice-fields pushed and stretched to the very gates of the two-room railway sub-station from which Rahoul emerged at sunset.

A *madhobi* vine curved arching over the narrow outer portal, great clusters of delicate shell-white flowers blossoming in rich profusion. But the earth was sun-hardened at its roots, and the leaves, pale and drooping, seemed to beg for sap. Rahoul stopped, fascinated, and pressed his nose upon a white cluster, filling his breath with the tender fragrance. That was Bengal— the thought came upon him—so much beauty could grow in such neglect and hardship only in Bengal.

It was good that the railway ran close to the village, even if the trains would not stop at the sub-station save for higher-class passengers at their bidding. Grandfather lived not far off—a half-hour's walk down the red-earth pathway. A light suitcase in his hand, Rahoul strode fast, lest darkness fall and he lose direction.

He had been fretful in his heart all that winter and spring-time. Science could not hold his thoughts. The new world order was an empty dream? The Allies fought for victory and nothing beyond? Only to hang their washing on the Siegfried Line? No higher ideals were visible in their proclaimed war aims—none.

As the first flush of dream faded and misgivings grew, Rahoul had a desperate need to see Grandfather and replenish his spirit from the other's simple, clear-cut faith. In his pre-Cambridge days Grandfather had cast a spell over him, moulding his ideas, stirring a fire in his heart. Fresh from college, youthful and eager, Rahoul had stood at the edge of the national movement that had flared up then, ready to plunge in at his teacher's word. His father, alarmed, held out a bait. Cambridge. Cambridge or prison—he put it that way and missed his mark. Prison had become a place of pilgrimage. He started a new line of attack. Should you not give your very best to your motherland? How better serve her interests than as a great man of science honoured by the world? And you would serve all humanity that way. What better training-ground than Cambridge? To break the Salt Laws and be rushed into prison—anyone could do that, tens of thousands had done that. Must you, with your great gifts (and who more certain of them than Rahoul himself?), rot in wasteland?

"Cambridge can wait," Grandfather had said, his voice mild as always, yet iron-like.

Rahoul shook his head. "This is my only chance. Later they won't give me a passport."

. "Then your son, citizen of a free republic, will proudly go to Cambridge."

Rahoul had laughed. His son! Marriage had no place in the picture of life he then saw for himself. To talk of his son!

"And shouldn't I know the people of England before I start my fight with them?" he had pleaded.

"Why should you fight the people of England? They are good people. The people are good everywhere. Our fight is with the rulers of England, who hold us in subjection for their narrow interests."

So there had been a keen struggle in his mind. Cambridge had won.

He had travelled far from those days. If he had lost the emotional stirrings he had known then, he was more honest with himself. Science, he would now admit, was his intellectual blanket, a refuge from chill winds. Friends had gone to Spain that time, undeterred by the work they loved, acting on the passion of the soul. What was more precious in life than that passion?

Grandfather, now past his seventieth year, so mild and so hard, had acted always under that inward urge. In this grave hour of decision what was he going to do with himself?

The track dimmed and divided, forking out south, southwest. In the old days Rahoul had known the village paths well, but he had not been this way for years, and he stopped, uncertain. He looked about, and saw two peasants, ploughshares on their shoulders, coming across the cropped bare fields. Rahoul put down his bag, waiting, and when they drew close he made his query; he spoke Grandfather's name. Devesh.

They stood scratching their heads in thought, then both cried together, "Not Devata? His house? There—two, three steps."

Rahoul gazed ahead. "Past the palmyra clump?"

"Past." They nodded their heads. "Two, three steps."

Devata? wondered Rahoul as they walked on. Grandfather's name was not quite that. Devesh. No one had ever been named Devata.

"Why call him Devata?" he said. "Only a god is so called."

"It is because of our love for him," said one peasant.

"Love? Surely Devata is to be worshipped, not loved?"

The man nodded as though in agreement.

"We are common folk, sir. We have no learning in our heads—our eyes cannot make out the shapes of letters. In worship we read love, in love worship."

"The divine bliss fills his heart with riches," the other man explained further. "When we call him Devata, our tongue and our soul earn Merit. We are only peasant folk, sir."

A silence, and then—"My grandfather," said Rahoul, his heart big with pride.

"Thine?" the men in wonder exclaimed, and stopped dead, and they put down their loads and bent their knees, heads knocking on earth. "We fall at thy feet." And they rose and reached for the leather case. "Master, we beg."

"No, no," said Rahoul. "This is no weight."

"Master, how have we annoyed thee?"

He turned to look at the pained faces and he smiled. "Have you not loads enough to carry?"

"Master," they begged with folded hands, and one murmured to the other, "*his* grandson to carry a weight when we are about! The village has no shame? The village has no honour?"

And Rahoul broke out in a laugh and yielded to their will.

"There!" cried one man as the palmyra clump was passed. "Himself coming this way."

Rahoul looked. A tall, straight figure in white homespun. Long, silver hair thinning at the edge of the high forehead, long, flowing, silver beard. It was *dadu*, Grandfather. He walked barefoot like the peasants.

"Rahoul!" he cried, clasping him in his arms as Rahoul was about to bend to Grandfather's feet in salutation. "What ages I have not set eyes on you, Rahoul! Not since the great day of the marriage festival." *Dadu* peered eagerly at his grandson, holding him at arms' length for a clear view. "Let me have a good look. You have grown much thinner. Not unwell? Worry, Rahoul?"

"A hundred worries." Rahoul tried to make a piteous face. "No fun to be the father of a girl. You wouldn't know. You have had only a son."

"So many worries? Poor boy!" Turning to the two peasants: "Binda, take the bag home. We shall be away a time."

Dadu had not changed at all, save for some deep wrinkles on his high forehead. The silver of his hair and beard gave his face a quality of light. *Dadu* would show him the way as of old, thought Rahoul, with renewed faith.

"Where are you taking me, *dadu*?"

"A little way. An invitation to a rice meal. You will see village folk."

"Unasked guest?" said Rahoul, hesitant. "To share their meal——"

"Rahoul, our meals are a very simple affair. We peasants do

17

not have elaborate courses with our rice—fish, meats, curds, sweets—we can't afford them. You'll be given a leaf-plate of steamed rice and lentils, a pinch of salt and a lemon, some baked sweet potatoes and a vegetable curry of sorts, and perhaps some thickened milk in a small brass bowl by way of a luxury. That makes a big festive meal."

"All the same, *dadu*, I am a stranger——"

"You are no stranger. It is my daughter's household. They have heard everything about you."

Rahoul gave him a glance. "*Hoon!* So you have a daughter in this village? And we never knew!"

"I have a daughter, Rahoul." *Dadu* made a guilty face.

So would they speak to each other in their light moments, free as friends, heedless of the half-century between them. But, with a swift change of mood, Grandfather said, his voice grave:

"I have scores of daughters and sons in Baruni. I am proud of my people. They are not bright and knowing and—civilized!—like you city-breds; but they are good people. Centuries of brute hardship and strain have not destroyed their faith in human values."

"Tell me about the village, then," said Rahoul eagerly.

"This is a fair-sized one, our Baruni—not very big, not small. Less than a hundred households. About a quarter of them hold land on lease from the *zemindar*. Another quarter are landless *kisans*, peasant labourers, who work for their more fortunate brethren, planting the rice and reaping the harvest for a day-wage and meals. A good many are fisherfolk. Life centres on rice-land and river."

"India's daily income," spoke Rahoul, "is less than two *annas* per head, so it has been worked out. The figure seems incredible. It does not tell much, though."

Grandfather agreed. "Facts never tell much unless they are seen in terms of human experience. On his petty income the landed peasant can have just enough of his own rice to eat, no reserve for lean days. And the *kisans*—they must always be hungry save for a spell of two or three months in the year, when they earn meals and a wage for field-work. The hundred million *kisans* of India must always be hungry. It is a rare gracious day to have the stomach full." He paused, and walked a minute in silence. "Hungry and half-naked, that hundred million—how can they afford to buy long *dhoties* touching their ankles? You see, Rahoul, the true meaning of the spinning-

18

wheel—the symbol of our national movement? The masses of India, with their less than two *annas* a day, can work the wheel and produce loin-cloths to cover their nakedness. People often don't realize this plain fact."

Plain enough if you knew the meaning of two *annas* a day. Rahoul could see the peasants of Bengal, men and women, making soft white yarn with a simple wheel, and the village weavers turning the yarn into a fabric—loin-cloths for the men and red-bordered *saris* for the women.

"Apart from re-distribution of land, science must be used intensively to raise productive capacity," musingly he spoke. "Our grainlands are weary and famished. Their yield is about the lowest in the rice-growing world. With proper manuring, seeding and ploughing—a new type of plough must replace the present prehistoric kind—that yield could be increased three-fold. That is the figure for Japan. We could have food for all and a surplus. The *zemindar* takes no interest in production?"

The *zemindar*! *Dadu* sounded scornful. And he spoke of the background of Bengal's rural life—of how, long ago, at the beginning of the nineteenth century, a servant of the British Trading Company made a "permanent settlement" with the landlords of Bengal, fixing for all time their annual payment to the Treasury. The value of land rose tenfold, the value of the *rupee* lessened, but the basic payment knew no alteration. There was no such contract, though, between landlord and cultivator, and with reassessments the cultivator's dues went up at a tangent. The landlord leased out his estate to by-pass the bother of rent collection, and lived care-free in his city mansion, his income assured. The lessee likewise farmed the land to sub-lessees, and so it went on till a village often had an hierarchy of overlords. The peasants' dues were payable in cash whatever the crop was like; why, then, should the overlords worry about production? The peasantry was not in their eyes a living mass; it was like a tract of coalfield out of which you hewed coal for profit and more profit, heedless of its exhaustion.

The peasantry of Bengal, said Grandfather, was on the edge of exhaustion.

"What sort of landlord have you, *dadu*, the chap nearest to you?"

"Bepin Ghose," said Grandfather. "Listen. It's a good story. Bepin was born in our village, the son of a rent collector. He, too, became a rent collector. Once it so happened that the peasants in a village near by, Vishnupura, formed a combination and refused to pay extra rents demanded. So their holdings were put to auction under a court decree and disposed of. But the new owners, creatures of the landlord, could not secure actual possession because of the peasants' united struggle. Then, one day, young Bepin Ghose appeared at the police *thana*, borne on a stretcher, groaning in agony, his clothes blood-smeared. He complained that he had been assaulted by the dispossessed tenants and the union leaders, and these men— he identified them—were at once rounded up, tried, and sent to prison. The peasants' resistance now broke down and the lands went under the new owner's plough. The case was a frame-up! Bepin Ghose later boastingly admitted the truth to his friends. He had volunteered to be secretly mauled by the landlord's men, so that the case could be framed. Forty *bighas* of land in his native village was his reward. That was the beginning. A man of such calibre must go far. What wonder that Bepin Ghose is now the overlord of Baruni and rides in a rich proud palanquin?"

"What hope is there for the people?" said Rahoul, pensive.

"What hope?" Grandfather paused, hearing the sound of feet on the road, and turning, he called: "Onu!"

"*Dadu!*" A boy of ten or eleven years came up the pathway. He cast a wondering look at the stranger. Onu wore clean white clothes, a short homespun *dhoti*, sleeveless vest.

"Good shoes?" said Grandfather, tenderness in his voice. "You are pleased, Onu?"

For answer the boy lifted his feet and walked ten paces ahead. "Listen. *Mush, mush!*" And he walked back with hard, firm steps. "What *mush, mush, dadu!*" His eyes beamed with excited pleasure. "I walked this way, that way. I walked the four corners—no one has ever heard such *mush mush mush!* The storeman? Not even he, the storeman, so he says, truly."

Onu would have started to delight himself again with the joyous sound, but Grandfather was stooping low to tie his shoe-laces. "Look, son, this is the proper way." He tied one lace, then the other, and he turned his face to Rahoul and spoke: "You have no such shoes, Rahoul—shoes that squeak so well as Onu's. I was at the district town yesterday. I brought back this pair."

Rahoul gazed at the tall, stooping figure, tying the shoe-lace of a peasant boy.

So loving, so gentle! And yet firm and majestic. A true veteran of the national movement. Three times he had gone to

20

prison, seven years in prison. Devata, the village called him. What wonder?

"Onu, run home. Tell Mother Rahoul is here—my grandson Rahoul. He is coming over with me."

"Yes, *dadu*." Onu bent quickly to the stranger's feet, head touching road dust, and rising, with a half-smiling, half-curious glance he dashed off on flying feet, excited bearer of news. But when he had gone thirty paces he stopped and cried, turning, "*Dadu*, what if the heels get worn out with the running?" And he pulled off his shoes, held them tight in his hands and ran barefoot.

"Onu, my daughter's youngest," Grandfather explained. "He has a brother Kanu and a sister Kajoli. Kanu is the first-born. You will see them. There is also Mangala."

"Another sister?"

"Mangala? No. The milch-cow. A friend of the house."

"And the father?"

"The mendicant is away. You will not see him. He is a peasant with some land, three fair-sized strips and a yoke of oxen. But his soul is given to song and wandering. Yes, he lives for song, and of an evening the whole village assembles to hear his voice. But he is often away, save in seed-time and harvest, going about Bengal, roving the roads with an *ek-tara* [one-stringed lyre] for companion. So we call him mendicant. He goes singing:

> "' When the call has gone forth and no one answers,
> Then march alone, and alone, march alone——' "

"What a lovely character!" said Rahoul, and his eyes tried to see the mendicant.

"No uncommon type in our Bengal villages," said Grandfather. "Song is a spiritual need of our people. Every village has its poet and mendicant. They hold the people's love and respect." He paused for a time as though his mind was far, then resumed: "Rahoul, I heard your question—what hope is there for the people? The national movement gives top priority to village reconstruction work, that you know. This is the very basis of our life to come. The Government do not like it, of course. They and the landlords have grown to fear the peasant masses. Once, not many years ago, odd to think, they posed as champions of the voiceless people as against the intellectual classes, the sedition-mongers who talk of freedom for all. But the times have changed, the mask has blown off, the real face lies revealed. I run a school for the village, an evening school. A spy has been set to watch the school. They are anxious to break it up. Mass literacy is a danger for the rulers. It would, they know, make the trampled ones conscious of their birth-right—the right to live as human beings."

"India cannot breathe much longer under the present system," said Rahoul. "The bitter cup is brimful. Our existence has stopped at a dead-end. But the situation has grown complicated because of the War. I am puzzled, and, *dadu*, I must talk it over with you."

Dadu nodded, smiling. "We are bound by the discipline of Congress. We cannot act without the call for action, Rahoul. We shall talk later—talk all night, if you like. That is the house of our mendicant." And there was the mush mush of Onu's new shoes greeting the visitors.

A lanky youth was riding on the back of a russet-skinned cow. He sprang down and cried to Rahoul, "I fall at thy feet."

"Kanu—Mangala——" *dadu* introduced.

"May you live," responded Rahoul, with a quick glance at *dadu*. Their eyes twinkled at each other, and it was as if *dadu* said, "You are picking up our old-fashioned village speech fast enough."

"Kanu has a dream. He would go wandering like his father. He, too, has the gift of song. But he suffers so from earache, poor boy."

A girl appeared at the low doorway, a shiny brass vessel in her hands.

"Kajoli," said Grandfather.

The girl put down the vessel, then went on her knees, stooping over Rahoul's feet. Her skin was light, her features pleasing. She was fourteen years of age.

"May you live——" The words stuck on Rahoul's lips. Kajoli was undoing his shoe-lace! Flurried, Rahoul pulled off his shoes—leathern shoes, he knew, were not to be worn beyond the doorstep. But the girl, Kajoli, was stooping still, now seated cosily on her bottom, and out of the vessel she poured cool water on Rahoul's feet to wash off road dust.

"No, no. What is this?" cried Rahoul, as he felt her hand on his ankle and drew back a step. "Let me have the water-pail." He reached out.

The strange hurt glance in the wide eyes that looked up, now at Rahoul, now at Grandfather!

Then *dadu* spoke: "Rahoul, she is a good peasant girl with nice clean hands. Why won't you let her touch your feet?"

He grew more flustered. "No, what is this? To touch my feet—I mean——"

"She is a well-bred peasant girl. She has a legacy of manners as old as India. How could she give up her manners and proprieties to suit your new-fangled city ideas? You are a respected visitor in the house——"

Then Rahoul saw how *dadu* was enjoying the moment. He gave in. He came forward a step, smiling. "Kajoli, have your way, then; there is dust a-plenty on my feet."

"*Didi!*" Onu gave a great shout. "A picture, *didi!*"

Grandfather held a coloured print in his hand—he had kept it rolled up somewhere in his garments.

Kajoli sprang to her feet, eager and jubilant, the visitor's feet forgotten for the moment. "For me, *dadu?*"

"For you, Kajoli."

And as he turned to speak to his grandson an intense warmth came upon his face, mellowing like a cloud its pure quality of light.

"This young girl has a keen fancy for pictures of bright colour. She hangs them up all over the mud walls. Her longing for beauty finds expression that way." And his eyes, deep with compassion, rested long upon the peasant girl, as though pouring upon her some speechless blessing.

CHAPTER IV

SAMARENDRA BASU had played his cards well. His firm faith in the Empire's armed might had helped. The Stock Market was divided against itself. The Soviets had marched into Poland before the Nazi python could swallow it altogether. Some thought that the Soviets had thrown a challenge to the Allies; others thought it was a check to *blitzkrieg*. The Stock Market was concerned only with the military implication. Would not the Allies come into conflict with Russia? They would, and nervous speculators unloaded their holdings. They wouldn't, and the speculators rushed to buy back what they had sold.

Samarendra bought at each reaction and sold at higher

levels. He had no fear of Soviet power, only contempt. Who could withstand the avalanche that was the Empire at arms? The Germans? Yes, for a time. The Russians? What had they to fight with? Russia would not dare make war, lest there be a counter-revolution—the oppressed peasants would rise as one man while the Red Army was hard-pressed elsewhere, and swiftly bring to an end the system that had confiscated their houses and land and liberty, their moral code, their God and their women—the women, it was said, had become communal property, like the land itself.

And Samarendra collected his winnings and threw them back into the game, with one simple formula to lean on, for with him it was an article of faith. The Stock Market moved like the swaying of a see-saw. Each movement shed upon his lap a golden dust of profit, and it grew, it piled, till Samarendra wondered if it was not too good to be true. Easy money. What if he neglected his practice at the Bar of the High Court? He had earned more in a half-year, much more, than he could earn as a lawyer in a half-decade! And if the rate of progress held! The brilliance of the noon to come seemed to daze his vision, still accustomed to the mellowness of dawn.

New ideas jostled in his mind. A mist of ideas. He would not rest on his laurels as a speculator. Big business? An economic shake-up would surely follow in the wake of war. Would not the vast man-power of India make steam for the war machine? What if the Middle East were involved, as well it might be? Samarendra leaned back in his chair and lifted his eyes to a gilt-framed picture on the wall, as if seeking enlightenment. The Emperor and the Empress. Not long ago this picture had replaced another, for the Emperor of those days had shrunk into a Duke after a brief reign. Not even a Prince. Samarendra had been bewildered and shocked. What had gone wrong? To marry a divorced lady. Was not divorce approved by British law and custom? He had not probed farther, though. None of his business. It was the crown that mattered, not the head under it. And he had shifted the ex-Emperor to a dark passage.

"You tuned in to the B.B.C. last night, Rahoul? The Secretary for Air made a great speech." Samarendra spoke to his son at morning tea one day. It was a fortnight after British forces had landed on Norwegian shores. Kunal had left the room, having taken his tea in three gulps, as usual. Mother had gone to the kitchen. Rahoul sat on awhile with his father,

24

separated from him by an empty chair on the back of which hung a black alpaca coat of ample girth, waiting to be worn.

"I heard him," said Rahoul.

"A thousand pities I missed it. If only you had told me! It's reported on the front page here." Samarendra tapped his paper and cleared his throat. "Listen. *To-day our wings are spread over the Arctic. They are sheathed in ice. To-morrow the sun of victory will touch them with its golden light.* He read on a line or two in an undertone, then lifted his voice and shook his fist dramatically in the air: *And the wings that flashed over the great waters of the North will bear us homewards once more to the peace with honour of a free people and the victory of a noble race.* He paused and drew a breath of pride and exaltation, then added: "I wish I could hear the great words spoken, Rahoul. *The victory of a noble race.*" The voice was rapturous.

"I throttled him in mid-speech," said Rahoul, his lips hard with contempt. "This champion of a free people conspired not long ago with a Frenchman of the same feather to sell off a free country while fanning its people with lip-friendship."

"Abyssinia?" The shrewd eyes were scornful. "Why, Mussolini would have taught them civilized living. You have been in Italy. You stayed there one full summer. You ought to know, Rahoul."

Rahoul knew. He made an impatient gesture, thinking of all the freedoms destroyed in Italy. And the Fiats that had given hell to open cities in Spain. Civilized living! But Father wouldn't understand. Born in England, he would have been a Tory diehard. Born in India, he was conditioned by the same spiritual bondage and something worse. It was his kind, bred in the decadence that overtakes a race at certain periods in its history—yes, it was his kind that had made possible England's long-drawn occupation of India. He had his full reward in material gain. A great War was putting the old loyalties to a fierce test. It was giving the age-long problems a razor's edge. It was a crisis of humanity. But not in his father's mind. That mind was unshaken as ever, insensitive. Sunk in slavery, it thought of the War only as a rare chance to reap a harvest of gold. Devata to have such a son! The bitter irony! Devata never came to this house—no wonder. Hurt, unhappy, Rahoul looked at his father. His reverence and his love winced under his scornful thoughts.

"This Battle of Norway," Father went on, "don't you see its true meaning? The enemy, as H.M.G. have said so aptly, *the*

25

enemy has put out his head to be hit." His face stiffened, and as he spoke he smote the table. The tea-things rattled.

That far-off battle was linked in his mind with one close at hand—the battle in the Exchange between bulls and bears. A crisis of British arms. A crisis of Empire. And share values were pointed sharply downward. Then the British landing at Narvik. The Royal Air Force spreading wings over the Arctic. Now the bulls would be avenged. Samarendra felt like laughing aloud. The enemy had put out his head to be hit; so they felt in the Exchange, the bulls. Yes, he would make a lot of money. Rahoul was not impressed by the Secretary for Air's broadcast. He seemed to have no clear idea of military strategy. A true scholar, the strategy of warfare was not his business. The boy had no idea, either, that his father was making a fortune out of his correct reading of the situation, his faith in the Empire. Yes, a big fortune. And it was all for his sons' sake—with wealth heaped at his feet, his own personal needs were still little more than a daily bowl of rice, as they had been in all those years when poverty had held him chained like a slave. Rahoul, Kunal—they would be shielded from those burning worries he had known in the hateful years of struggle and pain. And the little one in the house, she now in her eighth month, she would be reared in luxury; bejewelled and *sari*-ed like a princess, she would move proudly in society, and, when of age, have a big dowry and wed an officer high up in the Imperial Service.

Pleased with this picture of life, Samarendra gazed at the face of his son. His eyes were tender for his son.

An incongruous vision flickered. A tin of Nestle's Milk. A petty happening half a lifetime away. He had watched a fellow-student at the mess pour the thick strange milk into his tea. "What is the taste like?" he had asked, face and voice eager, eyes gaping, but the other had grinned, mocking, and put the tin away. How he had burned! And he had vowed that he would struggle out of his poverty and when he had money he would help himself to a full tin of condensed milk at a sitting. . . . Much money came his way, but it was too late then, and the tinned milk stayed in his deepest mind.

His sons should have all the condensed pleasures he himself had wanted in vain—he would take care of that. His fist had clenched: whatever the cost, he would take care of that. That way, through his sons, he would fulfil himself.

26

"*Policewala*, sir!" The startling word came from a servant at the doorway. Panic in his face: "*Policewala*, sir!"

"What *policewala*? Have you gone mad, Roghua?"

"Inspector, sir." The eyes gloated over master as though to communicate excited alarm.

Pale, struck dumb, Samarendra clutched the arms of his chair. He had made his name as a criminal lawyer, and police officers often came his way in the course of his work, but—police on his own doorstep! Dryness spread fast over his palate, with grim pictures forming in his fancy. The house being searched, Rahoul arrested. It was Rahoul, of course, for he had gone down to the village, involved himself in some act against his Emperor. A seditious speech. Father had urged him on, that was clear. In his advanced years Father had no feeling for his kin, and he would not have to think twice to cast his grandson into the tiger-claws of the Law, just for an idea, a crazy dream. And the boy—book-learned but inexperienced, with little knowledge of life's realities, needing good advice, needing protection. Bitterness welled from his heart against his old father and made a lump in his throat.

"I shall go down and see——" said Rahoul, perturbed by his father's silence, but Samarendra shook his head with a thick "No, no!", gazing at his son with eyes that misted with affection and despair and pain.

A voice calling in a shout from the foot of the stair: "Tell the master I have come from Government House. I have to make some inquiries."

Government House. It was almost a minute before Samarendra could interpret the words, and then the wave of relief came upon him in a rush, and he breathed, "Mother! Oh, Mother of Mercy!" closing his eyes, relaxing. In an instant he rose, crossed to the door in a stride.

Rahoul was leaving the room when the visitor appeared, but his father lifted a hand to his shoulder, introducing, proudly showing him off: "Dr. Rahoul Basu, my eldest son. D.Sc. of Cambridge University." And suddenly, to the amazement of the visitor, he broke into a chuckle, and his face was shining with a joy he could not hold, for the Vassal of Law had not come to make an arrest. The boy was safe, safe—no worry on his account!

Rahoul learned the facts. His father had gone and signed his name in the visitor's book at Government House—it was the custom for loyal, respectable citizens to drive to the west gate

27

of the House and put down their name and address in a book, then they would stand a chance of being asked to His Excellency's garden-party. Police headquarters, however, made strict inquiries about each visitor before the lists were compiled and the cards mailed.

The officer was scribbling in his notebook.

"Monthly income—round about fifteen hundred, so you say."

"Is that not enough to acquire respectability?" Adding in a half-amused, half-rueful tone: "What good is it trying to increase one's earnings? Income-tax would eat up all. Don't you see?" His wary eyes watched the officer's face while in his heart he thought: "When I tell Rahoul's mother what I've just gone through, how the quick fever came and went, she will rush to make a grateful libation to the Mother of Mercy at the temple!"

The officer gave an assurance before he left: "The function is scheduled for the 20th of next month; you will get a card."

Samarendra nodded and smiled, and there was great joy in his face. It was a glittering moment of his life.

"You, too, should be there, Rahoul. With your Cambridge D.Sc., your smart talk, your knowledge of tip-top English manners, you should make a strong impression. You will feel at home in high official circles. You dined with a Lord once, didn't you? Mention it in your talk, just casually, as though he were an intimate friend of yours. Listen. Why not take out the Ford now—I don't need it—and drive to the west gate of the House and sign your name, designation, address——?"

And Rahoul, for answer, only laughed with set lips, in his silent inward way.

"I mean it. Don't you see? We are living through an exceptional time. A god-sent opportunity for us, this War."

"For us?" Rahoul seemed puzzled. There was nothing to be done, one way or the other, till Congress issued a directive.

"For me, yes. It isn't only shares. I have other ideas." He paused and cleared his throat. "For you, certainly. A slogan has just shaped in my mind: 'Through Science to victory.' Technical superiority in arms would tip the balance in every battle. New weapons. Secret weapons. There must be something astro-physics could do that way?" His face was eager, expectant. "Think it over. Make it your preoccupation. Work day and night as though you have a severe test before you. And let people up there"—his forefinger made a vague
28

thrust—"know what sort of work you are doing: invaluable war work. Think of the glory that could be yours. Perhaps a title, and you so young. Don't you see?"

A title! As wealth grew, the dream grew, till it was now an obsession. A title for himself. *Rai Bahadur*. *Rai Bahadur* Samarendra Basu. And then in a flash he made a decision on the edge of which he had wavered for weeks. He would contribute generously to the War Fund. What if it were far more of a speculation than the share market? A big, bold stroke. He squared his shoulders. He would have to sell off a few share scrips. No matter. He had surely the right to spend a little for his inner satisfaction? And there were possibilities, material ones. He did not quite know what they were. A mist of ideas. They would crystallize. Meanwhile, he must prepare himself. First things first. A title was a tattoo-mark of loyalty. Having achieved that objective, his eyes lifted again to his Emperor, seeking enlightenment.

.   .   .   .   .

The Empire let him down, though.

From winter till spring-time History's feet had lain enchained. The chains now snapped, hammered by panzer fists. Europe lay dying. And deathless men gathered at Dunkirk to make an epic.

Samarendra should have deeply felt the impending doom of the Empire. He should have grieved. But the doom that hung over him overwhelmed all other feelings.

The Calcutta Stock Exchange had crashed.

For a while the market had marked time. The retreat from Norway burst upon it like a bombshell. Then the Nazi lance thrust into the flanks of Europe, digging deep into its vitals. The break-through at Sedan knocked down the market altogether. It breathed panic. The Allies were crushed: India would be under Swastika rule—the Nazis were well on their way here. The fate of India would anyhow be decided at a conference table, and the Crown's brightest possession would change hands with the ease of a cheque passing from account to account.

Samarendra would have escaped with a bare scratch, save for his vast faith in the Empire's might. Even after Norway fell he could have liquidated his stocks at no loss. But he read the cabled speech of a Member who had complained on the floor of the House of *the tendency to make a mountain out of the Norwegian*

29

mole-hill. The man had gone on proudly : *Thank God we are led by a Prime Minister who is not easily rattled, and who possesses the gift of patience which so many of us lack.* And the words stirred a responsive echo in Samarendra's heart. They strengthened his faith. "Sell!" the cry went, and his brokers begged of him to sell, but Samarendra sold no shares. He clung to them all. He would not be rattled, he would not lack the gift of patience.

There were the days when his fortune was dwindling at the rate of a thousand *rupees* an hour. Then it was too late to sell.

There were the days when, with Weygand, he stood in the mud of the last ditch, before Paris, and made the futile guns roar despair at the pauseless rush of panzers. With Reynaud he prayed for clouds of planes to come racing over the Atlantic. With Churchill he implored the Government of France to send away their Navy across the seas and continue the struggle to the last breath. But it was all in vain.

    .   .   .   .   .

Those were nightmare days when the bottom fell out of life and there was no knowing in what pit one would land, but Samarendra, unlike many others of his kind, refused to go to pieces. His large profits had been wiped clean as though they were a mere figure on a slate. The big bulk of under-valued shares he owned (holding a sick baby, they called it in the market!) had passed to his creditors as security. Even his house, built with his earnings in the legal profession, was mortgaged. Yet Samarendra walked with his head erect, as though nothing had happened. He resumed his practice at the High Court, working harder than ever before. He did not breathe a word about his misfortune to his wife, not even to Rahoul, lest they be unhappy on his account. The household expenses were kept up at their former level out of his current earnings. And on the day of Baby's Rice Initiation ceremony, in her eleventh month, he gave her a gold neck-chain and bangles, as was becoming.

Deep in the night, however, tossing sleepless in bed, eyes staring into dark, he would see the figure of his great loss thickly inscribed in crimson, his heart's blood, and he would slowly shake his head on the pillow, muttering to himself over and over again : "Blood, toil and tears!" Then the tears would spill from his eyes, or else it was a dry, half-suppressed sobbing.

Once his wife, who slept in the next room, heard the sobbing, and sat up in alarm, ears alert, and hearing it again after a

30

minute, she rose, slipped out of bed and peered through the door. But there lay her husband in bed, his eyes closed, his mouth open, sleeping peacefully, and presently the moaning sound repeated itself, and then she laughed and walked away thinking: "How he frightened me! He has invented a new snore!"

The Battle of Britain, fought in the clouds of a far sky, was re-fought, as it were, on the Market floor. Share values were resistant at their low level. The enemy would not find the rest of the War a walk-over. Confidence was flowing back into the Market—who did not know that England always lost all her battles save the last one? Prices had an upward trend. There were bargain-hunters about. They had waited long, but now that the tide seemed to have turned they feared to miss their chance, and rushed to buy before it was too late. And the bears, gorged with profit, having sold a great many more shares than they possessed, rushed in also to secure themselves with re-purchase.

Bright hope prevailed in the market.

Samarendra was happy again after months of agony, yet unhappy, too. If only he had sold off his shares as soon as the enemy broke through into Denmark! He would have had enough funds to buy them back at bargain rates. He would have become a millionaire! And Samarendra, happy that his doom was averted, was unhappy that he was not a millionaire. Was there nothing he could do now? He was getting back his value almost as fast as he had lost it. His debts were wiped off, and he had a good balance to his credit. Samarendra started his activities again, but with more caution, and with his eyes fixed far ahead. The American President had now signed the Lease-Lend Bill. The War was bound to be long-drawn. Samarendra planned accordingly. Before the crash came he had been looking over the economic field, assessing the prospects of each war-time business. Why should he not start some kind of production on his own? The enemy had been a great exporter of chemicals and drugs, and these would now be in short supply. There were other lines worth considering: pottery, brewing, toilet articles. He could set up a public company. Why not several public companies? Samarendra was immersed in his old dream of directing Big Business.

He had a plan for Rahoul, too. Pity that Rahoul was still determined not to call at Government House. However, he seemed to have taken his father's advice to devote himself completely to research: he had won his famous professor's approval —it was a wonder that he, reticent one, had spoken at all about that letter from Cambridge. He needed publicity and push. He needed contact with high officials. With the right word cast into the right ear he might be taken on as a Technical Adviser at New Delhi.

In a party at the House (he had been asked to three or four of them), Samarendra set his plan in motion. He had shaken hands with the lesser bureaucracy and was face to face with a Secretary.

"My son Rahoul took his D.Sc. at Cambridge," said Samarendra as soon as he had an opening. He knew that the Secretary carried 'Cantab' after his double-decker name.

"Which college?" The Secretary seemed interested.

"St. John's. He was there for four years, working under a world-famous professor. Astro-physics. Research work in astrophysics." The last words carried deep, clear emphasis.

"St. John's? I was at St. John's myself." The mask of gravity was relieved by a thin smile. He was a tall, wiry person with hair greying at the temples. "But long before your son came to Cambridge. He must be young."

"An old head on young shoulders." Samarendra was piqued that "astro-physics" had made no lightning impression on the bureaucrat. It needed elaboration.

"Rahoul is at present a Professor at Calcutta University. He is engaged in advanced research work on astro-physics. Trying to draw a secret or two from Mother Nature so that man may be armed with new power, tremendous new power. Of course"—his voice dropped—"in the present circumstances, while we're at war, that power will have to be destructive. The Voice tells us, Hindus, through the Holy *Gita*: 'When evil prevails and righteousness has crumbled to dust, I descend upon the earth, then, age after age.'"

The Secretary now seemed to be impressed. "Shall we have some tea?" He led his guest to a vacant table.

Samarendra followed him with his nose in the air. He felt himself the target of many eyes.

"Creation out of annihilation," he pursued his theme zealously while the other poured him a cup of tea. It was the moment for another appropriate verse from the Holy *Gita*, but the Secretary intercepted.

"Your son—just what is he aiming at?" he said.

Samarendra had no clear idea of his son's work, but he was

quick with his answer. Rahoul, he said, was determined to harness astral power. If his efforts were crowned with success —and so they would be, with facilities placed at his command and with proper encouragement from Authority, a factor of incalculable moral value—well, the present technique of warfare would then have to be scrapped altogether. Howitzers would be assigned a place beside the battle-axe and bow-and-arrow. Even aircraft would be unnecessary. The energy of the sun, the energy of a thousand suns, the energy that sends billions of stars hurtling in their cosmic course—a spark of it would be directed from somewhere in England right upon a division of enemy troops, and instantly, in one cataclysmic blaze, it would crumple up—tanks, planes, guns, men, all crumple up like burning rag. A few sparks of cosmic energy could destroy the entire armed might of a Great Power. This weapon of weapons was known to Ancient India—*Brahmastra* they called it. Rahoul was no visionary, though. A hard-boiled scientist, Cambridge-trained. It was all a question of time, preparation and moral backing. Just a tubeful of Death Ray!

"Tubeful?" The Secretary lifted a dubious eyebrow.

"Tubeful." Samarendra clung to his word.

They shook hands and parted. Samarendra had no notion then that his brief talk with the Secretary would have a more vital effect on his son's life than he had reason to expect.

The great windfall in his own fortune was still to come. The war spread to the Pacific. Pearl Harbour—Hongkong—Malaya—Singapore. But Samarendra acted before Singapore fell. One evening, as he listened in to the broadcast news, the loss of two great battleships was announced to the world. Samarendra was overwhelmed. He shook his head, recalling a threat that had lain stored in his memory: 'Blood, toil and tears'. He made a swift decision. In a minute he was speaking to his stockbroker on the 'phone.

In one great sweep Samarendra cleared off his holdings. Pity he could not be a millionaire. But he would not be a pauper either.

The Stock Market shivered with the smash of bombs in Rangoon. And as Alexander's ill-equipped khaki-clad army fell back through trackless jungle, the Market also fell back. Then the Market crashed.

It is strange how great inspiration comes sometimes from matters of no moment. One day as Samarendra was taking his

c (s.m.h.)

car out from the garage an old beggar whined: "A grain of rice, Father; only a grain." Samarendra offered him a copper, but the white-haired one shook his head with: "What good is that, Father? The goddess is gone from the copper bit, it is an empty shrine. The goddess lives nowhere save in a rice-grain."

The goddess lives nowhere save in a rice-grain, mused Samarendra in his car, driving to a Board meeting in Clive Street. And then the great idea flashed upon him. *Cheap Rice, Limited.* His plans had found an anchor.

It was a grand vision. India must mobilize for defence. Bengal would grow into a great military bastion. A million soldiers, perhaps, would be needed to hold the thousand miles of the Eastern Front. They would eat their fill. Millions would be engaged in war production, and they, too, would eat their fill. The grain supply from Burma was now lost. If a fraction of Bengal's rice-yield could be cornered—oh, Mother of Mercy, stupendous task! Anyhow, huge stocks could be purchased at the next harvest, laid up, frozen, till demand exceeded supply and the price level rose (one must eat, whatever the price); then the stocks could be slowly released at a huge profit.

He cast his plans. Big money was needed, and a vast organization. He must look for Directors and issue share capital. And as he trod his ground with caution he discovered, to his surprise, that the idea was not his alone; it was weighing the minds of some others who were in the forefront of business.

Samarendra had no other thought that spring and summer save rice: no other interest, no other dream. He and his colleagues worked feverishly building up the business. And nothing stood in their way until India spoke in the voice of a volcanic outburst in the fateful mid-August days.

CHAPTER V

"Have you done good ever to anybody, *dada*?" Kunal tossed an odd query at his brother.

"Hm-m?" Rahoul was taken aback. "What sort of good?"

They stood waiting at a bus stop near their lakeside house, Rahoul on his way to college and Kunal out for a hair-cut.

"The one sort that truly counts—helping to solve a fellow's *dal-bhat* [lentils-and-rice] problem. Well, then"—a smile as though of pride played on his face—"I have. I have resigned a post so that another chap may be free to rush for the vacancy."

Rahoul knew the facts. A Government post had been advertised. Every applicant had to send, as usual, a fee of five *rupees*. There must have been two thousand applications.

"And the selection had in effect been made before the fees poured in," Kunal laughed. It was strange how his laughter lent his face a gravity it did not possess. " 'Canvassing would disqualify a candidate'—so the legend went. Father arranged it all by plain canvassing. Government profiteering!"

"*Hoon*," murmured Rahoul.

And Kunal went on: "Anyhow, I am out of it, thanks to my commission in the Army. A needy, broken-hearted fellow will get a second chance."

Rahoul had his mind elsewhere.

"Kunal," he said, pausing to light a cigarette, "since you are now in the Army, perhaps you have asked yourself whom you will fight and for what?"

Kunal drew his brows, pondering.

"I know your thoughts. You are sorry for me, aren't you? A pawn in the imperialist game. A mercenary. Of course, I am no idealist like you; I have no philosophy of life, and the Army is to me just a career." He pondered for a moment, his brows straightened, and he spoke fast. "Yet, not quite. Believe me, not quite. It's an odd paradox, isn't it, that the alien imperialist is a keen admirer of our Indian culture? I mean, the culture of the old days. The imperialist applauds our spiritual heritage, our other-worldliness, so that he can quietly rule over us while we have our eyes fixed upon Beyond. It would make our rulers very uneasy if we were to adopt a materialist view of life. We can't help that. Science would fill our new life—science. That's where you come in. But that is half the story." He paused again for a deep breath, his keen glance intent on the face of his brother. "You see, we must cease to be escapist. Look at this War business. It will be good training for us. We are going to show that we're as good in battle as our proud rulers. We can play their game quite as well. We can rise to a crisis; we are resourceful, calm in the field; we do not fear to——" Kunal seemed to waver, and the inevitable word sprang in Rahoul's mind, his eyes filling with

35

concern. But Kunal said, "Live. We do not fear to live—dangerously."

That explained Kunal. He was, Rahoul knew, no opportunist—he had thrown up a safe permanent post for the perils of the battlefield and the uncertainty of an emergency commission. And the boy was not conceited, either: he wouldn't decorate his personal conduct with a colour-wash of social value. But he had over-simplified his problem, pondered Rahoul. It was as though he thought of war as cricket. War was mass murder. You could commit yourself to mass murder with a clear conscience only when you were convinced that you would be ridding the world of some evil pest. In the name of humanity Kunal and others of his generation were called upon to fight the pest in Europe. But the champions of freedom abroad were the eaters of freedom in this land. Kunal seemed insensitive to that side of the picture. He would be learning the game of war, and the experience would be worth while, for him, for his generation, for his race. That was enough. Kunal felt easy in his heart.

Not Rahoul, though. The misgivings that had preoccupied him often these days held him again as he stepped into the crowded double-decker and found a seat. If he could brusquely eschew the War as nothing but an imperialist adventure his problem would be ended. Was it not likely that the War would yet break out of bounds and give reality to the professed aims of false-hearted politicians, creating out of a world in ruins a new enlightened world order? His countrymen could not surely be detached onlookers of that historic process, which, as it developed, must draw all enslaved nations into its orbit?

That was Rahoul's dilemma. That was the dilemma of the national movement. That was the dilemma of every thinking Indian.

The national movement was harassed about England's war situation. Its fight was with England's diehard rulers, not with her people, who, defeated, would face enslavement, adding to the miseries of humankind. The national movement offered co-operation, pledging its full strength to the war effort, in return for recognition of the Indian people's right to freedom. Authority scorned the idea, hating to part with power, and it promptly answered by clapping into prison a great figure in the national movement who had decried the attempt to drag his people into a war that was none of their seeking, as though they were the humblest of slaves.

Rahoul was unhappy. That leader had often expressed Rahoul's own thoughts in words and images more beautiful and forceful than he himself could devise. Rahoul was no hero-worshipper. His ideas had been shaped on the anvil of reason, and emotion had no visible place in the process. Yet that one personage whom India knew to be her man of destiny stirred his depths—was it because (Rahoul had asked himself, wonderingly) he seemed so warmly human, even as he wrote and spoke and acted with relentless logic?

Rahoul tried to see a prison. He had no material with which to build his mental picture save the big, iron-barred gates and the long stretch of drab, towering walls which he had seen unseeingly from the street in Alipore as he drove past in his car. Odd that a noble-hearted person who had reached the peak of civilization and culture must share the grim lot of thieves, gangsters, cut-throats, for the sole crime of speaking out his true faith in democracy! And—the bitter mockery!—the prison warder was one who was pouring out his own people's life-blood in a struggle to rescue democracy from its chains!

Kunal nudged at his brother from a back seat. "Not getting down?"

The bus had stopped near the college. Rahoul hurried to his feet. "I thought you were out for a hair-cut, Kunal. You should have got down at Chowringhee."

"I have something better to do," said Kunal, glumly running his fingers through his hair. The way it grew! It was a bother, a hair-cut, needing much patience. To sit still, draped in a sheet, while the barber-fellow did things to your head! Kunal had decided to postpone the ordeal.

Prokash, the research student who worked under Rahoul, was already in the laboratory, fixing up apparatus. Rahoul gave him a surprised glance as he walked to his desk. However early he might come, Prokash would be there, deep in work; however late he stayed, Prokash would be the last to leave. The boy seemed to have made the laboratory his home! Had he no other interest, none?

On his table lay some typed sheets under a marble paper-weight. Prokash had submitted notes for his perusal? No! His eyes widened. *Statement of Nehru at his trial in Gorakhpur Prison.* Banned, it had not appeared in the papers. But the words of Nehru had found wings. They were everywhere, spreading from town to town. Rahoul had been eager to see the statement. Here it was, in cyclostyle, on his table. Rahoul turned

37

his head, his eyes intent on Prokash. Unconcerned, absorbed in work. Rahoul smiled. He did have other interests, that boy. None but he could have placed this paper on his table. Rahoul picked it up, reading swiftly with breathless interest, and then, the second time, slowly, pondering over words, images.

"I stand before you, sir, as an individual being tried for certain offences against the State. You are a symbol of that State. But I am something more than an individual also: I too am a symbol at the present moment, a symbol of Indian nationalism, resolved to break away from the British Empire and achieve the independence of India. It is not me that you are seeking to judge and condemn, but rather the hundreds of millions of the people of India, and that is a large task even for a proud Empire. Perhaps it may be that, although I am standing before you on my trial, it is the British Empire itself that is on its trial before the bar of the world. There are more powerful forces at work to-day than courts of law; there are elemental urges of freedom and food and security which are moving vast masses of people . . ."

He read with a strange mounting excitement he had not felt since the trial of Dimitrov. His heart was beating fast, a flush spreading to his ears. Something in him, deep and vital and suppressed, had found sudden release, as though by the lifting of a lid. And in that instant he was not a scientist in his laboratory, but a prisoner at the bar, and he, the prisoner, was calling to trial at the bar of world opinion his proud accuser, the mediæval-minded Empire. He was filled with an exaltation that made his breath quicken. . . . The strange mood held him for a minute, then drained off, and he felt restive, desolate.
"Sir——"
Prokash stood by the table. He needed advice on some detail of his experiment. Rahoul gazed at him in a blank way.
"Prokash," the irrelevant question slipped out, "have you seen a jail-house?"
"Why, sir, of course." Prokash gave him a quick glance. "So many times I have gone to Alipore Prison to see my father—four years he has been there." The young face saddened. "He can't stand it any more. He has a lung disease. Still one more year to serve."
Rahoul stared at him. "What has he done?"
The youth looked down at the typed paper on the table, and his eyes glinted for an instant. "He loves his country."

"And you? Prokash——" Rahoul seemed to be straining for words.

Prokash stood silent, his face intent, waiting, and he said, "I?"

"You do not fear to go to jail, Prokash?"

The answer came swiftly. "Yes, and no. You see, sir, I have to support my mother and a widowed sister with children. There's my research grant, and I have taken up private tuition. If I go, my dependants will starve. Otherwise——"

Breadwinner, at his age! All day he was in the laboratory. Evenings, too, had to work coaching pupils? A question echoed itself in Rahoul's mind: Have you ever done good to anybody? Unaware, he had done good to this one person. Prokash had won the grant on his recommendation. No favouritism, that. Prokash, if only he had the chance, would do valuable work in his field, so Rahoul believed. If only he had the chance! Rahoul, in a muse, pursed his mouth sadly. A consumptive father. A large family to support. The daily grind of tuition. The grant would run for only two years. Then Prokash, with his first-class M.Sc. and research experience, must look for work in a college, but he would not succeed —the police would see to that. A political suspect would make a dangerous teacher. And Prokash, with his brilliant mind and unfulfilled dream, would be struggling to secure a post, any post, and at last, with some luck, he might get a petty clerkship somewhere—keeping the ledgers or selling postage stamps. What more could one hope for with the police at one's heels and no man with pull for a father or uncle or father-in-law? He would be crushed quickly on the wheel of hopelessness and miserable living. Yes, a typical bit of India was he, Prokash.

"Otherwise, sir," Prokash was now adding after a silence, "when my time is up I shall not fear to go the way"—his glance touched the cycloscript with a kind of caress—"those others have gone. After all, we are all in a vast prison, the four hundred millions of us. What matter if a few hundred thousand have to be in a prison within a prison?"

Prokash moved off to his table, limping as he walked. Rahoul felt a new personal interest in his pupil, and asked a question he had withheld before.

"What happened to your ankle, Prokash?" he said, tenderness rich in his heart, for it was as though Prokash, brave soldier of the national movement, was his friend, his comrade, his brother.

Prokash looked back with a start. "My ankle?" His answer

was reluctant. "Oh! I was at a meeting. The police made a *lathi* charge."

And the gentle, quiet-eyed boy plunged into his notes, hurrying as if he had to make up for wasted time, eager to discuss with his teacher the physical nature of little-known beams hurtling from star to star.

But Rahoul was withdrawn in thought. The work that ever fascinated his mind ceased to interest him to-day. Grim, tall walls loomed ahead, the outer shell of man-made hell, blackening the beams of stars. His eyes were torn from a far vision to a vision near:

"It is a small matter to me what happens to me in this trial or subsequently. Individuals count for little; they come and go, as I shall go when my time is up. Seven times I have been tried and convicted by British authority in India, and many years of my life lie buried within prison walls. An eighth time or a ninth, and a few more years, make little difference.

"But it is no small matter what happens to India and her millions of sons and daughters. . . ."

That was that. The voiceless millions yoked to their master's ruthless will. You had only to claim for them the elementary rights of man, and you would be paying with all you held dear in life. Snatched from those you loved and needed. Snatched from your work. Swallowed up without trial in man-made hell. An evil stench struck the air—prison latrine. He sniffed the foulness out of his nostrils, he lighted a cigarette, drawing the smoke deep into his throat.

He tried to quieten his mind with work. He recalled, too, that he was taking Monju out that night to the *Great Eastern* for dinner and dancing. He loved Western dancing, and Monju, to please him, had learnt the steps. This would be her first dance in public. She was excited, alarmed. She had shown him the *sari* she would wear for the occasion: mauve crepe with broad gold-thread border, sleeveless brocade blouse. And he would be in his smart dinner-jacket cut by a London tailor—it suited him well, so Monju said. Good food, good music, good company—he loved all that. He was no ascetic. He loved the good things of life.

But the thought beneath all thoughts pounded in his head: How does one grow unafraid of suffering, like Prokash?

Monju alighted from the car.

"One minute," said Rahoul, pressing his foot on the accelerator, driving off to the car-park.

Monju stood forlorn in the hall when he returned. Her cheeks were flushed.

"I hated to be left alone," she said. "Next time we'll come in a taxi. You know what happened?" Her eyes were wide.

"What happened?" He edged nearer, full of concern.

"A man—an English soldier"—Monju gulped—"he winked at me, like this——" Monju snapped an eye.

Rahoul waited. "He spoke to you?"

"No. I turned my face. He passed on."

"That was all?" Rahoul was laughing.

They walked along the carpeted corridor.

Monju was angry. "Yes, that was all. You seem to be amused. I think you'd have liked it if the fellow had spoken to me."

Rahoul teased her. "Why, I have winked at scores of girls—in England. I can't grumble if a chap out from England winks at my lovely wife in return for my compliment to his sister or sweetheart!"

"You've done a lot more than winking over there—I am sure of that. But I am a Hindu woman. I hate to be winked at by anybody, not to speak of a stranger."

The music was in full swing when they reached their table. In a moment Monju forgot her grievance. She caught the rhythm, watching the steps of the dancers, while Rahoul ordered the meal.

He would make his evening out a release from the struggle that had possessed his mind all day. He would enjoy himself. The familiar music pleased him. The brandy he sipped coursed down his throat in waves of warmth. His feet fretted for rhythmic movement. "Dance, Monju?" he said in a while, for a quickstep was now on, and Monju could do it well.

But Monju shook her head, murmuring, "Not yet." Her eyes were bright, excited.

"That girl can't dance." She spoke of one gliding close by their table.

And Rahoul, to make her feel at ease with herself, shook his head: "She can't."

"Want that young thing for your partner?" A suppressed laugh on her lips, she indicated with her eye a short, fat woman with stubby legs, whose protruding buttocks made wistful response to the swift rhythm of her steps.

"Look!" she breathed in a minute. "Can you beat that?" Her lips, softly red, were amused again and laughing.

Rahoul cast his glance about.

"You don't see her? Madame Bare-back! The woman with her back completely bare. A Hindu woman—so unabashed!"

She was tall and well-built, with black bobbed hair and scarlet mouth, and she was swathed in scarlet silk from throat to ankle. She wore her *sari* in a way that left her arms and shoulders bare, and her blouse had a long V-cut slanting over the curves of her breasts to the hollow between them, with a longer V-cut at the back, leaving a wider stretch of white, smooth skin naked. Vivacity flowed from her as she danced nimble-footed as a fawn.

"Oh, that one? I know her. A curious story. Her husband is a colleague of mine. Not my own department. Chemistry. A timid, old-fashioned wisp of a man, years older than his wife and barely half her size. He loves her madly, so I have heard, and all his existence centres round that woman. He allows her every freedom. You can see how she uses that freedom!"

"She has such a white back—white as lime-plaster. Beside her I am a darkie."

"She is enamelled all over—the visible parts of her, anyhow." Monju gave him a glance from the corner of her eye.

"Uh-huh! You know much about her, it seems."

"She comes to the College now and then to see her husband. Then she is not so heavily painted. I have met her. She would hardly be anxious to know me in this crowd, though."

"Why not?"

"Position. Social status. She goes about with high officials. She is swallowed up in her social snobbery."

Monju looked amazed. "You hold a high place in the University. A distinguished scientist. You——"

"I am only a teacher. Not in the Imperial Service. She and her kind love everything Imperial. The rest of the world is common. She is a slave inside, poor woman."

Monju in a muse ate her fish. "No wonder she goes about with her back all bare!" was her meaningless comment.

"Our new life, still caught in the age-old slavery, is half progress, half decadence," said her husband.

"I wish I knew how to whiten my face like her——" said Monju, still in a muse.

42

"Monju, why should you whiten your face? I like you just as you are. You have a lovely complexion."

"You think so? With your background?"

"What background, Monju?"

"All the white girls you winked at!"

"They don't count. You are as pretty as the prettiest of them."

"Liar!" she said, but her heart was joyous.

The band now struck up a quickstep again. She put down her knife and fork on the plate and leaned over the table, and in a whisper said, "Shall we?"

Then he was leading her on the floor, and her face was pale, her feet dragging; but as they went round the floor and passed their table, and she saw the chair with her bag on it and the fork aslant on her fish, she was strengthened, the self-awareness dropping from her mind, the stiffness from her limbs.

She thought it was great fun.

She danced with her inherent easy grace of movement, and looking in her eyes, black and large and edged with collyrium, he saw them brighten with jubilation. It was a dream fulfilled. And the jubilation of her flowed into him like a current. The new perfume she used, soft and exciting, cool and warming, caught a fresh meaning—it was the very perfume of her person attuned to the mood of this moment. It was as though a great perfumer had studied her in this mood and then in the perfume he had created for her had given her expression.

In the lit pool of her enjoyment he abandoned himself.

Yet, for a fleeting instant, while his feet moved with the music, he was not dancing on the polished floor with a lovely woman in his arms, but stood a lone prisoner at the bar, and he, the accused, was the accuser: There are elemental urges of freedom and food and security which are moving vast masses of people——

It was only a fleeting instant.

Later, at the table, braised duck in his mouth, a thought crept to his mind: What sort of food had convicts to eat? And he fled from the thought and ate his duck.

His knees touched hers under the table, and he felt an instant thrill of delight, and, with a hunger for more, he let his knee caress hers again. She turned her head, unaware of what he felt, yet, with a woman's instinct, she knew he was upset (Kunal would be going away to war in a few days), and made instant response, reaching out under the table, gently touching him, and gratefully he took her hand in his fist. And it was as though that slim, soft hand, a folded lotus in his firm grip, was his defence from some elemental urge with its trailing shadow of a grim threat——

As he drove back home he drew Monju close to him, closer, and she edged contented against his ribs, laying her sleepy head on his shoulder, and so he drove slowly into the night. And the thought was beating in her heart: not for a day would she be parted from him, not for a day, ever——

Baby slept in her cot. He bent and took her in his arms.

"She'll wake up," Monju in a whisper warned, but he, unheeding, fondled the little one and gently touched her hair and her cheeks, and for a long moment he held her pressed against his bosom, as though he would not be wrenched from her, as though he found in her a second line of defence.

Cambridge, too, came presently to his aid. The mail next morning brought a letter from his professor at the old University, a physicist of international fame, a winner of the Nobel Prize—to him Rahoul had submitted a paper on the nature of cosmic radiation. The professor was deeply impressed by his work, so he said, and he offered to get the thesis published in *Science*. The future of mankind was bound up with the harnessing of new sources of energy, and one such source was the cosmic ray proceeding from the stars and continually bombarding the earth. Rahoul had a vast field of research, and the famous professor expressed his firm faith in his former pupil. Cambridge, he said, would offer him a Fellowship, though it would take some time on technical grounds.

Rahoul felt elated. He began to work very hard in the laboratory. He was resolved to make a great contribution to science.

And the days ran on, the weeks, the months. The national movement still stood inactive, uncertain which way to turn. *It will be an infinite tragedy if even this terrible war is carried on in the spirit of imperialism for the purpose of retaining this structure which is itself the cause of war and human degradation.* So it said, and yet it looked forward with hope *not to a victory of one people over another or to a dictated peace, but to a victory of real democracy for all the people of all countries.* There was no call, therefore, for an immediate struggle. The national movement would not hurt Britain in the grave hour of trial. That would not be *ahimsa*—true non-violence. The national movement had more morality than strategy.

44

Rahoul, too, caught that mood. He felt free from emotional strains. Suffering did not come easily to him, as it did to some persons, and his mind was not attuned to self-denial. But more vital was the fact that the urge of those days had not force enough to effect the necessary inward preparation. Prokash, an emblem of that urge, shrank into a mere pupil, not a comrade, not a brother.

The emergence of the Soviet Union in the field of battle reconciled him all the more to his country's half-hearted line-up in the War effort. The War would, after all, receive a new orientation. Whitehall, tied to the Kremlin by the chain of necessity, must now use a propaganda idiom which suited its need, one which at heart it surely abhorred. History, he told himself with an amused grin—history has recorded the tales of many strange bed-fellows, but of none stranger than Churchill–Stalin.

Out of the Atlantic rises the Charter of world freedom!

They, the rulers of half humankind, *respect the rights of all people to choose the form of government under which they live; and they wish to see sovereign rights and self-government restored to those who have been forcibly deprived.* Explosive talk! What of the sword hung bare athwart India? We have conquered our Indian Empire by the sword, and by the sword shall we hold it—what of that other talk? . . . *In the process of working and fighting for victory, we must never permit ourselves to forget the goal which is beyond victory. . . . We plan now for the better world we aim to build.*

The Rights of Man. The Four Freedoms. Shall the new world order yet prepare a hammer stroke, that is not words alone, to break the shackles of the old?

CHAPTER VI

THE SUMMER sky had cast off its glitter, cool winds from the Bay washed the pre-twilight hour, yet the two men had sweat on their chests. Their breath came fast. For the heavy fishing-boat driven by their two oars had sped fast down the winding length of the stream. Two oars had done the toil of four.

"Fear is left far back," said Kanu, wiping his bare chest with the corner of his *dhoti*. "A little way to go—a bare hundred oar-strokes. That thicket at the water's bend. A good spot. The boat will have a safe hiding."

"Take it easy, Kanu *bhai*," said the young fisherman, his

companion, with relief in his panting breath. "Let the boat drift."

The boat moved slowly down the creek as it ran inshore, farther and farther from the net of peril.

The battle fleet of Japan ruled the waves of the Bay. That was the great peril. The wide-thrusting bosom of Bengal lay bared to the sea, unguarded. The enemy might make landings. What then? Scorched earth, was the firm answer of tight-lipped authority. The thousand-mile stretch of land in the lower reaches of Bengal rivers would have to be scorched. You started with the lines of communication—the boats. In this riverine land boats were bullock-cart, motor-truck, goods-train—all in one. Without boats the enemy would be bogged, helpless.

Seize the river-craft. Destroy the river-craft. Bring away the big ones.

So into the village of Baruni, as into five hundred others, the boat-wreckers had come, agents of the rulers, with soldiers to help them. Fifty boats they had seized, but a few were missing. Runaways! The boat-wreckers carried a typed list for each village. Bengal's rulers did their job well.

It was no act of tyranny, no forced forfeiture. The owners of boats were compensated. The agents carried fat bags of money. But the ignorant fishermen became grumpy, not knowing what was good for them. If the Japs came, would they pay for the boats? And surely fishermen, too, owed a duty to the State as it stood faced by the great peril?

The fishermen, benighted folk, behaved as though the boat-wreckers were the greater peril!

The work was nearly finished. The captured craft lay piled in big dumps on the river-bank. But the five absconding ones?

Kanu had rushed to help his friend, the fisherman. In the lessening sun they had moved the boat from place to place along the criss-cross of channels, fleeing from the foe, evading capture. Now it was near dusk. At daybreak the boat-wreckers would be gone. The fugitive's life would be saved.

Kanu, the lanky peasant lad, had developed fast in these years, growing to the height of his tall father, with hair thickening darkly on his upper lip.

"Who may they be—Japanee folk?" asked the fisherman, wondering in his heart. A week before few in the village had heard that bogey word; now it was buzzing night and day in their ears.

"Aliens," said Kanu, and made a face. "Aliens all—Engraze and German and Chinee and Japanee."

"And Iranee and Turanee and Armenee," the fisherman contributed the names he knew. "Aliens all. Why don't they keep to their own hearth? What madness calls them across the seven black-waters to the homes of harmless folk whose door-sills they darken?"

"Greed," said Kanu, with a click of his tongue—"the big greed in the belly. They are out to get rich, more rich. And how may they get rich, more rich, if they do not grab and make other folk poor, more poor? It is like this: you fishermen have boats—each household has one. And there is the river a-swell with fish. A fellow armed like a rogue comes and grabs your boats—all. Then he alone can get the fish, no other but he; for your tools of trade are lost. The fellow speaks to you then, as though out of his heart's goodness: 'Folk, you catch the fish for me, and out of every ten you get you will have one.' You are helpless, you reach out your hands for mercy. The boat is yours, yet not yours, the labour is yours, yet not yours; the river is the good mother of all, yet for every fish caught nine go to the big man, and you get one, and for twenty fisher-folk each with one fish in his basket the big man has nine times twenty. You see the trick?"

Yes, the fisherman saw it, even if dimly. "Nine times twenty," he echoed, dizzied by the arithmetic.

The fisherman passed his hands over his boat as if he fondled it.

"What peril!" he muttered. "Worries plenty we have. Hunger and a hundred pains. And from cool stars flame pours! What could I have done without you to help me, Kanu *bhai*?" He paused, resuming in a moment: "Boats. Boats are the limbs of us folk. They are our legs, for without them we are lamed, we cannot move over the river highways from village to village or from islet to islet. They are our arms, for with them we reap the fish; and some fish we eat and some we give for rice and salt and things on offer at the market-place. Boats are more than limbs for us folk: they are our blood and bone and heart and soul and all." And his hands passed over the boat again as if he fondled it.

"It is as though the fish hide your naked body," said Kanu, nodding. "No fish, no clothes for you—you go naked."

"It is as though the fish light our huts," said the fisher-man. "No fish, no bean-oil for the wicks of our lamps; there is darkness upon darkness."

"Darkness," Kanu nodded agreement again. "Darkness, too, for the peasant folk. With no boats, how shall we move harvests up-river to the market-place? And the islets in the river, *han*? The islets become water-bound prisons." He clicked his tongue and shook his head sadly as he picked up the oar to guide the boat to the approaching thicket.

They jumped down in the shallow water. Now was the hardest task of all. They must drag the boat up as far as they could to screen it with the deep, overhanging shadow of bamboo and brushwood. Sun-warmed water rose to their waists and pried in their loin-clothes.

"Push—drag! Push—drag! Hein-o-o!" Their arms strained in unison.

"Save your breath," said a voice.

A man emerged from behind the thicket. Another man came forward—a soldier in khaki uniform, rifle in hand.

"I have been watching you, following you," said the boat-wrecker. "I have eyes that see afar." He patted his binoculars.

The fisherman was struck dumb by the catastrophe. The blood beat in his temples, the eyes bulged from his head. When he regained his voice he burst out in a pathetic wail: "Do not take my boat, master. You have taken all. Spare this one, master."

"We have orders. We do as we are bid. Why blame us? We have orders."

"Master, how may we live with no boats? What the plough-and-kine is to the peasant, the boat is to the fisher-folk. Better kill us all. Master——" The strangled sob in the voice froze as he felt his friend grip his arm and heard his tense murmur:

"Why speak? What use? Trees and rocks have a heart. Not men. Why speak?"

The boat-wrecker made a gesture of impatience.

"The same talk! Our ears are brimful. *Aré*, why this fuss? It's not as though we are taking your royal treasure for nothing. You get your value—the right market price. The Gorement are just and bounteous—they are your *ma-bap* [mother-father]; that you know. The money will see you through for a long time, don't you understand? You will sit at home like a lord and eat the good rice of ease and sleep a-plenty and speak the name of Hari and be happy. All for a few planks of water-eaten timber."

"Money is a winged bird. It will fly off. What then? Master——"

"What if the Japanee come? They will grab all you have, and not a *pice* in compensation. The Gorement takes your boat and gives you money, and save you from the monsters out there on the sea—the dread Japanee!"

"The boat is all we have. All. What more can the Japanee take from us save our life-breath? Master——"

The boat-wrecker silenced the importunate man.

"Enough. We have no spare time to throw away in *khitir-mitir*." With cautious steps, with his long *dhoti* drawn up to his hips, he climbed into the boat. His men pushed it into the stream, and they climbed in and took the oars.

"Come along," cried the boat-wrecker. "Your blood money!" He held up his bag with a swagger.

As the boat plied back the way it had come, the boat-wrecker handed money to the fisherman. "Look! No paper notes that get soiled and torn, all bright silver. Feed your eyes on the shine. What luck for you that Gorement is so bounteous to you, undeserving ones. Two *rupees* I have deducted as my commission—that is the custom. Now for your thumb-mark on this I-have-received paper."

The fisherman yielded his thumb and let its mark be pressed on the paper, but he seemed sunk in a daze. Once in a while his hands passed over the smooth wood of his boat as if he caressed it, and his dry lips muttered softly and piteously, "My boat! My boat!"

Kanu grieved for his friend. Barely a month had passed since the day of the young fisherman's marriage, when, overmuch joy in his heart, he had given a gift of fish—a *seer's* weight —to every peasant household in the village. No one had ever heard of such extravagance in the past hundred years, but the fisherman had won the girl on whom his soul was set, and because of his fulfilment he had taken his boat on the river for long hours, day after day, and made a big fish-harvest and, poor as he was, he had made his gifts of fish to his peasant brethren; and though some men might have laughed in private, Kanu had understood his friend's tender sentiment.

And Kanu hung his head and hummed a folk-song to himself because of the heavy sadness in his heart:

> Make a hymn, make a hymn!
> As stars and moon and sun make the hymn of light,
> As flowers make the hymn of hue,
> As birds make the hymn of melody,
> Spirit mine, make a hymn, make a hymn!

49

The huddle of captured boats lay ahead, dark shapes in the deep dusk. The fisherman made a last desperate protest in a voice hoarse with pain. "Must there be such dark tyranny in the reign of the great English *Kompanee Bahadur*, and no justice —none?"

The soldier in khaki uniform, who had sat silent all this while, calmly biting the droop of his moustache-end, now spoke. An up-country peasant, he had served twenty years in the Army and earned a stripe. It amused him that people in this far part of Hindusthan still believed they were ruled by the old East India Company, who had taken the country from Hindu and Muslim rulers.

"*Aré!* You are truly such an ignoramus? The kompanee was gone long ago. This is the rule of Victoria Queen. You folk live far from To-day in the dark pit of Yesterday."

Kanu gave him a scornful stare. The seething fury in him found sharp expression.

"Victoria Queen died years ago. This is the rule of her son's grandson."

Even in his burning agony the fisherman felt his heart swell with pride because of Kanu's knowledge, and it was like a balm on his wound that the audacious soldier with gun and fancy-cloth garb was humiliated.

"Young people must prattle," said the soldier, with a burst of loud, scoffing laughter.

"Facts of past ages are not a matter of shots and shells," Kanu flung back, bitter, and felt a keen satisfaction as he saw the meaning of his remark break through the surface crust of the soldier's thick mind. He grew bold, reckless. "No, knowledge is not a matter of 'Left-Right! Left-Right!'" He tapped his legs on the boat floor in mocking mimicry, then turned swiftly to his friend. "Brother, you have money tucked in your *dhoti's* waist-fold. Cast a look at the silver faces. Whose image do you see? Look. . . . There!"—he resumed as the fisherman unfolded his waist-cloth and peered at the coins—"Victoria Queen's on the old ones, but—the new shiny *rupees*?"

"Mother Victoria may not reign, but she *rules*," the soldier said in a shout. His face was flushed with anger, his thick moustache bristled. "It is the rule of her good old laws. Whoever reigns, those laws remain changeless; like the sun and the stars, they last for ever and ever."

Kanu was silenced, but the anxious fisherman hurried to lend his friend support as best he could: "It is still the rule of the great Kompanee Bahadur—who can deny that with tall talk?" His ideas were a muddle, his voice thick and lifeless. How he hated the one in fancy-cloth garb who gave himself airs as though he was the *Magister* of the district—no, the *Lat*, Governor, of the province!

Make a hymn . . . make a hymn . . . !

The boats lay in piles, broken up and heaped, and round each pile was a group of men and women, faces bent with heavy sorrow, eyes intense. All the fisher-folk had come to the spot. The boat-wreckers had put up for sale the fragments of boats, to be used as firewood. The rate was low, nominal, but there had been no offer from a single fisherman, not even from a peasant. The peasants would not have the wreckage of fishermen's lives, as it were, to light their kitchen fires. Not a scrap of wood had found a buyer. So the boat-wreckers had fetched cans of petrol from their motor-launch and poured it on the piles, and now, in the sacred cowdust hour, when the air was heavy with dust from the hooves of cattle returning from their graze and the sky echoed with the auspicious *oom-oom* of conch-shells greeting the dusk goddess, the good wood of fishermen's boats threw up a blaze.

"My boat! My boat!" the men cried in a murmur, with faces bent; but the women gazed hard and long at the funeral pyres, and their black eyes glinted with the rising, tossing flames, and they spoke under their breath:

"We curse you. We curse your dear ones. We curse your butcher masters. May you, too, burn like that; *nah*, may you, too, and your masters stand by and see your lives burn like that. We curse you all."

As the blaze died down and the boat-wreckers moved off in their motor-launch, the fisher-folk stepped to the burnt wreck-age, and each man picked up a handful of hot cinders and tied it to the corner of his *dhoti*. Then down the midnight path they walked back in utter silence, their heads bent, their bodies and souls burnt and destroyed.

But the end of one tale was the beginning of another. For, like a quenchless heritage of hate, the bonfire of boats was prisoned and ever-alive in each fistful of ash.

. . . . . .

It was in those hectic days, with the shadow of the foe deepen-ing from the Bay, that Girish, the grocer of Baruni village, found a wondrous lamp with which to light his way to wealth.

51

The grocery was like others of its kind, a petty affair, a cottage with two living-rooms and a front room fitted with shelves and turned into a store. Stacked on the shelves were bags of cereals, some salt, country tobacco, cans of mustard-oil and bean-oil, and various city goods—grain-bags, tin lamps, kerosene, brass utensils, cheap hardware. The peasants could not always buy or sell at the Saturday *haat* in the market village miles away on the river-bank, an outlet for the produce of five villages around. For centuries the grocery store had been a link between the peasant and the market-place.

But Girish was no chip of the age-old block of his forebears, who had pursued the calling contentedly, happy to make a subsistence. He had an itch to get on in the world. A man of ambition; an augury of the new times! He had saved some money, and this he loaned to needy peasants. He loaned rice, too, and goods from the store. Interest mounted on interest. Yearly his capital grew.

"A rice-grain saved is a rice-grain trebled," Girish had often said bluntly to his wife. "If we eat less to-day, to-morrow we shall have our bellyful and some more. That 'some more' will become a gold ring in your nostril, bangles for your arms, a cow, a room added to the house, a ricefield, why"—the voice dropped a tone—"even a store in the district town!"

A store in town—what an achievement! His eyes glistened with his vision. And Girish denied himself and his kin, reducing their mouthfuls, offering them vision in lieu of grain.

It was a remote vision, all the same, never perhaps to be fulfilled, even in his old age, even after life-long self-denial, unless a miracle happened. And suddenly it looked as though the miracle was round the river-bend!

The boats were gone. The village was crippled. Then Girish had dreamed of a boat for himself. He alone would have a boat, none else. He would command the transport of all the rice grown in the Baruni fields. He could pay his own rate— with no boats, how would the peasants market their surplus grain? It was not enough for a man to eat. He had to clothe his body. He had to buy other necessities. He had to perform rites and meet social obligations. He had to make offerings to his gods. And—why, above all he had to pay his rent to the *zemindar* in hard cash. Girish would pile up the stocks of grain in his boat, carry them to the market-place up-river, back and forth, back and forth, and sell all at a big margin of profit. That would be real high-class trade, and not this petty grocer's business of selling a half-*seer* of gram to this peasant and a *pice*-worth of bean-oil to that.

Girish had heaved a deep sigh of dismay. He could get a boat built with his savings, but Authority would know in an eye-flick and the boat would go the way of others—burnt, sunk or taken away. No, it was not for Girish, a worm of a grocer, to win the monopoly of food transport in the village.

Then one day a heavy blow had befallen him. Other agents of the Government had arrived, and had visited his store and weighed his bags of cereals and listed them in a book. They would buy half his stocks, they had said. The village people were allowed just enough to last them till the new harvest—the rest they must sell. That was an order. Thousands of *maunds* would be gone from the village at one sweep. Later the price would surely rise—with his flair for business, Girish could see that. But his luck was out—he would have little to sell when the market soared.

Big news had raced that day from mouth to mouth: under the aged banyan stands the wonder of wonders! All the village had flocked to the tree. A jeep stood parked in the shade, and around it was a display of pictorial posters. As the crowd assembled, a big voice started to boom from the jeep fitted with a loudspeaker. It addressed the village folk as brethren, and spoke of the dread foe approaching nearer, nearer every day. The barbarians thirsted for blood. They practised shooting at human targets. They bayoneted little children, the manacled parents looking on. They brought pollution on the wives and maidens, dooming them in this life and in lives to come. The belly sickened at the fearful tales! Burma had fallen. The British General, Alexander, was making a wonderful retreat through vast trackless jungle. Bengal would become a front line of battle if the enemy, choosing to strike at the rear of the defences, came by sea and made landings—they might land on the estuary barely three days' cart-ride from this village banyan. In that event the barbarians must be harassed at every step. That was, brethren, why the boats had been scorched. It was not enough, though. Food had to be scorched. The peasants would get a fair price for the stocks they sold to the Government. Understand? If the Japs came, they would not pay for the food, they would loot all they needed. You wouldn't, dear brother cultivators, have the greedy demons eat up the golden grain you raised with the sweat of your brow and the blessings of mother Earth?

The pictorial posters served to illustrate the theme. They showed the Japs committing atrocities, and the poster drove home the point with the caption: *Your property is valuable to you, isn't it? The soil of India is rich, isn't it? Your wife is beautiful.* A man from the city stood by the poster reading out the caption to the illiterate ones—his voice sounded like a challenge as he read the caption over and over again.

Yes, the Government did the good work with all its accustomed thoroughness.

Not that the village folk had much property to lose; not that their wives were always beautiful; not that the enemy could rob the soil of its richness. Yet in the simple hearts of peasants grim panic would be planted.

Farm doors would open, the big barge on the river would fill with rice, Girish knew, misery heaping in his heart. Never would he have a store in the district town. No gold would bedeck his wife's bare arms. No room would be added to his mud house. He was of the same commonplace clay as his father and grandfather, his life a drab copy of their lives. The defeat, the mockery, of such existence!

A city man came striding down the village path as Girish stood by his doorstep, gazing morosely towards the river.

"You have rice?" said the stranger, stopping, nodding his head in a friendly way.

"Grain by grain has it been weighed and reckoned up and placed in your book," Girish answered with heat. "Then why this new talk?" This man was the same agent, even if he had another face, another name.

"What book?" And the stranger walked into the store. His eyes prowled among the bags of cereals. He came out, lighted a cigarette and held out the packet to the grocer.

Girish concealed his amazement. He was a man of dignity. "*Gol Filik*," he said, with an approving nod, showing that he knew good cigarettes—he was no ignorant peasant. Once in every three months he went up to the district town to look round and get supplies—he was almost a city man. Why should he not share a good smoke with a stranger from the town?

"Those people who weighed up your grain—they are Government men. Nothing to do with me," said the man, the cigarette glowing at his mouth. "I belong to a Kompanee. We deal in rice. You are a grocer. You can help us."

Girish studied him curiously and shook his head. "How can

54

it be? What is a Kompanee beside a Goremen man? Those others will take all, fill their barge."

"A rat slips in through a doorway too narrow for the bulky elephant. I, too, have a barge on the river. The Law doesn't say that none but those people can buy." The agent paused, listening, as the boom through the loudspeaker came faintly from the distance. "You hear that? The elephant lays the road for a rat. There's an understanding between us——" A squinting look deep with meaning! "They will give me a chance. Look. You are a grocer. You know every man who owns a field, you know what quantity he can be made to sell. Get the rice. You will earn a commission. The more you buy, the more you earn. Pay in advance and buy up the crops to come, the winter harvest. Take all the funds you need . . ."

"Since you have blessed my hovel with the good dust of your feet, will you not sit down a moment and drink the cool water of a coconut?" Girish hurried to fetch a floor mat. He felt his moustache itch. What rate of commission would they pay him?

While Girish cut open the inner shell of the coconut, the city man talked. The Kompanee was going to have sub-agents in villages—one, say, in a group of five or ten. The sub-agents would work under a district agent—he was one. Over all the district agents was the chief agent at Calcutta, and he took his orders from the Kompanee's directors. Even the big *zemindars* would be drawn into the network of this great organization. There had been nothing like this in Bengal—ever.

"It would be the luck of your seven ancestors if you belonged to such a mighty machine," said the agent.

Girish was making rapid calculations. So much commission on each *maund*. On a hundred *maunds*. . . . On a thousand. . . . The yield of the next harvest. . . . Girish scratched his moustache because of his excitement.

And while in his mind he cast up the figures, he saw the arms of his wife bright with bangles, he saw his mud hut grow, he saw his city store crammed with stocks. The voice of the jeep, sounding nearer, distracted him for a moment. The jeep was touring the village, flooding it with its voice. And Girish had tears of joy in his eyes because of the sudden turn in his affairs, and he said to himself in a grave murmur: "There! Panic rides on rubber wheels! Truly does the mighty elephant lay the road for a humble rat!"

The storeman and the trader from the city had no inkling then that they would have to contend with the power of a word.

The word came, softly spoken, a mere murmur, but it rang louder far than the jeep's loudspeaker. Kanu straddled the russet milch-cow, Mangala, riding, yelling to the peasants who pushed ploughs in the summer sun, tossing the word from field to field.

"Devata spoke. 'Do not rush to sell your grain. Think it over.' So he spoke."

The word was a command.

Devata had pondered well before he reached that vital decision. True, the peasants had been offered a fair price, and they were tempted to sell off all surplus stocks. But what about the *kisans* who had no stocks at all? Where would they get their rice? And the fishermen, dispossessed of their boats? The artisans—the weaver who clothed Baruni, the blacksmith who forged ploughshares and sickles, the carpenter who chiselled the woodwork of ploughs and cartwheels? Devata was worried. If you let the rice above the growers' immediate needs be drained off, village economy would soon go to pieces.

Villages were going to pieces all around. Many had been taken over by the military authority as strategic bases to post troops, build airfields. The brick houses of the well-to-do had been rented, the mud huts of the poor purchased outright. The people had been cast out of their homes. How would they find new homes even with cash in their waist-cloth, the price of their ancestral roofs? And where find land for the plough, since the land, too, was gone? Cultivation would fall off, with so much land out of use. Parts of the coastal zone were being evacuated, lest the Japs should come and make use of the man-power at hand. Groups of the dispossessed were passing through Baruni, wandering about, men, women and children, with their cattle and possessions, homeless, aimless, dazed by the sudden evil turn in their fate. The cash they had been given in exchange for their life on the land—how long would it last? Food-grains they must buy anyhow. What if the growers of rice had nothing left to sell? The merchants who purchased to-day at a fair price—to-morrow, if there was a squeeze, what selling price would they impose? There was as yet no price control in Bengal—and battle rushing to its door! —no rationing, no way of honest distribution. The rulers with War in their heads could not worry about such trifles. And the third year of war was running its dismal course.

Devata stood on the ridge of his sunlit field and gazed across the ploughlands at the far curve of the sky, as though looking for some bitter cloud that might come upon his people.

They had scorched the boats. They had scorched the food. They would scorch the people. Devata feared for the people, who were the core of his being, his blood-and-bone.

CHAPTER VII

FOR TEN days the city was in the grip of revolt. A sudden thunderstorm on a dark, deadly gulf of Time! For at that moment the Jap stood firm on the doorstep of Bengal, poised for attack. The defences falling back, ever falling back. Would they pull out of Assam, pull out of Bengal? The national movement could no longer wait and watch the peril and mark time. And the word rang out: "A free India will throw all her great resources into the struggle against Fascism. . . . Free India will become an ally of the United Nations, sharing with them in the trials and tribulations. . . . Freedom will enable India to resist aggression effectively with the people's united will and strength behind it."

The historic *Quit India* Resolution!

"No future promises or guarantees can produce the needed psychological effect on the mind of the masses. Only the glow of freedom can release that energy and enthusiasm of millions of people which will immediately transform the nature of the War."

Alien authority would have as little truck with the national movement as with the Japs, for these two had the same purpose at heart—the end of the white man's Empire—even if one had a purpose within a purpose. The aliens would not arm India for defence and guerilla warfare, if need be, in the manner of China, Russia. Would the subject nation, once armed, ever again meekly bend itself to the old subjection? And the aliens could not let India's industries be geared to full production, even if arms and ships and ball-bearings were in desperately short supply—would the industries, once grown tall, ever lie low for the old economic set-up? Alien leadership, perched proudly on the debris of a dead century, would not win the war only to lose Empire.

The national movement "is anxious not to embarrass in any

way the defence of China or Russia, whose freedom is precious and must be preserved, or to jeopardize the defensive capacity of the United Nations. But the peril grows both to India and these nations. . . . Inaction is not only degrading India and reducing her capacity to resist aggression, but is no service to the peoples of the United Nations."

Lynx-eyed authority had watched every step of the national movement. All its competence through past decades had been sharpened for that one end. It had no strength to create values, but it could swiftly destroy them. If it lived in an old century, it used the tools of the new to destroy the new. It used science to smash science. It used thought to smash thoughts. And with a sudden surprise leap it took the national movement in hand-cuffs and chains.

Grim bureaucrats had prayed for this hour. To strike an avenging blow that the trouble-makers would never forget. The surprise they had planned was complete in its effect. Nehru to speak to the U.S.A. on an American radio link, waiting in his flat for the sponsors to come. The police came instead. Gandhi about to write a letter to His Excellency at New Delhi. He wrote it, a different letter, from prison. Black police-vans loaded full at one set hour in every city of India——

Then the people's revolt, unplanned, yet unsanctioned by the national movement. A swift flare-up of wrath against the despotism that had cast the people's leaders into prison. And Rahoul, like his people, had felt the flare-up in his blood. And events had snatched him along, forcing him in their frantic rush.

As he sat now at his desk at home on the third day of the raging storm, writing to Grandfather of his reactions at Baruni, his mind moved back to the huge demonstration of thousands passing down College Street. *Quit India!* the Voice flung out—and *Bandé Mataram!* [Hail, Mother!], the fighting challenge. Rahoul, watching from his laboratory window on the first floor, had seen a bigly-built European sergeant, pistol in hand, pounce upon the tricolour flag heading the procession and dash it underfoot, and as the youth who had been carrying it bent to win it back the sergeant charged him, kicking, trampling. Then other youths came forward, and yet others, armed with nothing but non-violence.

The police swung their *lathis* and cracked heads, and then they opened fire.

In that instant Rahoul lost himself. Emotion flooded up in him, and he turned and rushed out of the room, bounding

58

down the stair, and thrust his way through the jostle of the crowd, purposive, possessed by one thought: Hold up the flag. Nothing else seemed to matter. Five minutes before he, a calm scientist, could not have imagined himself in this picture. It was very strange.

The hard impact of a *lathi* on his leg, and as he crashed down two policemen took him by the arms, dragging him into the van. The leg burned like fire. And something deep within burned fiercer than fire.

His fellow-prisoners in the cell were students, young intellectuals. Some had seen Rahoul before, others knew him by name. They were deferential.

"Is it the hour at last?" eagerly they asked, and hung on his word.

That question had long harassed him. It had harassed all anti-fascist India and held back revolt. The War was one piece, indivisible, and India could not let the battle of China be lost on the Ganges earth. But then, freedom, too, was one piece and indivisible. Enslaved, enfeebled India would be a tiresome drag on world freedom.

"The hour is not just yet," he said, "but we are apart from it by a hair's-breadth. We must stand ready to carry out our leader's command: 'Do or die.' We must not let our strength run to waste."

He had spent the day in police custody. Just before sunset he was taken out in the black van, driven to the college gates and dropped on the street. Free!

He looked about, and saw a city scarred as though by battle. The streets were deserted save for men in uniform. Armoured cars dashed by. Troops stood at the street corner with a machine-gun. Burnt-out motor-trucks lay about in dead heaps. The wreckage of a tram-car was being towed off to clear the line.

Here he was, free, after a day in police custody. Had they set free all the prisoners? A rare gesture of goodwill? Unbelievable!

Later, he knew. Authority was bent on smashing every vestige of the movement which it had now outlawed. Authority was goading, provoking the movement so that, patience lost, it would expose itself, target for gunfire. The revelation was starker than ever before—authority's bitter hatred of the people on whose bones Empire had been built, great prosperity for the homeland secured.

He knew, too, why he was free. The Death-Ray! Father

59

had let fall a word in high places. His son, the brilliant scientist, was seeking to harness cosmic energy, and you could use that energy to run a railway train or destroy a hundred thousand enemy troops on the field—Father had figured it out that way, and Rahoul, when pressed for details, had said nothing to deny, nothing to affirm; he had only laughed.

Then one day Prokash had said, "They've set a spy on you, sir. He reads all your notes and copies them out."

Rahoul stared. "What for?"

Prokash did not know.

"Who is the man?" The voice came hard with anger.

"A student of yours. It wouldn't be fair if I told you his name. Please keep your eyes open, sir."

It was not long before Rahoul knew the spy.

What use were those notes to anyone? puzzled Rahoul. And his private correspondence with the Professor at Cambridge, since that, too, had interested the spy?

Then Prokash had said, "This fellow is on the pay-roll of the Special Branch."

Police spy! And in that instant his mind flashed its reaction: the Death-Ray!

"How flattering!" snapped Rahoul as he saw the shape of things and grinned. It felt good to be allotted such importance, so much more than his due!

But Prokash had a solemn air. "You must keep it up, sir. We'll do some fake notes. You are not far from the Death-Ray —a few more hurdles to cross."

"Why must I play false, Prokash?" asked Rahoul sharply, and they looked deep into each other, and Prokash lowered his voice and said:

"The tension grows. No one is safe in India. But the Ray will be your protection. There's no point in just being carried off to prison."

No point. That was why, months later, Prokash went underground at the break of the storm, two days before Rahoul made his first gesture of revolt.

"I have no mind to liquidate myself in prison. There's much work to be done." And Prokash went underground.

Rahoul sat at home, writing a letter, not knowing that Grandfather would never receive it. Terror stalked alike in city and village.

Little Khuku trotted in, nestling against Father, breaking into his thoughts.

"*Policewala* bad man, wild man, burnt-face ape." She exhausted her strong epithets on her enemy. Earlier in the day she had armed herself with a discarded Gillette blade and shouted a war-cry, but Monju had taken the blade away, and then Khuku had wept brokenly.

Rahoul smiled down at her. "Khuku will weep if *policewala* takes me away again?"

Her eyes blinked and she half-whispered, woeful, "Khuku weep." She was on the verge of tears.

Rahoul picked her up on his knees. She curved tiny arms about his neck and clung contented.

"The soul of a race, as the soul of a man, does not grow only in terms of time-space," wrote Rahoul. "Once in a while, through the catalysis of experience, it grows far more in moments than in years. This is such a moment of quick growing, and India after August will never be the India of before . . ."

The crack of a shot mingled with a groan, and Monju screaming from the balcony!

Rahoul sprang to his feet, rushing out, Khuku fear-dazed in his arms. "Monju, what is it?"

"Murder," she cried between deep breaths, her voice shrilling.

Monju had been leaning over the balcony rail, gazing down at the deserted street. The familiar figure of the lamp-lighter coming up with his bamboo step-ladder. This suburban street had still retained its gas-lamps, and the lamp-lighter would appear at the day's end, prop his ladder against the post standing close by the balcony and, reaching up, would light the gas. Even in to-day's turmoil he had not missed his round of duty. . . . A motor-cycle roars up the street. A police sergeant in a white uniform, a grey helmet of steel. He sees the man up on the gas-lamp. *Congresswala* destroying Government property. The sergeant pulls up in the instant of his thinking, draws his revolver and fires and races off.

Monju, lying on the balcony floor, was very still, frozen by the cold killing. A shot, a shriek, then silence.

"Ma!" wailed Khuku, snivelling, sick for the arms of Mother.

Senses dazed, the bark of the fire-arm fierce in her ears, Monju was filled with a vision.

"*Lamp-man, turn your lantern up this way, lamp-man . . .*"

Little Khuku, pressing her face to the grille of the balcony rail, peering out, begging for gas-light.

Queen-mother, the balcony is lit with your presence. What need of gas-light? No lamp has the joy of your face, queen-mother.

That was all. Just moments.

Odd that in this death-stained moment Monju had to see the lamp-lighter in the pallid setting of those trivial moments.

And growing possessed her, the alchemy that transmutes the metal of an individual or a race. Monju could never be her old self again.

.   .   .   .   .

Tucked deep among the banana fronds, the heavy-shadowed pool with its wide green moons of lotus leaves lay close to the dusty cartway that straggled off to the fields of corn and cut across them, then steadied itself and went ahead, companioned by the railway track. Kajoli, seated on a low, moss-grown stone step, her *sari* drawn over her legs as they lay plunged in water to the knees, her tear-streaked face cupped in her palms, now let her eyes brood over the pool, now lifted them, sick with concern, gazing afar through a clearing of the thickets to the road's dim end.

This way the village had gone hours before, three hundred men and a flag.

Kanu carried the flag. It was his flag. There were six holes in it—holes made by shots fired from a tiny gun.

The set faces. The shouted slogans. The hurried march up the roadway, like soldiers ready to make battle. In her heart Kajoli had known elation. She was not at all scared. Even earlier in the day, when long-barrelled rifles had barked together and the men of the village darted forward in angry defiance, Kajoli had not been scared. Only her heart had beaten so fast that it dizzied her.

A day before, an hour before, such happenings would have been unthinkable. Life in the village was calm, like the face of this lotus-pool. Who would fancy that the pool could heave in tall waves?

The tricolour flag, orange-white-green and a spinning-wheel, was his, Kanu's; but Kajoli had her part in its making, for both together had spun the cotton yarn for local weave. Then Kanu had gone to the market village for an *anna*-worth of dye, and returned with an excited face. "There is nothing in the *haat* save orange dye and green dye. No rice, no pulses, only dye. The whole world is out to buy the colouring. Scores of flags will rise in every village. But my flag"—he had stroked his chest with his fist like a braggart—"you will see."

62

And it was indeed a mighty flag.

Kajoli dressed herself gaily for the occasion. Under her white homespun *sari* with green border she wore an orange half-blouse. A living tricolour! But the half-blouse was tight on her figure because of her growing, and she hid herself with her *sari's* folds, heedful lest they be displaced, her eyes bending in a startled way lest her bosom showed unawarely.

The flag-salute ceremony under the aged banyan. Devata spoke the new mind, the new words, of the national movement. The village echoed those words, and she, Kajoli, stood beside her tall brother, her head reaching no higher than his chin, and she, too, echoed the words, for it was a business as much of the women as of the menfolk, so Devata said. The women stood apart in a group and made their *pronam* to the flag, but Kajoli stood beside her elder brother, with her eyes on Devata, who was close by, who passed a hand across his brow as though he was tired, very tired. He had not slept well? Kajoli, as she made her *pronam* to the flag, could not fix all her mind on the national movement, of which the tricolour was an emblem, even as an image of stone or wood was the emblem of a god, a goddess. Kajoli had an ache of worry on Devata's account. And what was wrong with it, since the movement, the flag, Devata—all were one? She would be true to the flag even unto death, solemnly cried her voice; she would not let Devata over-tire himself, tenderly cried her heart. Devata to others, *dadu* to her. While her eyes gazed at him and fretted, her lips smiled faintly with pride and softness.

The *Red Turbans* came early at dawn. A lorry-load. They forced Devata out of his sleep, put handcuffs round his wrists and searched the house all through, bundling up books and papers, slashing at the bed-mattress with bayonets as though to find some hiding sedition. Then they came to Kajoli's home and took her father, and Kajoli would have burst out crying, but her father gave her a calm glance and said: "Kajoli, you made your *pronam* to the flag; you are a fighter." And Kajoli squeezed back the heavy tears in her eyelids, pressing her teeth into her lower lip until they bit into the tender skin, for she was a fighter.

No one cried—not the mother, nor Kanu, nor even Onu, all having made their *pronam* to the flag; fighters all.

The village had heard the news in a flash, and now it stood gathered on the road up which the police van would pass. Hundreds of men, old and young. They shouted

63

in anger. They would rescue Devata. They came forward in a surge.

The *Red Turbans* fired a warning volley in the air. Their next shots would be aimed to kill. So they said.

The sudden thunder of fire stunned the men, but only for a moment. Then something snapped within them, some restraint. "*Kick out, kick out the Evil Thing,*" a big voice burst like a roar. "*Let them not touch our Devata. Kick out the Evil Thing.*" A shouting medley of voices lifted the cry, a banner of fury. In a split instant they, who were ever meek as lambs, became as lions. They dared the fire. They would fling back the Evil Thing even if they had to die. It was "Do or die".

Kajoli did not quite know how it happened that Devata stepped out of the van and stood in front of his captors and faced his people, and the wide sleeves of his tunic fell back as he held his long, handcuffed arms aloft. The surging crowd paused in wonderment. There was utter silence.

He stands there, the tall, white-clad figure with uplifted arms, and the pale silver of his hair and the pale silver of his flowing beard are touched with a light that is not of the sun alone.

"Friends and comrades, do not betray the flag. Do not betray yourselves. We stand or fall with our inmost faith: *ahimsa*. There is violence in your thoughts; that is evil enough. Do not make it worse by violence in action."

The men bend their heads. No one speaks, save for a murmur here and there that is soon hushed.

"Ours is the harder task. If we use the weapons of our enemy, we play into their hands. The supreme test has come. Be strong. Be true. Be deathless. *Bandé mataram!*"

He turns, he climbs back into the van.

All that Kajoli saw, pained, exalted, tears in her eyes, but a gleam, too, for she felt a power in her. And as she heard from others the rest of the tale her breath deepened and her fists clenched and unclenched.

The police van was passing by the aged banyan when it pulled up suddenly. The officer who sat beside the driver had sighted the tricolour. Fastened to a hanging root of the aged banyan, there was the symbol of freedom, a promise of hope and glory. He drew his tiny gun and fired six shots. The van passed on.

Then something snapped again in men's minds, and there was no Devata to hold them back. Frenzy possessed them, a

64

swift flame. With shouts of hate and fury they rushed the way the motor van had gone. Kajoli understood their feeling, for it was her feeling, too. Could you bear to see the pictured face of your mother riddled with shots? Or the image of your god smashed? There was a limit even to *ahimsa*. You could call forth strength to put up with all, suffer without retaliation, when they attacked your person; but not when they attacked your mother. That was the feeling of her people, Kajoli knew. She knew, too, what words Devata would say in reply. *Ahimsa* was not passivity. It was a weapon of war, more powerful than fire-power. True. Even so . . .

Alone on the mossy step of the pool, emptied of excitement and glory, she had let her pent-up tears trickle from her eyes. *Dadu* gone. Father gone. What suffering would be their lot in jail-house? When would they come back? Months, years? *Dadu* over seventy years of age, and the deep, tired lines in his face. Father with malaria in his bones. They had done no harm to anybody . . .

Her heart fretted as never before, her eyelids were swollen. The young peasant girl, newly grown to be woman, had reached depths of tender feelings. And how they hurt her! Kajoli was yet unprotected from herself. The face that would kindle fast with a gay laugh would fill as fast with a sad cloud.

Devata they called him, for his presence in the village had been a blessing, ever, for all. Mendicant they called the other —a happy wanderer who could not stay in one place for more than a time, who must walk the long roads of Bengal ever and ever. Restless feet chained up in jail-house.

She wiped her eyes and looked up, pricking her ears. The zooming of a skyplane. Planes often passed high up in the sky-ways, but they never came low enough to be seen so clearly. Her sadness was eased for a moment because of her wonder and fascination. To touch sky-blue with an outstretched arm—so! A length of sugar-cane lay upon her knee. She picked it up, and her full mouth parted wide as she tore at the hard green skin-fibre with her even young teeth. There had been planes in Ancient India, and she knew all about them from vivid ac-counts in the epic *Ramayana*. . . . The zooming was now loud, and Kajoli lifted her head, her eyes searching the sky. The far eagle grew swiftly bigger, bigger, as it dropped low. Never had Kajoli seen a plane fly so close—it could touch the palmyra tops yonder. In a while it was heading in her direction! With a shattering roar it was coming right upon her, the huge flying

D (S.M.H.)

thing. And Kajoli gave a shriek and flung herself into the water, and her bare arms slapped the lotus leaves as she dipped to the stalks veining the pool. . . . When she lifted her head, mouth wide, gulping air, the skyplane had passed on.

She staggered over the steps, pale and shaken, and shading her eyes with her hand she gazed at the receding eagle. How low and close it had come! As though it would pounce on her and take her away. She could still feel the swift breeze of its wings, and her heart was all tip tip tip! What evil had the plane in mind? What business had it to fly so low in this village sky?

Kajoli could not know that the R.A.F. pilot who flew the Lease-Lend Lightning on reconnaissance duty was worried, too. He was miserable about the task assigned him. At home, before the War, Flight-Lieutenant Brooks had been an engineer in a steel mill, and an active member of the Labour Party, with Left Wing leanings. He had seen the Battle of Britain. He had fought Messerschmitts in the sky of Libya. And here he was, trying to strike terror in the hearts of ill-fed, ill-clothed, unarmed people as though they belonged to an enemy country. A great patriotic urge was sweeping these people, he knew. Brooks was pleased about it. He happened to believe in world freedom. But what if he were to be ordered to strafe the village with machine-gun fire? Other pilots had, under orders, attacked villages nearby, Brooks knew. The dirty, brutal business! He had seen the crowd on the road and the small building ablaze. Brooks felt the sweat trickle down his nose.

Shame came upon Kajoli that she had been so affrighted—she, Devata's grand-daughter, who had faced gunfire. And she picked up her sugar-cane and put it between her teeth as if for solace. She must go home and change her *sari*—drenched, it lay on her body in wet spots. And her tight half-blouse was plastered on her breast. Kajoli walked up the stone steps to the dusty cart-way, blowing her nose and wiping her wet face. Then she sighted groups of people ahead, near the railway track. They were back, her people. Her heart trembled. What could they have done? Kanu—he was safe? The Evil Thing had not taken him?

No time to go home. Her loosened hair hung to her waist, dripping, and she squeezed it and gathered it back in a pile. She slipped her fingers through the neck of her blouse and freed the tight fabric from her skin. And she cut across the fields, yellow with sun-sodden paddy, walking fast, breaking into a run over a grassy footway.

The men came in utter silence. The excitement had worked itself off, and they seemed worn and unhappy. Kajoli looked eagerly for her brother. There he was, still holding the flag, his face shining damply in the sun, his steps tired, dragging. She took the flag from his hands, holding it aloft, and between panting breaths she cried, "*Bhai*, what happened?"

He answered after a silence, briefly, in a staccato way. They had gone to the *dak ghar*, five miles off, smashed up equipment and set alight the mud-brick house with its roof of corrugated sheets—it was only a sub-post office. The postmaster did not seem to mind. He only tried to save the cash-box, but they wouldn't let him. "Then let it go," he said, dropping the box into the fire. "Twenty-three postcards and six envelopes— that's the day's trade. Not a single Money Order." He drew a meagre pay, and had no love for his masters.

So the *dak ghar* burnt gaily, and the men felt consoled, having destroyed Government property and avenged themselves for the attack on their flag. But as they turned their feet homeward they thought of Devata, they thought how he would grieve if he knew; they had disobeyed him, and sadness was heavy in their bones.

"Sugar-cane," said Kajoli, passing the length of cane to her brother. He had not eaten that day. No one in the village had eaten a morsel.

He put the cane-end in his mouth, but took it out in a moment with a grimace of pain. His ear-ache. How he had been suffering this half-hour, since the excitement cooled off, so that it was hard pain even to stretch the mouth open. His chronic ailment, this, coming intermittently. Something had gone wrong with the roots of his left ear. He often lay screaming in unbearable torment.

"Let us hurry, then," said Kajoli, tender yearning in her voice. At home Mother would foment the ear with heated salt tied up in a bit of cloth. That would be relief for the boy.

But the ache was shooting lightning in his head even hours after, when the *Red Turbans* reappeared in lorry-loads—more *Red Turbans* than had ever been seen before in the village. With them was an informer who knew the bad men of Baruni, Devata's close associates. A truck was filled with handcuffed prisoners, ropes tied about their waists. The *Red Turbans* looked for the big flag, too, the flag of unrest and sedition— they would trample it with their boots. Kajoli, knowing their evil mind, had concealed the flag in the haystack. The blue-uniformed men who gave themselves lordly airs would not push their proud chins into a haystack.

No one cried this time, either—not Kanu in handcuffs, not Onu, not the mother; soldiers all, though there was a wrench in the mother's heart: "If only they would let me foment my son's aching ear for the last time before he goes——"

CHAPTER VIII

T HE PEASANTS had had bitter clashes with the Evil Thing. Men had been shot down. Men with bullet-wounds had been borne home by their brethren. Handcuffed prisoners had streamed out of many villages. Meek hearts long resigned to oppression were strengthened, not deadened, by Terror. Terror's fire-power wakened an answering spirit of fire. But a heavy immediate task was at hand. The wide landscape lay yellow with ripe corn vulnerable to rain. Many work-days had been lost. It was high time to complete the harvest.

Hot sunshine was falling on the fields, glinting on the sickles as they swished, and the tall standing paddy dropped, cut close to the earth, heaping, rice-heavy, at the reapers' feet. Kajoli could feel the rhythm. She knew the movements, like the beats of a tune, but she was unskilled at it, an unaccustomed novice. This was no work for a woman. A woman had her hands full at home, threshing the harvest, sun-baking the grain, drying dung-cake kindling, fetching pitchers of water from the pool, minding the hundred tasks that made a homestead. Father gone, Kanu gone, Kajoli had to take up a man's rugged work. She felt her spine grow stiff with long stooping; she felt the sweat smear her body and wash down her throat, down the neck of her white cotton jacket. She paused and straightened up to ease her back, and wiped her hot face with her palm. How many drops of sweat to earn each grain of corn? thought Kajoli in her heart, looking at her wet palm and wiping it on her *sari* for a better grip on the sickle.

Not that she was downhearted, defeated. *Dadu's* grand-daughter! Those last words he had spoken before the *Red Turbans* took him away: "Do not betray yourselves. The supreme test has come. Be strong. Be true. Be deathless." And she, listening, had felt a power in her!

Kajoli, lifting her hand to her sun-flushed face, jerked

68

her chin in a gesture of decision. Be strong. Be true. Be deathless.

Onu? Even more of a novice, he was far from strong, that boy. The hard work wore him out. The fatigue that filled his eyes! Kajoli ached for her brother.

"Onu, stop and rest some moments, *bhai*. Not three days since you had fever-heat. You are such a worry!" Kajoli heaved a big sigh.

"*Nah!*" said Onu, and he swung his sickle and saw the corn-stalks drop. He paused. His breath, like his sister's, came deep from the strain. "Tired? *Nah!* Three more sheaves you have done, *didi*? Look at my lot—maybe it will make three?" His face was eager and proud as he turned and gazed at his reaping.

"It is more," said Kajoli, measuring with her eyes. While gathering the cut stalks with her brother's back turned towards her she had quickly shifted armfuls of her own reaping into his lot. "Let me pile it up, then we'll see. Wait."

Onu watched. It made three sheaves and some left over. The young face lit up with pleasure.

"I'll work still faster, *didi*; you will see. Why, I am as good as Kanu"—he hesitated—"as good as Father."

"Onu," said Kajoli, throwing down her sickle, "the sun-god is up at mid-sky. See? It is meal-time."

"So soon?" The boy looked skyward. "The sun-god has rushed. I can't work so very well after rice, *didi*. Heaviness sits on me and I take it easy, I don't know why."

Kajoli pleaded with him. "Look at your belly. See how flat it is. Our *kisan* uncles—they, too, must be hungry. You can't sweat them, with no food in their stomachs. What am I to do with you?" Her calm eyes worried.

Three *kisan* sickle-men were at work at the far end of the strip. For years they had worked on this land, and they were as old as Kajoli's father. "Uncle", Kajoli called them. One, with grey hair, moved stiffly, awkwardly, for he had been crippled by a bullet in his leg. The men fed by custom out of their employer's kitchen during harvest time. Kajoli would fetch them their midday rice, and they would eat squatting in the shade of a tree.

So homeward they walked, the girl and her brother. Three fields off she saw the storeman talking to a peasant, gesturing with both his hands. The storeman saw her and called out. "Tell Mother," he said, wrapping his round face with a smile, "tell her I shall come and see her at sundown." The smile spread to the wide ears. "I'll bring a goodly length of blue ribbon for your hair, Kajoli. It's the new fashion in town."

Faintly she moved her head, saying no word. The storeman had come and seen her mother about the rice harvest. "We are not selling," said Mother; "we'll need the little we reap." But the storeman would be coming again to plead with her. A man of endless patience and persistence.

The storeman had no time these days for his old business. He had installed his wife's brother at the counter to sell the *pice*-worths, while he trudged the day through, field to field, house to house, in this village and in others—a group of them were under his charge. Tirelessly he used his glib tongue, pleading with the people.

"Brother, this is your true chance. Sell all you can. Eight *rupees* for a *maund* of rice. Ever had such price, brother? Ever heard of such price in a hundred and one years and in all the days of your fourteen generations? It is as though your paddy is dyed with water-of-gold! The dye will wash off, brother; it is no fast die! To-day the Japanee devil stands at our door. Our soldiers need to eat well. Our workers in mills need to eat well, for they toil day and night and night and day, with no moment for sleep, no moment to chat and stretch a limb. This cannot last over-long, brother. There are the British. There are the Americans. The Japanee devil will be crushed under-foot like a beetle. What then? Who will buy grain? Soldiers will be back home, soldiers no more. Mill-folk will sit on their doorsteps and scratch their bodies—scratch, scratch. I see rice rotting in the barns then. Why, Gorement will flood the market with its huge uneaten stocks. Cash in your hand, cash a-plenty; you can buy back your own rice. Sell to-day at eight *rupees* a *maund*, buy back at five. That is good business. I put this to you plainly as man to man: What harm is there if you sell your grain now and buy it back later, whatever you then need, at a cut rate? What harm if you make this extra profit and use it to get ourself a cow, a shiny ploughshare, new roof for the old one worn thin? Turn it over in your heart, brother.

" 'Do not sell'; so Devata spoke? Devata is wise, he sees all, he knows all; I bow at his feet. I lick the dust of the road on which he passes. If only Devata were here! He would say: 'Sell. Sell all you can, friends and comrades. Life is a game of cards, brother. With each new game the cards are newly shuffled. How can you play to-day's game as though you still

70

had yesterday's cards in your hand?' Alas, if only Devata could send you word!''

So he talked ceaselessly, the storeman, talked with ten tongues, and gestured with his hands. And while he talked, whole villages of folk were on the highroad beyond the railway track—people, cattle, all homeless, landless. For more air-fields grew—British fields, American fields. More villages were scorched. A wave of wanderers would turn from the highroad once in a while and pass into Baruni. "You will sell us rice, brother? Yes, we can pay—we are no paupers nor cheats; it's only that the military have taken our old earth. You will let our kine nibble a blade in your pasture? The rains are heavy, and grass grows a-plenty.''

Blue ribbon for the hair? That was the new fashion in town? mused Kajoli. She would like to have a blue ribbon in the braids of her hair-knot. But she could not take it as a gift from the storeman. She was not selling him rice. She would sell rice to the homeless folk, and to none else.

Not that there would be much rice to sell. This was a poor crop, this *aus*—a mere quarter crop. A stop-gap between the *amans*, the big winter crops. You planted with so much labour and reaped so little. Who could afford to miss these few *maunds*, though? *Aman* saw you through to mid-year and a little farther. *Aus* took you along to midwinter.

"A white rubber ball he promised me," said Onu. "As if he could get round me that way!"

Onu had not yielded to temptation. The sole male member in the family, had he not responsibility? The rice was not to be sold, so Father had spoken. A white rubber ball—huh!

"Race me!" cried Onu, suddenly breaking into a run, and Kajoli drew a full breath and ran, hands on chest, hair-knot slipping off in thick plaits.

That was their way every day. As they returned from toil, and home was well within sight, they would race to the door. Perhaps it was their youth. Perhaps it was nostalgia for Mother.

"Mother! Mother mine!" the eager voices cried together. The two whirled to the kitchen yard, then stopped short in amazement.

A stranger sat cross-legged on the veranda floor, stooping over a brass tray piled high with rice and curried pumpkin. His mouth was full when he heard the call and looked up from his food.

The mother came out through the kitchen door.

"There she is, my golden one." She looked at the stranger, then proudly at her daughter, and her eyes came back to the stranger. Swift anxiety lined her face. The stranger had not said a word, looking up for a moment, and now his head was bent, his fingers making a little ball of rice, dipping it in the gravy of pumpkin. It was as if he had no eye, no mind, save for his meal.

Kajoli watched him eat. That pumpkin had been in the house for a month, the last fruit of their old vine. Kajoli had longed to make it into a curry, but the mother had saved the good vegetable, so big and yellow-green, keeping it preserved for a lean day. What had come upon her that she had sliced it and cooked it for a mere stranger?

"Not two hours he has been here." The mother turned to Kajoli and spoke. "He comes and says, 'Mother, first cook me a meal, then I'll tell you all.' Father has sent him to us——"

"Father?" cried Kajoli, her voice leaping with eagerness: "he is not in jail-house, then?" She was trembling on the edge of joy and fearing disillusion.

The mother nodded her head, and her voice was toneless.

"The Evil Thing has him still. That boy was in the same jail-house. A full month they were together. Father is well. There has been a terrible massacre——"

"Massacre?" gasped Kajoli. Her eyes flew wide to the stranger.

The youth now looked up and spoke, his lips suddenly unsealed.

"They opened fire on the prisoners. We used to sing. They told us not to sing. We sang. The warder slapped one of us. That one slapped him back in return. Whistles blew, bells began to ring, the jail-house was soon a battle-ground. Warders, guards, opened fire on us, unarmed ones, who had nothing to fight with save our fists." He dropped his face and voice. "Fifteen killed. Twice as many more wounded. It all came out in the papers."

"Father is unhurt." The mother spoke quickly, lifting her joined palms in a *pronam* to the gods.

"What song was that?" murmured Kajoli. Such massacre because of some song!

"A song of revolt," said the youth, with a sideways look at Kajoli. The corners of his mouth were stained with curry.

"He will tell you the words," the mother said. "He has spirit, the same as your folk. Our Kishore will teach you the

72

song of revolt. In good time." Her sad face grew wistful and bright with some thought. "*A-ha-reh!* His parents dead. Poor boy! Five hard months in the jail-house. It is Fate's writing— else why should he be in that one jail-house of all the thousand in the land, and in the same cell as Father? And, save for the revolt, he would have come out of the jail-house two months back; then Father would not have known him." She paused, and her face saddened again. "Who knows where my Kanu has been taken?"

Onu was looking at the stranger with new respect in his heart. As silence fell, he seized the chance to open his mouth.

"My elder brother, Kanu by name—he was born in jail-house." Onu spoke in a boastful way.

Kishore looked up, too amazed to speak. Kajoli explained: "Our mother went to jail-house twenty years back. Gandhiji's *satyagraha* movement that was——"

Onu added in a rush: "And our brother Kanu was born right there, right in jail-house." He had a secret feeling of defeat that he himself had not been born in jail-house.

"A little more rice, my son?" said the mother, her eyes on Kishore's emptying plate.

"No, no, Mother," pleaded the youth. "I am full up to the throat. I cannot eat one more grain, Mother."

And Kajoli, standing with eyelids lowered, felt his clear glance upon her, now eager and intent as he looked up again, and something in the glance made her blush, turn her face, abashed.

"Just one mouthful, my son. Do you not like the curry?"

"Why, Mother, look at my plate. Not one grain of rice left, not one drop of gravy. The crows will curse!"

Mother smiled, and passed into the kitchen saying, "Just one more mouthful," and Kajoli followed her, leaving Onu to chat with the stranger.

"The very image of my Kanu," said the mother in a low voice, a new excited light in her eyes.

"Who, Mother?" said Kajoli, though she knew whom Mother meant.

"My new son. You have not seen the likeness?"

My new son! The girl stared in plain amazement. What was the meaning of this swift fondness? And what likeness was there between Kanu *bhai* and this stranger? They were about the same age. But this one was light of skin, and Kanu was dark—Kanu took after Father, and was dark like him, unlike

Mother. Happy, smiling face; not sad, not bemused, like Kanu *bhai*. They looked different people, even if they were one in spirit. The strange way he looked at her, as though with great joy, till Kajoli felt her face grow hot and she turned her head. But she must make him tell her the song of revolt that maddened the guards in jail-house——

"You have not seen the likeness, Kajoli?"

She hastened to ease Mother's heart. "Of course I have, Mother. Who can miss it? He is the image of my *dada*, in his face, in his ways." Kajoli was grateful to the stranger that he had brought Mother some happiness—secret unexpressed sorrow had been wearing her out ever since the father and son had gone. And Kajoli thought: Father was not too miserable in jail-house? The stranger would know. Kajoli would ask him and find out all. Father's companion in jail-house—her eyes softened for the stranger.

"Three months he had been a prisoner when Father came in. There was a strike in the mill. The boy was a worker in a big cotton-mill. He led the strike. The manager had him in handcuffs. When his term was done, Father gave him a message for us. They got hold of a pencil and a slip of paper——"

"A message from Father?" Kajoli cried eagerly. "A letter?"

She nodded her head with a smile. She gave Kajoli a deep, curious look.

"Kajoli *lo*, I have not told you yet. The boy has brought us a note from Father."

"Show me, then. You have kept silent all this time! A note from Father!"

Rice-bowl in hand, the mother walked off to serve her son. When she returned, Kajoli was pleading again, impatient, "Mother, that note——"

The mother rinsed her hands with water from a pitcher and reached up for a thick old book resting in a niche in the wall. The niche was high, and the mother had to rise on tiptoe, for she was not tall—she was like Kajoli in that way. Between the leaves of the *Ramayana* the letter lay pressed. Kajoli read.

And her face tensed as she read, and in her eyes the black pupils dilated. The mother watched her with excitement and pleasure, and nodded her head gently with some thought. It was a good thing that her husband had taught her to read and write—few womenfolk of the peasants had the gift. The mother read haltingly, spelling out words. But these words were plain

74

enough: "Kishore is our new son. Our Kajoli is yet unbetrothed. Not to be wed till near-sixteen, so Devata said. She has grown up, our Kajoli. I pray to the gods that the boy takes it in his heart to wed our Kajoli."

If only he approves of our Kajoli! the mother mused, keenly watching, and she picked up a fan of palmyra leaf and waved it over the girl's face to dry the smears of perspiration, anxious that she should look her best, clean and sweet, before the boy saw her again.

"What has come upon you, Mother?" Kajoli snatched away the fan, between her deepened breaths a half-laugh. She put the letter, now that she had read it twice, back in the leaves of the *Ramayana* and rose on tiptoe to replace the volume in the niche.

"Before he casts off prison dress he folds up the precious scroll and slips it into his mouth, so clever he is, that son of mine. Else the guards would have taken away the note." The mother was anxious to pile credit upon the boy.

Lips mute, eyes cast down and turned from the mother's glance, Kajoli washed, scrubbed her feet. Earth stuck all about her, earth of the rice-field. On her face, neck, hair. She was like a thing of brown Bengal earth.

What bride had ever stood before her groom-to-be with such sun-wet face? Call it her fault that she had to do a man's work in the field, reaping the corn? Hold her to blame that she let the stranger from a city cotton-mill see her earth-smeared, like a wild one? Shame bit, and tears grew in her eyelids.

She washed her face clean till the skin was pink with scrubbing, and as she loosened her braided hair, combing the dust out of the long, thick tresses, she thought suddenly of the ribbon the storeman would bring her in the evening. It was the new fashion in town. If only she could have that blue ribbon to wear in her hair! sighed Kajoli.

. . . . .

What chance had a peasant bride to keep her face clean and cool when the grain hung ripe in the fields, asking to be gathered in a rush, lest it should be plucked off by heavy rain?

A bare minute he had seen her, face washed and hair combed well. A minute and no more, for a bride had her shame, and held herself away from her groom; so custom commanded.

Noon was not far gone when Kajoli was back in the fields handing food to the *kisans*, then picking up her sickle, the sun beating fierce on her bare head, on her neck and hips, till the perspiration grew all over her again in beads and smears, from the upper edge of her brow down to her shins. *He* (you wouldn't speak your groom's name even in your heart, you said *he*) would be chatting at home with Mother as she whirred the spinning-wheel, or he would be sleeping on a cool grass floormat (and the floor swept neat with a wash of dung)—the walk of six miles from the railway station had filled him with heavy tiredness. Yes, he looked spent, Kajoli had not failed to see. The months in prison; the hard labour, yoked like oxen to a shaft and crushing oil-seeds; the struggle with the guards. Out of prison, he had not stopped for a minute: he had come rushing to the village, as though there was a call, a great urgency. With what great love and respect he spoke of Father! A city youth, yet so simple in his heart; and no superior airs, none. No bravado, though he had faced the fierce guards who had guns in hand. How he had enjoyed the rice and pumpkin, calling it a festive meal, not leaving one grain of rice on his plate! Why, if he truly cared for pumpkin, Kajoli would plant a few more vines and train them up to the thatch roof, where they would bear fruit. Kajoli herself would make the curry this time; she was no less of a cook than Mother. There was a way to make pumpkin a delight, a trick of seasoning it, while it was being boiled, with the right spices and chilli-seeds so that it was hot, yet not biting—just hot. She would cut down the slim plantain tree in the backyard and slice and cook the white inner core, the soft, delicious tube.

The sickle moved slow in her hand. The strokes came uneven. The way *he* had looked at her, with her face washed and hair neat, and the great joy in his eyes, and he could not take his eyes from her, shaming her. Yes, you will have a comely bride; no worry on that account——

And as she smiled with the thought, the bright, sunlit corn over which she bent became a looking-glass that showed forth her proud, smiling image!

"*Didi*, look!" said Onu, triumph in his voice. As he sheaved the reaping, he had more to his credit than his sister—a good deal more.

She looked. With a sudden gesture she flung out her arms and drew the boy close. She wiped his face with her *sari*, she smoothed back the uncut hair plastered on his brow.

76

"So hard you toil, Onu *bhai*, so much you reap; your arms do not ache?"

And she was mindless and slack in her own reaping because of the strange new tenderness in her breast.

"*Didi reh*, look!"

Look again? Which way this time? Turning round with an air of languor, she gave a start. Not twenty yards away was *he*, striding across the stubble in her direction.

The chaos of feelings that overwhelmed her! Sweet shame to be seen with her groom even before they were wed. Sour shame because of her glistening face and earth-smears. Pleasure at sight of him. Pleasure, too, that he was concerned enough to come—how he cared!

With her fingers she wiped the sweat gathering about her eyes and quickly turned back to her work, while Onu hailed the newcomer with a clamour.

"This earth is all ours"—Onu made a sweeping gesture. "Those men over there, our men, *kisans*. This is rice of the finest kind, do you know? *Sonamukhi* rice. Father brought the seed-grain from Mursh—Mursh——" He struggled with an unfamiliar name.

"Good rice," agreed Kishore, with a knowing look as he stood between the two young reapers. "You can tell from the skin what's inside. Shape—colour——"

Onu was amazed. "All paddy is not the same colour, then? Fine, middling, coarse——"

"A matter for the knowing eye," said Kishore solemnly.

The girl smiled, and could not hold her tongue.

"Rice grows plentiful in cotton-mills, fine *sonamukhi*. You didn't know, Onu?"

"My grandfather was a farmer," said Kishore, and his grey eyes twinkled.

"Then of course he ought to know everything about rice, Onu," Kajoli said playfully again. "The worthy grandson." Her mouth had a twist of light mockery.

Kishore grinned in answer. He was well pleased with himself, having drawn his bride out of her reserve into good, sharp talk. Now he reached for a sickle. "*Bhai*, let me try my hand. Good strokes—shush! shush!"

"*Didi*, he wants your sickle——" Onu cried with concern, gripping his own and slashing at the corn. Would he lose this great chance to show off his worth to the man from a city jail-house?

The girl handed over her sickle and watched it swing swiftly in Kishore's hand, and she cried out in alarm, "Take heed. You will cut your own leg."

Then Onu broke into a giggle. "Why, he doesn't know how to cut grain. He can't hold the sickle the right way. *Didi*, look!" Onu gave an excited shout.

"Onu! Owl!" Kajoli chaffed him, but her eyes were bright with fun.

Kishore paused and scratched his head, then he began to laugh. "Why, it is the truth," he admitted good-naturedly. "What do I know of rice and reaping? Machines I know. Spindles that make cotton yarn I know, and looms that weave. I'll know the earth soon enough, the earth and its output. Two good instructors, one on each side." One thumb lifted, pointing at Kajoli, the other at Onu.

"Look, this is the way." Onu, loving his new instructor's role, wielded his sickle with pride and energy. "So simple. You need practice. Just a little practice."

Kishore watched awhile, then tried his hand. The corn began to heap at his feet.

The *kisan* reapers at the far end of the strip were looking this way, Kajoli saw; they were puzzling about the stranger. Kajoli did not heed. She watched Kishore reaping. What did he think of this peasant's work? she wondered. Out there in the mill the big machines toiled for you like giants. You only had to feed them with oil or coal and keep them content. You could take it easy while you sat protected from the hot sun. No wonder the mill women, daughters and wives, could preen themselves, hair gay with ribbon!

"Silly folk!" She spoke as if to herself, but meaning her words for her groom's ears. "Silly folk, cotton-mill women."

"Why silly folk?" he said, looking up at her, smiling dimly.

"Phoo! They put gaudy tapes in their hair. The new fashion. Like little children. Don't they know it when they've grown up? Tell me." And her eyes glanced, eager.

Kishore would not agree—how could he read the deeper purpose of her words? Why, in the big May Day demonstration, he said, the women marched along with the men-folk. "Waken, workers!" sang the women. "Unite, workers! What have you to lose but your begging-bowls? Do not beg. Demand. Workers, arise!"

She listened, and her face burned suddenly. How he admired the mill womenfolk! They were truly his people, and he liked them, he belonged to them. Here in the village he was a tourist, an alien. She, Kajoli, meant nothing to him—an object of curiosity, pity, nothing more. Nothing more.

She drew a quick breath, and could not speak for some moments. When her voice came, it was hard with scorn.

"You folk need to be wakened, and the poor girls have to be on the job. Call it manly! Here in the village our folk do not sleep like old cronies, we rustics have no need to open our mouths and shout: 'Waken, peasants!'" Kajoli lifted her voice a tone or two. "Arise, peasants! What have you to lose but your good sleeping time? Nothing, nothing more." Her lips set in a line and opened for a moment—"Manly!"—and set again.

Kishore burst into a laugh, low at first, then free and loud. "Nothing to lose but our good sleeping time—nothing, nothing more!" he cried, and grew more exhilarated for no obvious reason. He was laughing so heartily, with such obvious delight, that Kajoli lost her hurt feeling, looking at his face. And their eyes met and forgot to withdraw. And there was such joy in his glance, such worship, that it shamed her, and she caught her breath, flushing, her eyes darting away. She stood in dumb silence, looking down.

A jerk of her chin, the gesture of decision.

"My sickle. Where is the time for gossip?" Reaching out her hand.

He gave no response. He held on to the sickle.

"My sickle?" Insistently.

But he shook his head. He stooped, swinging the sickle in a neat stroke, and he lifted the fallen paddy like a banner. He could see the march of life. He cast his eyes over the yellow acres and the figure of men reaping. He smelled the rich earth, his lungs filling. His eyes came to rest then on the one who was a daughter of earth, with the earth's mellowness, the earth's exuberance and rich yielding.

With her woman's instinct, Kajoli knew his vision. She felt her blood quicken. "The reaping? What if the rains come?" her voice pleaded, and her eyes lifted skyward, as though she saw dark clouds of rain hidden in the glare.

The answering words were firm and grave, yet a caress.

"Never again. You will never again hold the sickle to reap. Not as long as my arm has strength. Not as long as my body has breath."

CHAPTER IX

SHE, TOO, had once held the rich gift of laughter in her heart; she, too, could once laugh out of plain delight, laugh till the tears came. But the Evil Thing had killed her young gayness. Gravity was heavy on her face and spirits. So Kishore had known all these days—two moons were gone since they were wed. She laughed, if ever, only with her lips—half laughed in a strangled way, as though with the threat of a hidden hand upon her throat.

And now this sudden miracle! The utter abandon of gay, ripe laughter as it spilled out of the hand she cupped over her mouth, the helpless laughter that drew tears to each eye!

The blood rose and heaved under his ribs so that he felt his heart toss crazily, like a paper boat in an eddy, because of Kajoli's laughter.

It happened thus. Kishore had toiled with the *charkha* the past month, two hours every day, to fulfil his heart's fancy: to see the girl, his wife, wear a *sari* out of his spinning. The *sari* was made, ready to be collected, and this day at sun-up they had gone, he and the girl, his wife, to the weaver's hut on the river-bank at the edge of the village. As they walked back with the soft, white *sari* neatly folded in Kajoli's arms, Kishore was mad to see her put it on. He was impetuous, like a boy; he would not bide the time for her to be back home; she must wear the *sari* that moment for the joy of his eye. There was the tall bamboo clump off the roadside to screen her as she changed.

"*N-nah!*" Kajoli had cried in shame; but he had begged and cajoled so hard that she had to give way at last. "Stand guard, then, lest someone drop from emptiness and see me bare." And she had slipped off her old garment, now worn so thin, and it seemed to him, looking at her, that the new *sari*, white and soft and chaste, loved her slender yet well-made body as she draped herself, the folds neatly spread, the red border drawn over her head and edging her forehead.

"Silk and satin are shamed," said Kishore as they walked into the village, passing by the aged banyan. "And the rainbow colours the city girls wear, those also. In white you are like a lotus, shaming all the flowers that bloom ever."

80

"*Nah!*" Kajoli said huskily, flushing, embarrassed by this hymn.

Yet he would love to buy her a city *sari*, too, a mill-made one of fine texture, when he had some money. Why, one day, when he had money, they would go to the city of cities a-visiting, he and the girl, his wife. What streets! What crowds! Like people in a fair. And the illumination! So many lights on each street. No lamps of oil, mind: lights of great power, lightning-white; so many lights that night was no darker than daytime. And the cinema plays! How he would love to take the girl, his wife, to a cinema play!

"There is a fear, though," he added, his eyes twinkling.

"*Han?*" A shade of anxiety in her voice.

"I fear to take you to the city. What if you pick a fancy for some smart-like city chap? What then?"

"How can it be? Am I not married? Tell me."

"What if you are married? It happens in the city every day. The cinema play shows it happening, all like life."

Between the slant of her eyebrows a frown came.

"Then I'll never see a cinema play." She spoke in flashing anger. "It is evil. What a lie! Such things cannot truly happen." And her nose puckered with disgust.

Kishore cleared his throat as though to speak boldly.

"Take it the other way, then. What if I pick a fancy for some wench of the city, winsome?"

Kajoli had stopped dead and stared at him, her black eyes very wide, and then all unexpectedly it happened. "You?" she cried, and her eyes lit and danced and she broke out first in a giggle, then in her blithe laughter. And she said again, "You?"

Flurried, he had scratched his head. How well she knew him! He pick a fancy for another, he whose very soul was tied to the *sari*-end of this laughing one! He, too, could have laughed a bellyful!

Yet, if words could be weighed, those thoughtless, fanciful words of his would tip the scales against a goodly measure of gold or of wisdom! Had they not raised her drooping spirits? Pushed aside some thick fist in which her heart lay clutched and choking? Kishore could have cried out for joy! But he walked in silence, only smiling to himself, and then, from his great happiness, he hummed a snatch of a city song:

> I know, I know, beloved,
> Not in this life will hungers be sated—
> I know, I know, beloved!

"What hungers, then?" Kajoli broke in abruptly.

"*Nah*. It is a way of talk, à song from the phonogram."

But Kajoli, pondering for a moment, yet read meaning in those words.

"Woman, wed, has no hungers left to be filled. It is not so with man," Kajoli said in a murmur.

He mused in his turn. The pathway wriggled through fields big with harvest, goldening in the hard sun. He cast his eyes about, turned and said, "Man has a hunger that his rice be heavy on the stalk." One idea led to another. "Man has a hunger that he may look tall in the eyes of his kin and brethren. Man has——"

But Kajoli broke in again, abruptly.

"Woman, wed, has one big hunger for home—no other. Little hungers make part of the big home hunger; they belong to it as the spokes belong to the cart-wheel. Woman, she has one big wheel of hunger. Man is a single spoke in that cart-wheel—*nah*, maybe he is the axle. And——"

He waited. "And?"

But Kajoli walked on, not saying a word, smiling a little, dimly, to herself—absently, as if in dream.

Such moments came often, when she seemed far apart, and Kishore would never then break her self-absorption. He was content to look at the face, look covertly. A woman must have her strangeness—else, would she be woman?

"Coo-oo!" A kokil sang from its tree-top perch, and there was such passionate joy in the bird-voice, deep yet penetrating, that it was like a sweet, throbbing ache.

"Coo-oo!" an echo answered, and, hearing it, Kishore held his breath and stood rooted, amazed at the full-throated cry, bewitched by richness. The laughter first, then the kokil cry! Kishore was discovering this girl, his wife.

"Why stop?" asked Kajoli, turning round.

He spoke no word, only gazed at her, his eyes intent, and he came a step and lifted his hand and passed it gently over the smoothness of her throat, the dip of the collar-bone and the curvature.

"Why——" she began, then losing her voice, joying in the tender caress of his fingers, closing her eyes because of her inward flutter.

"Like a kokil is thy soul-bird, girl." He who spoke so was no peasant lad in Baruni village—a hero, unawares, of the cinema plays he knew so well!

82

"Listen. What if people see? *Hoon?*"

"Who cares?" Yet he looked about quickly, and there loomed a figure striding across the fields on the criss-cross of footways, not fifty yards off. Sunk in each other, they had not seen the man this while.

"Agony!" moaned Kishore, and drew apart.

Startled, she turned, and her eyes narrowed, and the brows moved closer in thought, and as the figure crossed the strip of field edging the road she drew a quick breath and cried, "Yes, it is he!"

"He? Who is *he*?" The quickened breath, the eager cry. Kishore felt sudden heaviness press upon his chest. "How do you know city folk?" His voice came drily.

"S-sh!" said Kajoli, a warning finger to her lips. "He is the grandson of my grandfather."

"The grandson——"

But Kajoli said again, "Sh!" and Kishore, now easy in his heart, closed his mouth and looked ahead with interest.

The stranger stepped near and spoke. "I am looking for the house of the mendicant. Three years I have not seen this village path."

Kajoli felt a pang in her heart. He had forgotten her altogether? She cast down her face, while Kishore stole a tender glance at her. Poor Kajoli! How eagerly had she spoken often of this grandson of her grandfather, who did not seem even to know her.

"Pray come this way," he said. "We are of the mendicant's house. He is gone. The Evil Thing has taken him, you maybe know."

Yes, he knew. In each province the national movement, now outlawed and hounded, had secretly compiled a list of the victims of Terror. Rahoul had been busy these days on a committee that kept track of the prisoners, arranging defence for those who were brought to trial—youths barely out of teen-age were facing the hangman's rope. Save for that work, Rahoul would have made time to rush to Baruni long before.

"This one is his daughter," said Kishore, his voice anxious. She would be so hurt if he still failed to know her. . . .

Of course. Kajoli. She was a child when he saw her last. She had grown in these years. He almost knew her even at first glance, only he could not be certain.

"You are wed, Kajoli?" he said, warmth in tone and smile,

83

having noted the vermilion streak in the parting of her hair. "This is the groom?"

Her face lit. Forgotten her? He even remembered her name. And she smiled back, and then dropped her eyes, shy, as they walked along the pathway.

"It is only two moons," said Kishore, happy again. "Two moons we've been wed." And his eyes deepened with some sudden memory. "In the jail-house we were wed." He saw Rahoul stare, astonished, and with a light laugh explained: "Not wed in the jail-house, truly—that is just a way of talk. We occupied, Father and I, the same cell. Father set his fondness on me, why I do not know, and he wanted me as his son-in-law. I drew him out with talk till I had a mind-picture of the daughter. Why, whenever I was tired, homesick, I had but to close my eyes and I could see her, big as life, threshing grain in the barnyard. I could hear her voice call: 'Onu! Onu *bhai*!' or, a bucketful of cow-feed in her hand, 'Mangala!' When I left the jail-house and came to Baruni and set my eyes on her, she was no stranger. Same face as in the mind-picture, the big eyes and light skin, a smallish person. So I always say, in the jail-house we two were wed. Not truly, just a way of talk."

So he spoke, as though he were thinking aloud, and he turned his face to look at the girl, and her eyes were shining for him, and in that instant one gay thought struck two minds: the gift of coloured prints! He had brought three with him from town, knowing how she loved to put up pictures on the walls—the father had not missed telling him that. The next instant Kajoli dropped her eyes. Sudden melancholy swept her face. Her father, the very soul of goodness, held behind bars like a felon. And Grandfather. And Kanu *bhai*.

"Will they not release *dadu*, considering his age?" Her voice was strained because of the choke of misery in her throat. She was so lonely for him, so wretched!

"Release *dadu*?" Rahoul shook his head. "They have taken him far out of Bengal. To Dehra Dun, a thousand miles away."

They walked in silence for a while and then Rahoul said, "This village has suffered much?"

Kishore answered him. "Devata has laid the *ahimsa* spell on Baruni. The people burnt down a *dak ghar* in the heat of great anger, and then they remembered his teaching, and the fire in them cooled off. But other people of an outlying village across

84

the meadow burnt down a police *thana*. Truck-loads of troops came soon after with rifles and machine-guns and fired on the village folk, fired and fired. Many of our folk died. Many lay wounded, crippled for life. Then the Evil Thing set fire to houses. Like hungry tigers they bestrode the village, like fierce robbers they looted, like murderous maniacs they laid brute hands on the women——" His head hung down in anger and shame.

"They out-Japped the Japs," cried Rahoul, and the anger in his heart was like a pain. "The Evil Thing! There couldn't be a more fitting name for this Quisling Government—the Evil Thing!"

"They shot down a boy of ten years because he cried '*Mahatma Gandhi-ki jai*'. They beat a villager to death before the eyes of his wife and children——" said Kishore, and his voice broke.

"The *Red Turbans* are not our people, folk the same as us, with dark-blue coats on?" Kajoli spoke in wonder. "Their mothers and sisters are not like us?" Her lips had a way of parting when her heart wondered.

"If you serve the Evil Thing and eat its polluted salt you sell your very soul, you sell your mother and sister for the salt," said Kishore, rubbing his face, which felt warm and prickling with the angry rush of blood under the skin.

Coo-oo! sang the kokil on the tree-top, showering the bliss of joy on a dismal world, soothing the hurt of pain-torn spirits. *Coo-oo!*

Kishore looked swiftly at the girl, expectantly, but she drew a slight smile to her lips and her lips remained mute. All the same, she was echoing coo-oo! in her spirit, thought Kishore, and the silent song in her spirit came upon his ears in rich, passionate throbs, so that he felt restive, he felt his chest ache with a wanting—a wanting to be alone with her: he and the girl, no other; he and the girl, his wife——

A hundred yards from the house door Kajoli could not hold herself: she hastened her feet, and after a few quick steps she broke into a run, heedless of her new wifely dignity because of her strong excitement. She heard her companions laugh and, shamed yet challenging, faster she ran on her bare feet, the fresh smoothness of her *sari* writhing in folds, and her hips swaying a little, having filled out with two months of married life, grown womanly.

The relief that Rahoul felt! Grandfather in prison worried

about these helpless, woe-struck people who were truly his own, nearer to him than his blood kin. The girl wed. In the blackness of many sorrows, her joy was a shining jewel. Kishore would care for the household. The mendicant had chosen well. *Dadu* would have peace of mind.

Presently, in a breathless rush, Kajoli was telling the mother about the newcomer, and as Rahoul bent his head and passed in through the low doorway the mother came stepping across the barnyard.

"Father is well? Mother?" she asked out of politeness. "*Bau-ma* [daughter-in-law]? The little one?"

"Yes, Mother, they are well."

Mother! The word had slipped his tongue without thought. Happiness came upon him that he had broken out of his class sophistication and called a simple peasant woman mother. What was there in this woman of a Bengal village, not unlike others of her kind, that he had the urge to call her mother?

The peasant mother had tears in her eyes because of his kindness.

"How have you named your little one, my son?"

He laughed, his lips pleasant. "We are looking hard for a name. It's no simple business naming your child. Meantime we just call her *Khuku* [Baby]." He pulled off his shoes and stood in bare feet, as was becoming.

The mother nodded. "Kanu, Onu, Kajoli—Devata gave them their names. Those children could not bear to be away from their *dadu* even for one day." Her eyes were filling again. "Our homes are burnt. Our life is broken up. And we used to be happy folk. They have taken Devata. Kanu. The father. Who knows if our kin will be back—ever?" She wiped her eyes with her palm.

Rahoul consoled her. "Mother, when the War ends your kin will be back home. There is no fear. They are political prisoners, soldiers of Free India. The love of all the people of the land flows for them. They will live in history."

Meantime they stayed in prison, sixty thousand men and women, and the bulk of them were peasants. A thousand killed, twice as many wounded. Many had been hanged after a hurried trial—peasant lads had gone to the rope crying with their last breath, "Victory, victory to freedom! *Bandé mataram!*" Even a year before who would have thought this possible, this struggle of the common people to break their chains? It was the miracle of the age. How fast had history moved! You would not measure historical time in terms of years—a day could be more spacious than a decade. So Rahoul thought.

Kajoli emerged from the kitchen, a pail of water in her hands. She went on her knees, pouring the water on Rahoul's dust-filmed feet. Rahoul smiled, recalling another day.

"Kajoli will have to pass a severe test," he said, mock-serious.

She looked up, her eyes questioning and eager.

"She will have to produce her very best cooking for my benefit." And he lowered his glance upon the girl. "What is your best, Kajoli?"

"Pumpkin curry," she answered promptly, and then hung her head in shame. Peasant food, pumpkin. He was used to city dishes—fish and meats and game—he would laugh. She recalled the hundred delicacies of which her husband had spoken.

"What better eating than well-cooked pumpkin? Not too much trouble to you? Is there a vine on your thatch?"

"We had a fruit so big that I couldn't carry it down from the roof by myself," the girl cried, breathlessly eager.

"I feel hungry because of the pumpkin," said Rahoul. "Why," and he made a face, "I can smell the curry in my fancy!"

"Kajoli, hurry then," said the mother, gazing at the city youth, a smiling tenderness in her ever-sad eyes.

Kishore held his glance on Kajoli as she poured water from the vessel on the feet of the honoured visitor and washed them with her hands and dried them with a napkin. His lips pursed as he watched the ritual, and something like envy furrowed his smooth brown forehead. Had she washed his dusty feet—ever? Not once. The eager way she touched the feet of this grandson of her grandfather! If he, Kishore, held out his feet to her, she would say—so had she said that time—"Why, no, better you wash mine." But as he took her at her word and touched her feet, she sprang back as if bitten, and she dropped quickly to her knees and bowed low and pressed her cool forehead to his dusty feet, crying, "You think it is great fun? You don't care if sin touches me? You have no heart, then?" And she lifted her face, powdered with the dust of his feet. And her eyes were wet.

She was like that, Kajoli. The strangeness of her. But he would have enjoyed washing off with his hands the road dust that clung to her ankles. Yes, he would have loved it.

Rahoul spoke. "While the pumpkin cooks in its brass pot

I'll go round the village and speak to the brave folk who fought the Evil Thing, those few who are left. Kishore will take me round. Come, *bhai*."

Bhai! He was amazed at his progress. There in the city could he have called a millhand brother? It was easy enough to call them brother workers when at a meeting you addressed the mass from a platform, and there was no reality in the word then, no true warmth. With all your keen socialist faith, you had no great urge to call an individual worker *bhai*. Here in the village you cast off your intellectual snobbery without strain, you felt yourself as of one clay with the common people of the soil. Life became truer than life's trappings.

"Now let us start, *bhai*; for I must catch my train back to Calcutta well before sundown."

An unaccountable vision crossed his eyes for a fleeting instant, like an omen. The brave *madhobi* vine arching over the station gates was without the rich clusters of blossoms like white sea-shell, without foliage. The *madhobi* vine was dead.

. . . . .

So the storeman's words came true!

"The collective fine is marching down upon us like a giant. Gorement is no gout-eaten peasant man, brothers. Gorement does not lie down on its belly, brother, scratching the buttocks, scratching. The new *dak ghar* is all ready on paper. Who must pay for it? You, you who burnt the old hut. Every man who has land pays, so much for each *bigha* of holding, and I, who have no land, brother, only a store, I also pay my share. And the order goes: he who does not pay shall have his goods and chattels taken and sold off for the collection. Sweat the interior of your head, my brother, that you may understand. The winter crop is gathered. Mother Earth has been bounteous. The Evil Thing will seize your paddy-crop and cart it away to the market village and sell it in the *haat* there for no price at all— the price of well-water! Better sell on your own before the calamity comes, the giant marching down so fast. Sell and keep your money. Pay the fine or do not pay—that is your business, your headache. I only say: Take cash for your crop. Cash you can hide, not crop."

The peasants had not believed him. A collective fine! Was there no end to the dark tyranny? The peasants shook their heads—it could not be true. But in their bones they knew it was true.

And here was the tax collector himself, a dozen policemen at his heels, and a drummer going about the village, beating to the four winds the dread news of the punitive fine.

Kishore was wandering in a wood at the edge of the village, collecting "frogs' parasols" (wild mushroom) for Kajoli. Odd occupation! Kajoli would cover her mouth with her palm and laugh when she knew. A man, you, and you go about finding frogs' parasols for your fool of a wife who has silly fancies! A man, you! And she would laugh her fill.

Let her laugh her fill. As the child came in her body and grew, she gave up her rice, she hankered for oddities: lotus seeds, young bamboo shoots, frogs' parasols. A pregnant one had her fancies—it was a law of life. Kajoli would laugh to cover her shame. What was there to be ashamed about if it was a law of life? And then, was a man less of a man if he looked about for wild bits of food for the pregnant mother of his son? Kishore felt a warmth inside his chest as he considered the words—the mother of his son. That Kajoli girl a mother! Mother of his son! His lips hung open with pure wonder.

Then he heard the beat of drum—*doog doog!*—and the yell of the drummer, and anxiously hurried out of the wood, the mushroom slung in the waist-fold of his *dhoti*, and he came upon the tax collector himself, speaking to a group of peasants who had come rushing from the fields, all angry and alarmed.

"What have you to complain about, village folk? Have you no sense in your stomach? It isn't as if the tax-money will go to fill the belly of your Gorement. It will be spent, each and every *pie* spent, to build the grand new *dak ghar* that is now ready on paper—not the old-fashioned mud-brick house you burnt down, a steel-and-cement structure strong as a lion. It will be a proud sight. You are on the path of progress, village folk. You will slap red-cement floors with your bare, dusty feet, you will stand blinking at a counter of timber and brass where you will buy your postal cards and book your money orders for any place in the world and open savings-bank accounts and send a telegram to the *Burra Lat* [Governor-General] or anybody! Why, men, you may even have a B.A.-pass postmaster."

Somewhere in the tax collector's face menace glinted behind the wide, suave grin. He had tact enough not to give it out that the levy was also meant to pay for a punitive police force to be imposed on the rebel villages.

He would not hurry them, he said. They could take their

time. He glanced at the storeman standing away from the crowd, and something perhaps passed between eye and eye. He would be back in a month's time. "A month to find the cash to pay your punitive fine, village folk."

No way out. Trapped! Who would speak the word of wisdom? Devata in prison. The village elders in prison. And the storeman was the self-appointed trustee of the national movement! "The Evil Thing will seize your crop, my brother. Sell your crop lest it goes for a song! Why, in the villages beyond the river so much grain has been seized and sold that the bottom has dropped out of the price level—the rate has sunk and sunk. Sell off to-day, for to-morrow you must sell at a lower rate."

The storeman had eaten the good salt of *Cheap Rice, Limited*, and he would not spare himself; his legs toiled and his tongue toiled, and scarcely would he allow himself a moment to catch his breath.

When the fines had been paid and the rice drained from the village, moving off in big city barges, a new problem arose. The *kisan* field-hands could buy no rice at the *haat*—the *haat*, once so well stocked, was suddenly empty! And the *kisans* were in a terrible plight. The peasant brothers would not sell them grain? They would close their fists and see their men starve?

"Our own stocks cannot last till the new crop, Mother," said Kishore. "How feed other mouths? The *zemindar's* rent is due, Mother——"

The mother was silent for a minute with some thought, and when she spoke her voice was firm and compelling.

"If we eat, our *kisan* brethren and their kin shall eat. The rice is as much theirs as ours, Kishore; for it has grown from the pouring sweat of their chests. The money we have paid them as harvest wage is nothing. Man eats food, not money."

Kishore lowered his glance, shamed, humbled. But he fretted about the land rent that had to be paid, and the stock of grain soon to dwindle every day.

Presently the rice-hunger that was a thin stream was swelling into a mighty flood. Fisherfolk needed rice. Craftsmen needed rice. And all this while uprooted villagers were trekking over the village, victims of the Army order of evacuation.

And the mother would not deny anyone who came to her begging. "*He*, now in jail-house, would not have eaten while men hungered at his door; how can I let him down?" So she said, and her eyes were far and brooding, and her will had a new edge of iron. She seemed possessed by her perilous faith.

Kishore made his grave decision. He would go to the city and find work. He would work very hard and never eat his fill, pinching himself to save each copper *pie*, and he would send a big money order to his kin every month. It would break his heart to go away from Kajoli in her pregnant state, but there was no other way. Perhaps he would come back when she was in her child-pain. . . .

The new *dak ghar* would, after all, have some use for him, Kishore thought with a sore smile.

No trains stopped at Baruni station save for higher-class passengers at their bidding. Kishore must walk to the junction six miles away.

The day of agony came.

Kajoli took off her eardrops, thin silver filigree work, a marriage gift from the mother. They were all the trinkets she owned. Kajoli slipped them into her husband's hand. "Listen. Sell them in the city. Food and shelter you will need before you find work."

"No—no—no!" Kishore almost shrieked in woe.

"Yes. You must. Can't you understand?" She lowered her eyes as they moistened. "Trinkets! What use to me? You gone, who would look at them?" Then she lifted her glance, soothing him because of his misery, a smile like sunbeam breaking through the tear-haze: "Why, when you come back home in the winter you will bring me silver loops of the new city fashion. And bangles for my arms? *Han?*"

And she bent her head, flushing because of the look in his eyes—eyes gazing unsatedly.

At the moment of parting she struggled to hold back the big drops of tear—tears were ill-omen—and her lips made the semblance of a smile as she said murmuring, "You will write a letter every week? A long one?" And she took his hand in hers and laid it for a moment on her belly, where the child nestled, invoking the father's blessing on the unborn one.

As she sat down to her noon meal two hours later, suddenly she gave a violent start. She sat very still, frozen, eyes flickerless, as though listening with all her soul, and then she slumped on the mud floor and buried her face in her arm and burst into broken-hearted sobbing. Ceaseless floods of tears came streaming down her face.

In that instant Kishore lay dying across the steel track, a

bullet in his spine, within sight of the railway station a furlong away.

His Excellency was to pass that way in his special train, and armed guards had been posted as usual all along the line, ten to a mile, for hundreds of miles. As Kishore climbed the embankment and set foot on the track by way of a short cut, a police guard challenged him, and Kishore in sudden panic started to run. The guard took aim and fired.

CHAPTER X

FROM SOMEWHERE in the Libyan desert Kunal had written to his brother. Letters from him were all too rare these days. Heavy battles had engaged him. Mersa Matruh, Tobruk, Benghazi. After El Alamein, Kunal wore the oak leaf signifying that he had been mentioned in despatches. He stated that casually in his letter, as if it meant little to him, for there was a deep thought in his mind and a keen feeling.

"Our soldiers from India have won a great victory, I am proud to say," he wrote. "I don't mean their victory over the enemy, I mean their victory, as it were, over themselves. You see, *dada*, they have killed their old foe—the sense of race inferiority. Over a long period of history the European has stood as a higher being because of his fighting power. Now what has happened? The soldiers from India have fought and defeated white troops in pitched battles even against very heavy odds. The white man's bubble has exploded in the African air, as a literary chap would have it (would he?). I have sounded men of my unit, and that is my clear impression. Perhaps you know? The men write to their people at home, and with pride and scorn they rub in this defeat of a white race. The myth that has been the spine of empires lies in pieces on the desert sands.

"Do I sound somewhat dramatic, *dada*? But this is my plain feeling. And this, I can tell you, is the feeling of other Indian officers. You know I cannot write all about it, but when men and officers return home, believe me, *dada*, they won't take things lying down."

One good thing, then, would come out of this War, mused Rahoul. Meanwhile the War had brought a calamity over the land. One day, late in the spring, Rahoul recalled, a lone straggler on the eastern seaboard stumbled and fell and never rose again. He had died for lack of food, so it was reported, and the brief news flashed past almost unnoticed. A mere beggar. No one then felt that he was a premonition, a symbolic shape of things to come. Other men sank down and died. Then women. Finally, children. Husbands and sons had tried to shield with their blood and bones the dear ones at home, and failed. All were decaying together.

And the avalanche had moved fast. How suddenly it smashed down upon Calcutta, sweeping over the congested chaos of the north districts, overflowing the centre, pressing as far as the pleasant lakeside where Rahoul lived!

Authority took little heed. A passing phenomenon. A situation over-dramatized by the Press. The dying ones who lay huddled on monsoon-wet pavements were refused admission to hospitals—the regulations did not provide for people who were not diseased, only shrivelling because of an empty stomach.

The empty stomach was due to no blight of Nature, no failure of crops. It was man-made scarcity, for the harvest had been fair, and even if the Army bought up big stocks, with rationing at the right level there could be food for all. But there was no rationing. The belated law against hoarding was a dead letter, never put into force against the food profiteers. Forty thousand country boats wantonly destroyed. Many villages evacuated. The uprooted people pauperized. Inflated currency added the finishing touch, eating up the people's purchasing power, reducing the small savings of a lifetime to a fifth of their worth. Nothing was left of the foundations of life, the roots deep down in the soil.

Yes, it was all simple enough. They paid the peasants and took their grain. They took land and houses and the fishing-boats. They always paid well. And how smug they were about it! And then they worked their printing-presses to death, making money out of paper and printer's ink—big money. They flooded the land with promissory notes, fifteen hundred million swelling soon to seven thousand million! They devalued money in the process. The peasant who had two hundred *rupees* in exchange for his ancestral home found that the sum fell to a fraction of its former value. The outward look of money showed little change. The same face of the British King, the same print-marks. Only the value fell; every month the value was less. The bewildered peasant did not know how it happened. His rulers knew. It was economic banditry practised on a staggering scale.

Such was the picture of Bengal's economy at the crisis of its life, Rahoul knew. And there was the colossus of authority, cold and inhuman, to steer the stricken people through the great hunger with the aid of its fawning puppets, the hired quislings. And the quislings incompetent, negligent, sunk in apathy, utterly insensitive. The administration leprous with corruption from neck to heel.

Corruption had grown like an epidemic. Money had become a mad hunger. Flowing in great swollen streams, it made private lakes for the rich, who grew vastly richer. The poor grew proportionately poorer. Never in the land's history had the process that made the rich richer, the poor poorer, gained such ruthless intensity.

Destitute humanity groaning about the rich city in tens of thousands—misery's overflow from the countryside. What impenetrable distress had overwhelmed their homes? No one knew the full details, for the contacts were few across the tall walls of isolation. A Minister of His Excellency of Bengal had suggested that rural foodstocks and the people's needs be officially assessed. His Excellency had promptly scrapped the idea. Waste of time. It would not help the war effort. The real thing was scorched earth, not collection of food figures.

His Excellency, who bit into the people's bread and their life, smug in the comfort of his mental sanctuary, was also a symbolic shape, mused Rahoul, pencil in hand, drawing lines on the blotting-pad, making that symbolic shape.

The post that had brought a letter from Libya had brought also a money order from a Bengal village, mailed to a peasant mother and returned to the sender—the addressee could not be traced. What had happened? wondered Rahoul. Where had they gone—mother, Kajoli, Kishore? To some city where Kishore had found work? Kishore knew his city address, and if things were bad he would surely have written, he would even have come to Calcutta—he knew the city. Rahoul was worried. If only he had gone to the village when the letter he wrote brought no reply! Remorse lay in his heart like a thorn. If only he had left his work and gone down to the village! He had enclosed money with his letter lest they had been caught in lean times. (How could Rahoul know that the letter was never delivered? That the postal censor who opened it—all letters mailed to rebel districts were read—had to tear up the letter

so that the enclosed money could be transferred to his pocket?)
Two months Rahoul had waited, and then sent a money order
—that, anyhow, would bring back a signed receipt. But the
money was back, lying beside Kunal's letter in a little heap.

The armed forces of India who fought the battle of civilization were thinking new thoughts, and would not take things
lying down when they returned, so Kunal had written. But
what of the people? There was no hunger riot in the land, no
angry demand for food, the birthright of every man. Rahoul
knew the reason—it had been revealed in one illuminating
flash. A group of destitutes dragging their legs along College
Street paused near a cookshop, sunken eyes avidly gazing at
the arrays of eatables behind the plate glass. Rahoul stood by
and watched.

"Why don't we break the glass and eat?" said a voice of
excited anger.

A half murmur of approval. Jail-house? Why, they would
eat in the jail-house, they would keep alive. Then an old man
with hunched shoulders spoke quietly.

"*Chih!* my sons, *chih!* Are you men or thieves? How can
you take by force what is not yours? Have you no faith, no
tradition, no true principles of living? Are you wild beasts?"

"Beasts?" shouted the young destitute who had spoken.
"Those others who lay by so much food and deny us crumbs—
they are the beasts."

Silence followed. Then the bent, grey-haired man stepped
forward.

"My son, I have saved a morsel from yesterday. Eat." And
out of a fold of his loin-cloth he produced a piece of coarse
bread. "Eat, my son."

Two other hoary-headed men hobbled up and they, too,
produced stale pieces of food from their loin-clothes, saying,
"Eat, my son."

The youth stood dazed and blinked his eyes, and suddenly he
burst into weeping and turned and fled from the people. And
the three old men gazed at the receding figure, and they looked
at each other with their sunken eyes and smiled faintly, as if to
say, "He is saved from the evil in him," and they lifted their
folded palms to their God in grateful salutation.

Barely a year had passed since these men, or their brethren,
had risen in anger against the tyrants, the robbers of freedom,
who had swept the people's leaders into prison without even a
pretence of trial. But they would not rise in revolt that their

95

stomachs could be soothed—a selfish personal end! They would fight and die over a moral issue. But hunger was their fate, an expiation of the sins of past lives. The peasants' hands were manacled with their antique moral tradition. The tyrants, rice-robbers, were safe from peril because of the peasants' tradition. Yet one day the hungry millions would see the truth and waken to their right to live, and then they would make tyranny tremble with their wrath——.

Rahoul rose, bemused, and paced the laboratory floor, his feet restless, his heart now sinking with the hopeless apathy of the people, now tensing with the vision of the people's wrath.

Why could he not forget the woes of this pebble of an earth and commune with the stars, the far earths whose untapped secrets he sought? Why could he not fly from the oppressive darkness of Bengal far into cosmic light? That was his true concern. Not the people's hunger for food or freedom, for he had his own separate hunger. His own hunger was his true concern. Why had he lost his intellectual poise?

He could not help it. He was made that way. He knew in his spirit the hungers of his people. They were his hungers, too. In his blood and spirit he had so many hungers!

His mind flew to Grandfather. How he looked forward to the day when he would meet him in the Central Jail at Dehra Dun—he had received permission for an interview. *Dadu* would strengthen his spirit, *dadu* had strengthened him ever in the past with his clear faith and vision. And Rahoul would tell him of Kunal's new feelings and of the awakening of India's armed forces. *Dadu* would be full of joy. Strange how *dadu* had always expected much from Kunal, though there had been no contact between them, no common ideas to share.

As he walked past the half-open door he saw a figure slip by, and in swift anger he was about to cry out: "Rat, I have not gone yet; I am taking my time." He controlled himself.

He must write down a few notes as though he still pursued the Death Ray. That spy creature would be in the laboratory as soon as he was gone, reading the notes, copying them, perhaps, so that he could make his report to his masters. To the Evil Thing. Rahoul recalled the peasants' epithet—so appropriate!

How much did they pay him for his unclean work? wondered Rahoul. He would not have to hunt for a job, that one. When he passed out of college, the Evil Thing would find him a good post. And the brightest boys of the University would go

96

jobless, that provision could be made for spies and such other riff-raff armed with certificates from highly-placed riff-raff.

The students were on the edge of revolt, and, fearing them, the Evil Thing watched them like an ogre. Their hatred of fascism alone held them in leash. But the danger was that, once out of restraint, they would take up terrorist tools, as they had often done before. That was not the way. Mass action, pin all your faith on mass action, and make yourself one with the common people—so Rahoul urged on them. The student movement was gathering pace. Rahoul had to play his part. The star-beams must wait till freedom came.

But he had better shield himself with fake notes. No use being buried away in prison. The spy creature had to be duped. The Death-Ray was round the corner!

CHAPTER XI

Kajoli had prepared her vegetable patch with anxious care. She would take no chances. She had dug the moist, dark-brown earth, loosened the clods and picked off grass and weed and let air soak into the soil—the rootlets of plants drew life from the air they imbibed. Then she had flattened the soil with the manure she had prepared in a trench—Mangala's dung cast in the trench and covered till it became a rich earth sustenance—and she had turned the soil again for more air to soak in, and over again. She had cut ridges for drainage and sown the seeds of egg-plants. The egg-plants yielded a vegetable in common use, a round, swelling, smooth-skinned shape, white at first, gaining a purple hue as it filled out, ripened. Barely knee high, the plant bore a dozen fruits, and these, baked on a slow fire, were good to eat. Kajoli knew the secret ways of egg-plants, and her crops had always been plentiful. Strange that a plant, like an animal, had its own secret individual way, and would never look well and become rich with fruit unless it could fulfil itself.

All along the hedge she had planted bean seedlings. Beans were easy to grow. They were filling, nourishing. Between the egg-plants and the beans were a row of *bhendi*—ladies' fingers. Spread over the roof-thatch were the pumpkin vines, now withering at the season's end. Kajoli had used every inch of earth that was her own.

So in her small way Kajoli grew food for her kin and for herself. The stock of rice would last barely a month more, even though they saved each grain, eating a starvation diet, dreading the day when there would be no rice left in the big-bellied earthenware jar—none. All day she went about with mother and Onu, collecting odd bits of food: shrimps from the ponds and water-weeds; green wild figs from the tall trees; berries and soft, edible roots from wasteland. But the whole village, from dawn to dusk, was absorbed in the same pursuit, and the stocks of Nature's free food fell off every day.

Once in a while some trader or other appeared in the village with a bag of rice, offering a bowlful or two for the peasants' few possessions: ploughshares, axes, picks and shovels, petty trinkets, kitchen brass. That was the only new rice to come into the village. Not quite. For there was good cash paid for cattle, and with that you could buy food-grains from the *haat* at five times the past summer's rate. (A shadow of the old *haat* that had sat every Sunday for a thousand years, its trade was now but the bartering of grain for trinkets and household brass.) There was a big demand for cattle. The Army ate cattle. But no peasant sold his cattle till his knees gave way— how would he ever turn his earth with his plough-pair gone? The dealers bided their time with patience. Every peasant would have to sell his cattle—one day. What good were your cattle when hunger ate you, ate your dear ones? Time was a foe of the stricken peasant.

And the land? Many peasants could not sell freely the land they had under plough because of the *zemindar's* lien on it, but even the others, tenant-proprietors claiming the right, would die rather than sell Mother Earth, so they said. The land-greedy folk who prowled the villages listened and narrowed their eyes and smiled darkly, and they, too, bided their day with patience.

The Battle of Bengal intensified. Human endurance ebbed. Hungry children cried themselves to death. Streams of desperate men ventured out of their ancestral homes in search of food, hanging on to the footboards of railway trains, riding on the sunbaked roofs. But the police threw up barriers. Then the men trekked the meadows and roads, ten thousand village streams flowing citywards. Ahead was the city, shining bright as a lighthouse. The city had never grown a blade of corn. The city had eaten out of the green bowl of the peasant's fields. The city, having taken the harvests, would spare a little
98

for the peasant folk who had ever filled the bowls? The city would not let the food-growers famish? Move on to the city. Move on. Drag your sore feet and move on.

Kajoli, a dozen times a day, bent over her plants, watching the purple blooms turn into fruit-shapes, and the tiny white shapes grow bigger, bigger. The eye could not see the day-to-day growing, but Kajoli had a sight that was not of the eye. She knew the growing of each plant on her land. And she bided her day with patience.

This was her fifth month. A long time still before her child came. Oh, if only he could be here earlier! The arms of the girl ached to hold her child, the tip of her breast tingled for his mouth. How could Kajoli wait so long for the coming of her son, sunk as she was in woe, hunting for food from dawn to sundown, and hearing no word from her child's father, whom the Evil Thing (so Kajoli felt sure) had cast into prison? It barely crossed her mind that the new-born one would be ill-fed —that she, with her famished frame, would not be able to nurse him much. She worried, though, about her child's clothes. A pink frock—that was her dream. It was strange that she saw her child always in a pink frock. Perhaps she had seen a picture somewhere, in one of Grandfather's books, and it stayed on in her fancy? An impossible dream! She and Mother had two *saris* between them, and no other clothing. The two *saris* were getting worn; a few months more, and they would be ragged. The village had become ragged as never before; no new clothing for almost a year, since the starving weavers had sold their looms to the trader in desperation and wandered away. What would happen when these two *saris* became rags? Other village women, Kajoli knew, slept naked in the dark of night, these days, to save their *saris*, but she and Mother had not cast off shame to that extent. They must, some time. Else . . . Kajoli closed her eyes because of the shameful vision.

Kajoli, haunted by the dread that the only *sari* she possessed would fall into rags, yet dreamed of her child dressed in a pretty pink frock.

One day, as she rose at the break of dawn and bent caressing eyes over her egg-plants as usual, her face turned very pale. Ants! Red ants, the dread foe of egg-fruits. How save her treasure? She hurried to the kitchen and brought out a basket of wood ash, sprinkling it all over the plants. She waited, watching, her heart fluttering.

The ants wavered, fell back. They moved about in distress,

blinded by the ash, keeping away from the plants. Kajoli heaved a sigh of relief. But half an hour later, when she returned to look at the plants, there they were, a bigger army of ants, in their thousands. Kajoli sprinkled more ash.

So it went on all day. Kajoli could not go for her usual food hunt in pond and meadow. The night grew, the fray continued. Onu helped her and Mother also. A million ants seemed to be about. Perhaps they, too, had had a famine. Man had robbed them of their food, the roots that grew wild in wasteland. They seemed desperate. At last Kajoli broke down in tears, admitting defeat. She let Mother collect the few lean, half-grown fruits yet uneaten, and the plucking twisted her heart.

Early, at daybreak, she rushed out to the garden. The ants were gone. But they had completed the pillage, and chewed away the egg-fruits just peering out of purple blooms.

She covered her face with her hands, emptied, utterly spent.

The beans remained, and she tended them with renewed, ever-alarmed care. The healthy stalks climbed up the hedge and cast out looping tendrils, full and proud with the rich promise of fruit-bearing. Beans were a sturdy stock, no easy prey to insects. They would surely bear well.

Kajoli was cooking a meagre meal in the kitchen when she heard Mother scream in the backyard. The girl dashed out in alarm. The mother was trembling with rage as she stood gazing down at the cow, Mangala, and lifted her hand and slapped the face of the animal.

"Mother!" cried Kajoli in sharp protest, and then she saw what had happened. Stalks hung limp on the hedge, their leaves and tendrils ripped. "Mother!" cried Kajoli in a shriek. "My beans!"

For a moment or two Mother could not answer because of her anger and pain.

"Mangala ate them, the witch." Her voice was strangled.

Mangala ate them? Mangala, who was one of the household, sharing its weal and woe? Kajoli could not believe her ears. Her pained, amazed gaze rested upon the cow. Mangala stood very still, her head cast down, agony in her large eyes.

Mangala was famished, the russet skin a loose, hanging garment over her bones. There was little fodder for her. The village pasture was gone—the *zemindar* had put it under plough because of the grow-more-food campaign. The village had sold off its cattle and lost its right to a common pasturage. But what good was it if they grew more food, since it was not food for the people? And what was to happen to the few cattle that remained? No light job to take them to the grassland miles away in another village. The old plough-pair were gone for fifteen *seers* of rice—not a tenth of their true value—and Mangala alone was left. Mangala had not eaten well for months. And day after day she had stood in the yard, watching the beanstalks grow, the young green creepers with shooting tendrils and broad, luscious leaves. Day after day she had watched and craved and suppressed her hunger. Suddenly, to-day, Mangala had lost herself.

Kajoli, in a flash of understanding, knew all.

The unhappy mother was raging at the animal.

"Mother," pleaded Kajoli, "do not take her to task. Do you want to break her heart? Look at her eyes, Mother." And she flung her arms over Mangala and buried her face against the rough russet skin, weeping brokenly.

The mother looked at her girl and she looked at the eyes of the cow, and though there were no tears in the large black eyes, the mother knew that Mangala, too, wept.

.   .   .   .   .

The fig-trees were all stripped of their little green pellets of fruits, save for a few twigs here and there on the topmost branches far out of reach. But the boy could climb like a squirrel. He knew the strength and resilience of every tree-limb and could tell by its feel if it would bear him—it was strange how a thin, frail-seeming bough would often bend under weight, yet not break. The boy was the envy of his companions, who sat scattered on the lower branches, each with barely a dozen half-grown figs in his waist-cloth, while Onu crawled about high above their heads, hands busy, pocket bulging. Onu was no waster, though. This was the last figstock. It should be held in reserve, plucked with niggardly care. He took none but the fat, well-rounded ones—they would be faintly yellowing in a day or two, losing juice and flavour.

"Pluck us a few," said the boys, looking up at him with injured pride, but helpless.

Onu plucked a bunch and dropped it on the ground. The boys clambered down the tree-stem and stood with faces lifted, eyes harassed by the sun. But the boy, perched high on top and half visible through screens of leaf, was plucking no more. He was creeping down.

"Drop a few more, Onu," shouted the youngsters, scowling, wondering what was his game.

Onu had made up his mind. Those figs which he alone could reach were his own secret treasure. The others had no right to them. Let those boys help themselves if they could.

Selfishness had been alien to his nature. He had always loved to share his best gifts with his friends. But hunger had debased his warm, innocent spirit. He had become a hoarder. He hoarded for himself and his sister and mother the wild green figs on tree-tops which none but he could reach.

He came down, turned away from the boys and began walking off across the field. A moment's amazed silence, and then the boys broke out in a chatter and yelled, "Stop, thief!" They surged forward in a rush.

His face burned with shame, for he knew he had been mean, and his shame found relief in anger. "What is it you want?" His voice was a challenge.

With hatred they eyed the bulge of figs in his waist-cloth over the flattened belly, and one cried, "Thief!" and the others echoed, "Thief!"

"I am no thief," said Onu, with a jerk of his head. "I plucked my figs. You pluck yours—plenty left. You have gone mad, mad!"

The others hissed in answer, "Thief!", and in an instant, as though by a word of inner command, they fell upon him, hitting, pulling his hair, trying to snatch away his figs.

His bulging waist-cloth he clutched with one hand, fighting with the other. They were boys of about the same age, all bony-faced from hunger, friends a minute before, now torn wide apart by their need for survival, three ranged against one. Onu fell, sprawling flat on his back, desperately struggled and sat up as he felt hands prod, dig, at his waist-cloth till the threadbare fabric came apart. His sweat-smeared ribs panted hard while his teeth found a grasping arm. A howl of pain, and arms pushed him back, pushed madly. Onu fell again. His head bumped on the edge of a half-brick, his eyes closed and he lay quite still.

The youngsters gazed down, pale with fear, silent. Then they turned and fled.

One came back, though. He looked down at his friend as he lay senseless in the hot sun, dust on his lips and nostrils, a trickle of blood on his scalp. The youngster mused and wiped his nose and shuffled off to a pool nearby, plunged his *dhoti* corner in the water and came back and bathed the injured head. He watched the closed eyelids and, bending, spoke in his ear: "Onu! Waken, *bhai*." A sob in the voice. "Onu, do not get killed, *bhai*."

And the boy woke in a while and moved his head, his eyes blinking in the sun. He was dazed still, but he soon remembered the figs, and sat up in alarm lest they should be all gone. There they lay, scattered, bright spots on the pale grass. His *dhoti* was ripped, and at sight of the damage he pressed his lips together in anger and glared. "Rogue!" he said, and tightened his lips again.

The other did not feel the abuse. He smiled, joyous, and started to collect the figs. Having collected all, he put them in his friend's waist-cloth, first tying the ripped ends, and he shook his head, murmuring, "I never hit you, Onu *bhai*," and he shook his head over and over again, as though by repeated denial a lie would cease to be a lie.

"It is all for the little one," he gulped spittle to ease his mouth—"only four years old. Her stomach isn't strong like ours. She can eat no wild roots, no water-plant. She can eat fig boiled soft." The smile was gone from his face and his eyes began to fill. "Else, why should I fight you, *bhai*?" He hung his head, rubbed his eyes and sniffled.

Onu knew his friend's little sister. The father, like Onu's, had been taken away in handcuffs for warring on authority. Robi, like Onu, was the breadwinner of the house.

Onu loosened the strips of his waist-cloth and took out half the figs to offer them to his friend. "Every day we'll go halves, *bhai*, halves. That tree has plenty left." He seemed to be heartening himself rather than the other. "Every little branch at the top I can reach with my hand."

Robi sniffled more because of his friend's kindness. "No, not so many. Just one fistful, *bhai*. There." He cupped his palms together.

"Take all this lot," Onu insisted. He, too, sniffled. It now came upon him like a shock that the boy who had flung him down with a mad push—that boy also had a little one in the household, a baby brother. The *kisan* father was a cripple; a police bullet had hit his thigh-bone and his leg had wasted. Babies had to have figs. Vishnu had fought so hard only to earn figs for his starving child of a brother. Onu felt his heart sink.

So many mouths to feed. Onu could see in his mind the figs

that still hung on the tree, and he cast up accounts. Soon the figs easy of access would be gone, and then he would have to creep along the outspread branches and reach for the far, thin ends. But he was so frightened! What if he fell and broke his head and died? Or broke his legs and became a cripple like old Hori, who, too, had fallen from a tree—doomed to drag himself about on crutches? These days he could not climb to the tree-top with his old ease, because of his gnawing hunger and weakening—his hand shook, his head grew dizzy, his eyes dimmed, and he had to grip hard lest he fall.

Seized by dread and despair, Onu blinked to hold back his tears. He would not let his mother and sister live only on wild roots and herbs. And the babies, the tiny brothers and sisters of his friends, they could not eat wild roots at all. Onu must crawl to the tips of thin, perilous tree-limbs rocking dizzily under his weight. He was caught, helpless, in the snare of his own inner feelings. There was no escape.

CHAPTER XII

THE PEASANT mother smiled sadly to herself because she had been able at last to find Mangala this tract of green pasture, even if it was far away from the village. She had tramped a weary hour with her animal, reaching the river's edge, and there lay the grass in its young luxuriance, unhedged, open to access. The old pasture in the village had been put under plough to grow more food under Gorement's orders, so it was said; but others, farther away, were unaccountably closed to the village cattle—it looked as though the men who were buying up cattle in their scores used this device to force the hands of stubborn peasants loth to sell.

If you could not graze your cattle, you sold them in desperation. What good were they to you, those bundles of skin and bone? Milch kine? Their udders hung dry and shrunken. The animals were a sheer wasting asset. Die they would in a while, losing all worth. Then why not sell them for the rice you needed so badly for your shrivelling bodies and the bodies of your sons and daughters? How could you be so selfish as to deny the dear hungry ones?

But the peasant mother had not the heart to sell Mangala, and, even if she had, her Onu and Kajoli would not have let her—they would starve and die and yet not touch the rice taken in exchange for their Mangala. Rightly so, for it would be like eating the meat of Mangala, who was no animal to those children; she had become human for them by their long association and fondness. They had grown up on her milk. She knew their voices, and would answer their call with an eager low. Big-uddered, she had let them play with her new calves (herself born in this house, a little heifer calf), looking down fondly with great, black eyes. And who did not know that the men who were buying up cattle needed the animals only for their meat? A great Army, it was said, was covering all Bengal, *paltan* of all castes, all races, many eaters of beef. Cattle drained swiftly out of villages. The traders had money; but they wondered sometimes at the selfishness deep in the peasants' marrow-bones: to hold on to useless cattle while your children famished!

Luck seemed good to the peasant mother to-day. She had grieved to see Mangala low piteously for a bite of grass (and those well-guarded pastures where cattle had grazed since time-less time so thick with tall, sweet, monsoon grass, no use to any-body!), thick bones sticking out of her russet skin, eyes afraid and begging, even her pair of strong curved horns looking oddly emaciated. For months Mangala had been fed with the rice straw that thatched the house roof; the straw, too, was now spent, and the house was roofless save for one room where the family had to shelter from the heavy rains that might pour all day, all night, for days on end—the peasant mother and her children, and Mangala, too, all huddling together on the wet mud floor, while the rain pattered and the seven winds of heaven raged about like seven maniacs. But now that the mother had ventured afield across the railway embankment, gone to the river-side and found the unclaimed pasture owned perhaps by the Railway Company, Mangala would not have to famish. She would greedily eat a bellyful, more perhaps than was good for her, and in a week or so the loose skin folding and creasing over her flanks would smoothen as of old, tighten.

The mother could not afford to sit long, relaxing her limbs and watching Mangala graze contentedly. She must go about her day's task of finding edible roots for her children and for herself. She walked on by the edge of the river, and once in a while she stopped to dig up the thick roots of wild *kachu* or some unfamiliar plant (lumps of clotted clay hanging on them), to be cut and boiled and consumed with salt. Some roots tortured the stomach, and you learnt to discard them; but those that only made you uneasy, resting in your stomach like a stone load, had to be retained in your daily fare—you could not afford to pick and choose, and it was good, after all, to have something inside you that ate up your hunger for a long while. When you had to choose between the ache of hunger and the ache of indigestion, you would often choose the latter, so in her heart the mother knew.

Walking, she felt with her cupped palm the rice tied in a corner of her *sari*, and knew a thrill of pleasure. The last word in luxurious fare was rice. Once it had been the common staple diet. The fields of Bengal grew enough rice for all. But now that the peasants had been robbed of the grain (Gorement and traders took away the harvest, paying the market rate, but the cash dwindled in worth with each flick of your eyelid, and presently you were paying tenfold to buy back the rice you had to part with!), a rare commodity it was—each grain a grain of gold. A gift from Mangala, this rice. They were passing by the village store when Mangala suddenly stopped, shook her head with a jerk. What is wrong with you, Mangala, mother? No insect tormenting her eyes. No crow pecking at the grit in her ears. What, then? Mangala repeated the movement. Her neckstring of little brass bells tinkled gaily. They always tinkled as Mangala walked—now she stood still and made the bells tinkle. Mother looked into her eyes, and knew in a flash. "How can I take your trinket, Mangala?" But Mangala jerked her head again, insistent. So with heavy heart the mother untied the red-thread neckstring, holding the tiny bells in her hand. Mangala seemed content. She lowed softly. The mother walked off to the store.

"Cow-bells!" The storeman was scornful. "Who wants cow-bells?"

Mother felt relieved. "True, true," she said, nodding, hurrying off, when the storeman called out: "One moment, Mother." It had come upon him that cow-bells might fetch a price at the city store. Toys were in short supply. The children of the rich longed for them.

The storeman paid her with rice—five palmsful. The mother had not earned so much grain for weeks past. A space of time grows vastly in the convex mirror of intense experience, and these weeks were like years.

The happy-sad mother could not look at Mangala as they
106

trudged out of the village. No bells tinkled—Mangala had lost part of herself.

And then the mother had discovered the unclaimed, unguarded pasture, and her shame had eased. A gift of grass for a gift of rice. Kajoli, Onu, they would dance and leap with joy when they knew!

At the bend of the embankment a woman crouched, digging the soft mud with her hands, a tiny child by her side. The mother drew near, curious. She had collected enough roots for the day. No use digging for more, since they could not be stored, they would stiffen and become wood-like. The mother was curious to see what the other had found.

The young woman, about Kajoli's age, seemed intent on her work. She did not hear the stranger's feet or feel her presence. It was a trench she had dug, a cubit deep, and the mother watched her in amazed silence. The woman turned aside and picked up the bare-limbed baby boy, rocking him in her arms as he whimpered faintly, and coaxing, warm and tender: "No more hurt in the belly, my sweet one, my godling. You will sleep." And she laid the child in the trench, folded his reed-like arms over the bony chest and pushed the eyelids down as though to put the child to sleep, and then with hurried hands she began to pile the earth back into the grave.

Knees frozen, the mother could not move, she could not even speak a word. When the earth had buried the child to the chin, she made a desperate effort and shrieked in terror.

The woman was not startled. She turned, looked with distraught eyes, then resumed her terrible task. "No more pain, my godling," she said, coaxing, warm and tender.

The mother darted and swooped upon the child and snatched it from its grave.

"Witch! Murdering a child! Your own! What hell would hold the like of thee? Witch!"

"My child, give me back my child," the woman whimpered. "Hungry, he has no sleep in his eye; he stares, only stares. Let me make him sleep—sleep in peace." She reached out her arms, gesturing as though there was need for hurry.

In a burst of anger the mother lifted her hand and struck the woman across the face. The woman looked on with blank eyes, but her arms dropped. The mother seized her matted, dust-grey hair and pulled hard. The woman made no protest, did not cry out in pain. Her mind was empty—as empty as her

107

stomach. The mother knew her. A fisherman's wife. Hard to
see in her the gay bride of yester year.

"Poor godling, so hurt with hunger! Look, my breasts have
no milk"—lifting the tatters that half covered her bosom—"he
has no throat to cry. If he sleeps a little! Where is sleep? He
is hurt, and hurt all the time with his hunger. In his cool earth
bed he can close his eyes, sleep."

The mother shivered, looking at the grave, and held the
child to her bosom. The little one gazed with eyes that seemed
without light, dead.

"Come." She dragged the woman by the arm, walking with
hurried feet.

"For shame! Such a tiny one. What if I hadn't come in the
nick of time? God's will!" She folded her palms and touched
them to her head, and as she did so she felt the child press
against her face. In that instant she recalled the baby boy she
had lost many years back when she was young—he had been no
older than this one. She laid her mouth on the cool cheek.
Her heart beat with emotion.

"Your man, where is he, the fisherman?" She spoke with a
deep sigh. She knew the boy. A friend of her son Kanu. On
his wedding day the young fisherman had made a gift of fish
to every peasant household because of the joy in his soul. His
bride, his little son——

"Gone."

"Gone? Where?"

"Who knows? Yonder——" The woman pointed vaguely
with her hand.

The mother knew her meaning. There was not a youth left
in the village. All had gone off in search of food. None was
known to have returned. Her own son-in-law—— The mother
heaved another sigh. Her Kajoli six months pregnant. What
had happened to the boy? Three months he was gone——

"I'll give you rice." She held up the corner of her *sari*,
revealing the treasure. What better solace on earth than
rice?

But the woman was not tempted.

"How can he eat rice, poor childling? So young. I have no
milk for his mouth. No copper to buy milk. If he lives he will
suffer more, more. How can I see him suffer so?" And all at
once the tears began to pour from her eyes and she broke down
in a fit of sobbing. "Oh, Mother, why are you so cruel to my
child? What has he done to you? Why won't you let him sleep
108

in peace? In my arms he only knows pain; he dies slowly, slowly, slowly——"

The mother's hand lifted to her mouth in an accustomed gesture of helpless bewilderment.

"Why, girl, you can go to Calcutta city; you never thought of that!" she cried quickly, as an idea struck her. "They are all going hotfoot to Calcutta city—hundreds have gone. Your fisherman is already there, maybe. You will get milk a-plenty in the wonder city, and rice, and a new *sari* to put on. Calcutta city has money to spare. The people have kindness in their hearts to spare for poor folk. You will be looked after. You will find work, big wages! Nothing to worry about—nothing. One day when your child has grown and he is employed in a great jute mill—think of that proud day! Look." The voice had a begging tone. "Go to Calcutta city, girl." She held her eager eyes on the woman as though her own peace of mind rested on the other's decision.

"Calcutta? Long, long way. He will not live; he will die on the bitter road. How to live so many days with no milk in his mouth?"

The mother stared ahead, anguish in her heart. She saw Mangala lying on the grass, chewing her cud. Then a voice that could not have been her own spoke hoarsely from her throat: "Take my cow. Sell her. Go to the wonder city and be saved."

The woman gazed at the cow, gazed back at the mother. In her dull, sunken eyes there sprang a light. She was like a drowning person in her last gasp who, as she has no more air to breathe, sees a boat rush up to her, arms reach towards her. She flung herself at the mother's feet, and sobbing, her bosom heaving under the rags, she beat her head upon the earth over and over again. That was the way she showed her gratitude and her pain at taking away the cow from the mother.

The veil of stupor had lifted from her feelings. She was living again. And how she needed the little one, her child, her godling!

The mother saw all. She drew the woman to her feet and gave her the child—"Go, hurry!"—and saw her put the hungry mouth to her empty breast. She took a long look at Mangala, but dared not go near to bid her farewell, to touch her face for the last time—she felt she would not be able to stand it. Quickly she turned and walked away.

How show her face to her children, with Mangala gone?

They would not touch the rice; they would think it was Mangala's skin and bone. Then why carry the rice home? She stopped, turned round and hailed the fisher-women, who was walking in a burning hurry towards the cow.

The woman trembled. She thought the mother had changed her mind.

"Take this rice." The voice hoarse, dead.

The woman removed the rag from her breast and held it for the proffered rice.

As the mother walked back to the village without Mangala for companion, she was the loneliest woman on earth and weary beyond measure. She felt at each step her knees could not bear her any more. She longed to sit down by the wayside and weep.

So with dragging feet she trudged homeward, taking her time, the fear heavy in her heart: how would her Onu and Kajoli bear the blow? She paused on her way to speak a word to a village woman passing by the roadside with her young daughter. Mother and daughter wore new *saris*, one white with a broad crimson border, the other dyed with the bright indigo of a rainbow. What luck had come their way? Such garments! Once, when the earth was near-heaven, the weaver had them a-plenty; now they were as scarce as rice. You had to drape your limbs as best you could with old rags, patched all over. She had seen a woman wearing a piece of old sacking. When the woman walked, a grain-bag walked, or two grain-bags, one on top of the other, only the bags had been emptied of half their grain! What if one day her Kajoli had to drape herself with gunny-sacking? The *sari* she wore was ragged; no fit garment for a grown-up girl, pregnant. How could she bear to see her Kajoli wear sacking? The land? Even if she had the heart the land was not hers to sell. Only her husband could sell the land by his signature and thumb-mark.

And here was Neeri of marriageable age, but unwed, preening herself like a *zemindar's* daughter!

"What honey-eyed fate has smiled on you, sister?" she said. "Back in the Golden Age! It is good to see such stuff." She picked a fold of Neeri's indigo *sari*-end. "*Han*, it is good to feel such stuff." Her fingers traced the cloth with pleasure and with pain.

The mother of Neeri lifted her hand to her forehead saying, "The writing here." And she closed her mouth.

"Gifts have poured into your bowl. A wealthy groom? Our

Neeri is to be wed? And the son is mindful of his mother-in-law as of his bride?"

Neeri wed. Wealthy groom. The woman's mouth twisted and trembled, and a sudden nameless passion took hold of her. "Why do you stick your eyes to my kitchen' pot, mother-of-Onu? I have my woes, you have yours. I can't help you, you can't help me. You, too, have a daughter. Go your way. Leave us alone." She gripped the arm of her daughter, who stood with face averted, and her voice grew hysterical because of some secret emotion: "It is not your business. I must eat. Neeri must eat. Eat rice, not roots. You, too, will eat one day, for you have a daughter. Go your way, mother-of-Onu. Keep your eyes away from my rice-pot."

The woman walked off. The mother felt overwhelmed. She could not understand what it was all about. She had said nothing to annoy that person. Her angry talk made no sense at all. And the mother's sadness, softened in a moment of diversion, rushed back upon her. Mangala gone.

The house looked gaunt with the straw plucked from the roof, and the bamboos, famished ribs, sticking bare in the thatching. Strangers by the doorstep: a wiry man of middle age and a stout-bodied woman—city people by their appearance and dress. The mother approached with wonder in her heart. She drew the *sari* over her face, as was becoming, for a man who was a stranger sat in front, but the man rose and withdrew a little way, and the mother could now uncover her face. At this moment Onu came bounding out of the house.

"Mother, look!" he cried excitedly. "Eat." His eager hand held out a pudding-like milk delicacy that had been rare in the village even in the golden age before the famine.

"Onu, my son," the fat woman from the city cried fondly, "that bit of *sandesh* is all yours. I have plenty here. Your mother has walked a long way, let her rest her feet and cool herself. She turned her face, smiling, "My sister, you too will eat."

The mother felt her heart thump. *You too will eat*—she had heard those very words out there on the street flung in her face as though in sore contempt. She felt relieved, though, that Onu had not noted Mangala's absence—he had been much too excited with his milk sweet.

"Kajoli," the mother called out, "why, you have not offered these folk a jug of water to wash their feet. What negligence is this?"

Kajoli said a word from the kitchen, and the city woman cried, "No need, sister. She offered us water to wash with. Our feet are free of dust. We have shoes on." She paused a moment, and went on: "Kajoli? No girl like her in this village, in the seven villages around. I go about much, handing food to needy folk. I have seen ten villages in one month, and Kajoli—why, she can beat a city girl flat with that comely face of hers; unadorned, no red on her lips, no touch of black on eyelids, no powder to whiten her face, she can beat a painted city chit. What luck that I have come to this house! It is the will of God." She lifted her folded palms to her head, grateful for the divine will.

The bewildered mother stared at her visitor. What goddess of mercy was she to go about the villages handing food to needy folk? Would she not give her some handfuls? The mother's heart quickened with her expectation. Perhaps she belonged to a relief society? There were such societies at work here and there, so she had heard. But the bounteous one had riches enough of her own. The gold bangles, the trinkets in her ears, the bit of shining glass in her left nostril. Her *sari* impressed the mother more than her jewellery. To wear a *sari* of such length, reaching down to the ankles, and such ample folds! Here in the village it could be cut into three pieces and worn by three women. To waste so much cloth! And the texture, and the border!

"Taste this, sister." The woman lifted the lid of an aluminium box packed full with the sweet, and the other answered faintly:

"No, no, later. Is this the hour to eat sweet?" But her mouth was eager.

The woman insisted: "A city delicacy, sister. Eat. Sweet can be eaten any time of the day. Why, I eat the stuff at any time, four times a day, more. Look at my size!"

"What size?" said the mother, protesting out of politeness. "You are healthy, just what a woman should look like. Why" —she lied to please her gracious visitor—"I was more plump than you before the lean days came upon us."

And she sat down and ate. The wonder of it, as the milk-and-sugar lump lingered between her teeth and passed slowly down her throat. Her limbs grew languid, her eyelids sank with enjoyment.

Onu whispered in her ear: "Mother, *chal* [rice]! Mother, *dal* [lentils]! *Ghee* [clarified butter], Mother!" His wan face beamed excitedly. "*Didi* is busy in the kitchen, lighting the fire, washing the grains. Mother, I'll eat three bellyfuls. I'll——" He felt a cramp of hunger in his stomach and winced.

The woman overheard the talk, thick smiles creasing her plump face.

"Why, I shall leave rice to last you full three months. And there's the cash, twenty *rupees*—a fortune for mother and son in these lean days. That girl has a hard time in the kitchen trying to light a fire in the oven, bringing tears to her eyes. I peered in. No cowdung cakes for kindling—the eyes stream as the mouth blows and blows on the poor fuel. Is this a life for a young girl?" She shook her head. "Tell me!"

"Cowdung? Our Mangala has so little to eat——" The mother bit her tongue. Fool! To speak Mangala's name! She turned anxious eyes upon her son. What if he made a scene in front of the strangers? But Onu had not heard her. He was dreaming of *chal*, *dal*, *ghee*. The stuff was being cooked in a pot-ful of water. Oh, if only *didi* would hurry with it! Hurry, *didi*.

The man who sat thirty strides apart, smoking a cigarette, now called out in a loud voice: "Is it not time to speak?"

"Later," said the woman. "When they have eaten. Later."

The mother could not hold back her concern. "Speak," she begged. "The food won't be ready yet a while." And she waited breathlessly.

The woman cleared her throat. "Listen." Her small, keen eyes darted about and her voice was low, secretive. "She will live like a princess, your girl. Such features, such beauty! They will go crazy about her in the city, just crazy; they will lick the dust of her feet. She will eat all her stomach can hold. She will have *saris* in dozens, scores, not to speak of jewellery—gold bangles and bracelets and pearl necklaces and diamonds for her ear-lobes. Look, I have a *sari* for you, too"—she opened a parcel and revealed two *saris*, and one was white with a broad crimson border and the other drenched in the bright indigo of a rainbow—"you need it so badly, sister. It's God's mercy that I have turned up; else what would you have done when that much-worn piece of yours fell in threads, as it must?" Shrewdly she had guessed that it was the only *sari* the mother possessed.

As the meaning shaped slowly in her heart, very slowly, the mother stood rigid, too dazed to speak a word. It was as she had felt an hour before when she saw a woman bury her child alive in the river mud, and she, watching from behind, could neither speak nor move. Her lips trembled and were stilled.

"She shall have a room of her own in a grand household. Only good people are allowed—good, rich people. Through their fingers money goes pouring like water—so! There is a stream of money flowing these days; no one has seen its like in the past thousand years—not since the Mughal times. The rich don't know what to do with it—they must spend, spend with the right hand and spend with the left. What else is money for? Our good girl must learn a trick or two—I'll tell her what she must know—and all will be well. Rich, she will pay this fat, ugly woman with an open hand because of her heart's gratitude." One eye closed in a wink. "This woman was not always so fat and ugly, sister. She had her day. She had soft, pretty features like this girl Kajoli. One of her patrons was no other——"

The mother found her voice then. "Away with you, woman," she shrieked. "Away with you, witch."

The woman scowled, but resumed her placid speech. "Take it easy. Turn it over in your heart. I am not asking to have her this very minute. We have a boat on the river. We do not leave till to-morrow night, for we have more business to complete. Why be vulgar? Hot words, hot eyes, what good would they do you? What have you to lean upon? Even the cowshed" (the startled, guilty eyes of the mother!) "looks empty. If twenty *rupees* is not enough—it is the rate I have paid ten times in ten villages—I'll give twenty-five, even thirty, no more. There are big people at our back. I only get a commission. Times are bad. The whole country is dying. You can't feed your daughter, can you? Roots? In a month there will be no roots left anywhere in Bengal, trees will be shorn of leaves, even the green grass of the fields gone—gone into human bellies. Why not let your daughter live? How can you, a mother, watch her dying, day by day, till the skeleton of her dies altogether?

"Away with you, witch," the mother shrieked again, but her throat felt strangled. The woman smiled knowingly.

"Yesterday I took a girl of six into the boat. Ten silver *rupees* I paid the mother. She will be looked after in the household till she ripens. She will learn to sing, dance, make whiteness on her face. But the mother—oh, the way she howled at me at first, like a tigress, three weeks ago! Yesterday, when I visited her again, she cried her heart out, poor woman, and knocked and knocked her head on the hard earth till the skin was all bruised, and then she gave me her child. But I was

114

angry; I paid her two *rupees* less because of my temper. That was all she gained by making overmuch fuss." Her face hardened and her eyes glowered at the mother.

The mother was trembling. "A word more from the filth-dropping tongue"—she looked about frenziedly and found a stick of bamboo that had broken loose from the roof framework—"a word more, witch, and I'll bash in your mouth." She brandished the stick in the air, while Kajoli, who had come rushing from the kitchen, wailed, "Mother, oh mother!"

The stout-bellied one glared at the image of wrath, measuring the famine in her face: the hollow cheeks, the sunken eyes, the naked collar-bone breaking through the parchment skin. How long could she brew in her false pride? And the eyes came calculating upon the daughter. Starved, she had grown in comeliness. The eyes big in the face that was lean from hunger. The breasts ripe because of the pregnant womb, yet small from famishing. A type of beauty unknown to the city before the famine came. And the city liked it for a change. Yes, the fat one reckoned, the girl was worth fussing about.

"Have you cooked the rice, Kajoli?" Warm honey dripped from her tongue.

"Take your grain and leave us." The mother ran to the kitchen and emerged in a moment with the bags of rice and lentils and the tiny pot of *ghee*. "Do not pollute my doorstep ever again."

"Indeed! indeed!" The woman's eyes rested on Kajoli like a hawk assured of its prey, rested on her rising belly. The thing that grew there was an instrument of her own will. One day the girl would yield herself, that her child could eat and live!

"Keep that other rice boiling in the pot. Have one good meal anyhow." The voice was half soothing, half mocking.

But the mother emerged again, the heated cooking-pot in her hands, held by the rim with a piece of sacking. "There—it is no food, only dirt. Filth." And she overturned the pot, pouring on the ground the simmering, half-cooked *chal* and *dal*. The heat of the rim burnt her fingers.

The woman's face then dropped its mask, showing ugly lines. She was pleased. That meal would have delayed the good day ahead, building some little flesh over the bones, strengthening the bones. Aha, it was God's mercy.

"Come along!" boomed the wiry man, who stood apart, watching, the cigarette slanting from his lips. "Peasants!" he leered. "Peasants' brain-box! Even a sparrow would laugh and spit!" And he spat.

And the woman gave a parting kick as she collected her bags of foodstuffs and handed them to the man to carry: "Animals have no tongue for rice. They prefer roots."

Onu was sobbing bitterly. The rice gone. The cooking-pot empty—as empty as his ever-hungering body. Only the fragrance of cooking grain lingered faintly in the air. Kajoli sat with her head down, biting her lips hard, unshed tears heavy in her eyelids. And the mother stood staring at the backs of her visitors as they receded. A sudden thought startled her face. "I ate dirt from the hand of a whore." She bent forward, a finger into her throat, trying to vomit. Nothing came out of her empty stomach, only her famished frame was convulsed with the strain. She dug her fingers deeper, and shaking with the fury of her effort, ribs breaking apart, she vomited.

Onu was trotting off on his spindly legs.

"Where do you go, boy?" croaked the mother, a gasp in her breath.

Onu looked back a moment.

"To the fig-tree. Where else? A handful left far on top." He sniffled, woeful, and wiped his nose with his hand. "I'll climb and climb and the thin branch will snap——" He rubbed his eyes and, with a sobbing breath, heartbrokenly: "I'll drop like a fig; I'll be killed."

CHAPTER XIII

FAR ACROSS the rice-green carpets of fields the vermilion sun gleamed bright on the brow of dawn as the high-road lay revealed, a little way from the embankment, keeping stride with the track of steel.

It was the high-road over which uprooted humanity dragged sore-foot towards its destiny. One of a hundred high-roads. And the destiny was far and misty and incalculable. You had no yesterday, no to-morrow. You lived from moment to moment, breath to breath. You died as you slept, and you woke to life, and you died again. For your home was the high-road which had no visible beginning, no visible end. You were the dust of the high-road, inseparable. They called you a destitute.

So Kajoli knew instinctively. So the mother knew.

The mother paused on the high-road, looking back village-ward. The embankment bearing the track of steel stood ahead like a great baffle wall. All she saw was the green pasture she had discovered for Mangala, and, having discovered it, she had sent Mangala to her doom. Mangala would have died willingly for Onu and Kajoli, but the mother would not let her. And she had sent her to her doom lest a child be buried alive, an unknown baby boy. Why? Gazing at the pasture, the bewildered mother asked herself for the hundredth time, why?

Yet it was better so. What could a destitute do with a cow? She would have been stolen. She was aged. She had had her time in the house. *She* would not have to be a destitute.

It had been agony to leave the house—unutterable agony. Torn from the earth in which lay her roots and the roots of her husband; for, though the police had taken him away, his unseen presence filled the house, his singing voice and his clear laughter. The house had been their temple, with the sacred *tulsi* plant in the yard, the image of a god in a niche of the wall, the breath of ancestors in the air.

The temple became a death-trap. It had no hope, only hunger. They had clung to it while their neighbours and friends left one by one, and in groups, and now they would have no company on the high-road, she and her pregnant daughter and a mere boy, so helpless, unprotected. All had gone away save the men crippled by police bullets; they and their wives and children would linger and cast their bones to the soil.

In the hour of twilight yesterday the mother had blown the white conch-shell thrice, hailing the dusk-goddess as she had been hailed in the village for a thousand years, and Kajoli had blown the conch thrice, and Onu, too. Then the mother handed it, her last possession, to the trader to whom she had sold it for a fistful of grain.

The trader would stay in the village, buying land, buying things. He was not of the people. He was a vulture feeding on the miseries of the people.

That vulture had set his eye in greed on her strips of fields. But he would not get them—ever. The land lay safe for the menfolk when they came back one day. Only the autumn crop was mortgaged, all, at a bare fraction of the market rate, to pay the *zemindar's* rent. The land lay green with the blades of growing corn, the corn ripening for the trader.

117

"Why, you have eaten your autumn crop well in advance," the trader had said, laughing. "You have done the eating; for the trouble of reaping."

The trader had caught Mother Earth in a snare and held her in strong chains.

"Mother!" Kajoli called sharply, knocking on her rambling mind. "Look!" She pointed at a group of people who were coming up the road in their direction.

They came, men and women, boys and girls, their backs bent, their heads bent, each bearing a rag bundle, feet dragging slowly, slowly. They seemed all of a piece, figures in a frieze. One asked, not lifting his head, not pausing on his way: "Calcutta, Mother—how far still to go?"

The mother was startled. She was filled with pity for the wretched ones and fear for her children and herself, who, too, would be pulled down to that level.

"Far, far," the voice was a murmur.

"Far," echoed the man, and passed on.

The mother stepped after him. "Whence have you come, son?"

"Vishnugram."

"Long have you walked? How long?"

"Long. Who keeps count? There was a growing half-moon when we set out."

And now the moon was a pale blade in the small hours. How would they ever reach Calcutta city walking at that pace?

"Let us walk," she addressed her children, and the three gazed village-ward again through the tear-haze in their eyes; they choked the rising sob in their throats and set off, keeping some way from the strangers ahead. Those destitutes, more worn than they and no use to them, yet gave them strength, for those were people. In the lone days and nights ahead you would need people. Even if you had to die, you would rather die with others who were people.

They moved, and the house moved with them, holding their thoughts. They had been sleepless the night through, their last night under the sheltering roof, fretting about in the dark—it was weeks since the earthenware lamps had had bean-oil to burn—lying down now on the bedroom floor, now on the veranda, in the yard. And as the night lifted they had washed their faces and eaten a little of their last grain and passed down the doorstep, pausing to drop on their knees and rest their heads on the sill: "May we return soon to thy merciful shelter."

Now that the house had shed its habitation and companioned them, an airy spirit, the pains it had brought were gone, the happiness it had given through the years remained, along with one aching thought: What if one by one the menfolk come back—Father, Kanu, Kishore—and find the house empty, and each returns, broken-hearted, the way he has come?

They passed a group of people who sat at the roadside in the huge shade of a tamarind, cooking what looked like leaves. The sun hardened. Kajoli was panting because of the heaviness of her womb and the bundle she carried. Each carried a bundle. A cooking-pot, an iron ladle, petty chattels, a tiny quilt for Onu just wide enough for his back. Mother and Kajoli would sleep on bare earth, but Onu would have the quilt to lie on, lest the hard earth scratched his protruding backbone. And so they trudged on. A second group of people appeared ahead. Strange how one group was the image of the other, all of one piece, all figures in a frieze. Late in the noon, when hunger gnawed hard and the knees weakened, they stopped, gathered twigs and made a fire to cook the *kachu* roots they carried. Those were savings from yesterday. To-morrow they must find fresh roots. But the mother felt fear clutch at her heart. Many destitutes seemed to have passed down the road, living on the roots they dug, the edible leaves they plucked. The terrible words of the woman from Calcutta echoed in her ears: "Roots? In a month there will be no roots left anywhere in Bengal: trees will be shorn of leaves, even the grass of the fields gone——" Those words were a month old!

The mother had no notion yet of the vast starving masses that had gone ahead and the others who followed in their wake —hundreds of thousands hunger-marching city-ward. Not many would reach their goal. Each dragging step would take a little of their remnants of life. Dehydrated sticks of humanity. Humanity, all the same—all Kajolis and Onus and their mothers and their aged fathers. All people, with minds, with the capacity to feel, an inner gift that was now a curse; for the agony of the spirit was even harder to bear than hunger. Mothers would have given themselves to their fate with less pain if they did not have to see the shrivelling of their children, the day-by-day dying, not from illness, not from the Japanee foe, because of whom the grain had been taken away, only from long hunger, and there was nothing to be done— nothing.

No one would help. In the good years the peasants had given so much of their rice harvests to the *zemindar*. He would not help. So much grain was growing in the fields, a bumper crop was expected—the mockery of it! And what of Gorement, the people's *ma-bap*? The trader had answered the question that had been on the lips of every villager, and he had said: "It is your job to feed Gorement, not Gorement's job to feed you. And you warred with Gorement just a twelvemonth back, remember? You called it the Evil Thing, remember? The terrible sin of calling your own *ma-bap* names! What wonder that you suffer?"

Your own *ma-bap*—Gorement! True, not many years had passed since that had been common parlance. But those years were a century apart and a world apart. The old familiar parlance would now sound strange and mocking!

Your own *ma-bap*—he, the great one of Gorement—had come to a big market village three hours' walk down the river-side, not so very long ago, and before he came the drummer had strutted the fields and pathways of Baruni. Doog, doog! Go, brothers, early to-morrow morn, and gather you all by the old banyan at Rangamati. Doog, doog! The great one of Gorement would come, would bring you word. Doog, doog! . . . And, having listened, all Baruni, a-throb with new hope, had walked to Rangamati with empty stomach and heart pounding. He, the great one, had come at noon, riding a jeep, and he had sat in majesty on a cushioned chair placed up on a high pedestal covered with red *salu* cloth, and he had addressed the five villages assembled. And he had spoken of the Japanee foe and the Great Killing and the might of India's own *paltan*, who were our brethren, who were just us, so he said, and he had spoken of a hundred and one things, but not the Word. When would he speak the Word? As he stopped at last and sipped the cool milk of a green coconut, the five villages burst into a cry like a wail: "Master, the Word?" Hours had they sat in the blazing sun, quite still, tense, hoping every moment for the Word to come. And the wailing again: "The Word, Master?" Food, food; there was no other true word but food. The five villages had swallowed the great one's five thousand fake words that they could have the one true word: food. Then the old *zemindar* of Baruni had bent over the great one's shoulder and spoken to him in a hushed tone, and he, the great one of Gorement, had looked flurried and drawn his thick brows as though in anger and mounted his jeep, grave as a rock, and gone.

120

There was to be no true word, no food for the people's hunger. In vain, in vain had the five villages walked the three hours' way to Rangamati's banyan and the three hours' way back in scorching sun, and five thousand fake words in their empty stomachs.

. . . Vultures perched on the trees, vultures wheeled or hung poised in the sunlit air. A myriad vultures gazed down upon the countryside. Late in the noon the mother saw how well they did their job.

Corpses lay by the road, huddling together. Picked to the bone, with eyeless caverns of sockets, bits of skin and flesh rotting on nose and chin and ribs, the skulls pecked open, only the hair uneaten—fluffy baby's hair, man's hair, the waist-long hair of women. A family group had sunk into sleep; and beyond the sleep was—vultures.

The mother trembled, and gripped the arms of her children and hurried on.

Vulture-eaten corpses kept them company, now revealed by the roadside, now some way apart in the shade of trees and screens of brushwood, always huddling together. Some were half-eaten, and vultures perched on them, still pecking, and flocks of crows gazed on, a little apart, awaiting their chance. Small possessions lay all about: earthenware pots, women's combs and tiny wooden vermilion cases and knick-knacks, shabby rag dolls, quilts, pillows. Even in their homeless wandering some people had carried pillows.

A bare hundred yards from the high-road ran the railway track on its high embankment, now long and straight, now sickle-curving into the sky, and a line of dark-brown wagons trundled by—people, hundreds, clinging to the narrow footboard like apes. That way you would travel to the city? No, no, the mother thought, shuddering. What if her children slipped and fell? The mother clutched their arms, her heart thudding with alarm. They would walk the high-road, so, her Onu on her left, her Kajoli on her right, and even if it was three weeks, they would manage. Better than three hours on the footboard. If Onu, restless one, slipped, wrenched by the speed? If Kajoli grew dizzy and fell? The mother clutched their arms tighter.

New wicks of strength burned in her. In desperate crisis she had made herself strong for her children. And her children, too, were strong for Mother and for each other. Weakness in one would have destroyed all.

When the night grew they ate the left-over roots with some grains of rice they had boiled at day-time and lay down under the outspread branches of an old tamarind, and they, also, like the corpse groups, huddled together for warmth and for comfort in each other, and Onu wrapped an arm round Mother, and Kajoli too. The pitch-black night hung heavy on them, weighing on their spirits. Owls hooted and jackals shrilled in unison—scores of them seemed to be about. Familiar cries, but fearful as they lay unsheltered in the black meadow. What if the animals sniffed at them with their snouts, bit them as they slept? What if the red ants came? And creeping things—scorpions, snakes? Half an hour crawled by. Suddenly a thin, mournful sobbing filled the air, pouring down from the top of the tamarind. Then it was as though a dozen ailing babies sobbed their hearts out. Onu shivered as he pressed himself against Mother, and Kajoli, too.

"No ghostlings," the mother soothed them, looking up at the impenetrable dark of the tamarind and shielding her boy with one arm and her girl with the other. "Those are the young of vultures."

As they drew up their legs and settled down to sleep, they felt eyes glare at them in the darkness—the eyes of vultures on the tree-top, the eyes of beasts in the meadow. Are you dying? Are you dead? all seemed to ask. Razor-sharp beaks were poised to peck. Tongues lolled between grinning teeth.

The mother slept fretfully, lying awake often for long stretches, guarding her children. Deep in the night a great swarm of fire-flies sprang up suddenly, glimmering about, a myriad sparks. The mother gazed, and her heart was comforted by the tender beauty, and it was as though the tiny points of light were a sign, a message from the Image of Light. On to the city of a million lights! The city of humanity. The city of civilized living. If only your knees will take your weight and bear you till you tread the kindly streets!

In her breast was one throbbing hope: Devata's grandson—he was there in the city, he would help, even though they would not beg of him.

Kajoli had scorned the idea, her lips curling. "Mother, he is a rich man. He wouldn't know us. They have poor memories, rich folk."

"Kajoli, you forget whose grandson he is? If he only knew our misery!"

But Kajoli shook her head, smiling. "He doesn't remember us, Mother," and her smile was like weeping.

When dawn was about to break the mother dropped her eyelids and fell asleep because of her fatigue. Kajoli awoke then, limbs languid with the wet of night, and as she sat up she felt the child stir in her womb. "You awake?" breathed Kajoli, touching her navel, as though caressing her unborn one. Life had shed its young dreams, all save this. Kajoli still wove a dream around her unborn son.

Song-birds were twittering a hymn to the goddess of dawn, casting their joyous cry over soft fields where corn grew lush and green, and hunger corpses lay stiffened. Coo-oo! said one, sweet-sad. Kajoli did not hear. The kokil inside her had died.

Roots—berries—that was her anxious thought, that was her song. It would be good to find some roots and berries before the day grew. Let Mother sleep. Mother had aged so in these months, her lean face wrinkled, her hair a white mass—you had to look hard for ten grey streaks a twelvemonth back. Let Mother sleep. Kajoli gazed at her with eager affection as she touched the thick white hair, lightly with her finger-tips lest Mother was wakened. Then she rose quietly and walked off to the meadow glittering with the night's dew.

There were no roots anywhere. The meadow had been plucked bare. What would happen to them if they found no roots to eat? Better perhaps to have stayed in the village, to have died on their native earth. Kajoli wiped the tears crowding her eyes. Why had her husband never sent her word? He could not get into that railway train, he walked this bitter road all by himself and lay sick in the dust? The *Red Turbans* took him to prison because of his spirit? If only she could know he was well. Then would she be easy in her heart. She would ask no more than to know that he was well. Then would she bear calmly all misery that came upon her. And more tears welled to her eyes, edged with the dark of pregnancy and fatigue.

As she passed a jackfruit tree she stopped. She might as well go round the great trunk to see if any fruit was left—one chance in a thousand. She drew near; then a groan reached her ears, and she gave a violent start. A terrible sight met her eyes.

A woman lay stretched by the tree-trunk, groaning, while a jackal crouched and ate her body. The jackal saw Kajoli, grunted and slunk off, unhurried. It paused a moment, turned, then walked off with another grunt.

Kajoli stood frozen. She could see the gaping wound where

123

the jackal had fed. She closed her eyes and pressed her bosom with her hands, sickness welling to her throat. Go near and tend the dying one, said a small voice inside her, but Kajoli turned and fled. Gasping, holding her belly with both hands, she plunged across the meadow in mad panic, as though pursued by a maniac.

The mother was coming that way, looking for her girl. Kajoli rushed into her arms in a frenzy of sobbing. She sobbed bitterly, hysterically, unable to stop herself, while the mother soothed her, a nameless dread in her heart. "Tell me, Kajoli. Do not cry. It is bad for the child if you cry. Tell Mother."

At last Kajoli controlled herself. She turned and said, "Mother, come."

When they were within sight of the jackfruit tree, Kajoli, walking with a hesitant tread, said, pointing: "There! A jackal was eating her." And she struggled with hysteria. She would not go a step nearer. The mother walked on.

The jackal had eaten the woman's left armpit and breast and a part of the ribs. She was breathing still, her eyes wide open, but vacant. The mother felt her blood freeze.

There was a pool a few paces off. The mother rushed to the water, drenched the corner of her *sari*, and rushed back and let the water drip into the woman's mouth. The woman gazed at her long, fixedly. An expression, a tender cloud, came to her eyes. It was as though she was soothed to have a fellow being for companion in her last moments. Then her eyelids dropped close, the water spilled out of her lips and she died.

The mother looked up and saw the vultures overhead, circling, ready to swoop down. Heaven's scavengers. Save for them the air of Bengal would be putrid with the rotting flesh of man. Fellow humans had ceased to care for the living; how, then, could they care for the dead?

Then the mother saw the green, pimpled body of the jackfruit sprouting out of the trunk almost at ground level—it was big and about to ripen—and even in her wretchedness in the presence of the mutilated corpse the mother felt her heart grow faint with joy. The jackfruit would sustain the lives of her children and herself for two or three days. It lay very close to the dead one, almost touching her feet. That woman had found it, and she was about to light a fire to boil the treasured food (the heaped twigs under the cooking-pot had a story to tell), when her strength failed and she laid herself down, the jackal's prey.

Kajoli was too sensitive still. She would be sickened at eating the jackfruit; but she would eat it all the same.

. . . . .

Chill blew the wind, wet and sharp with recent rain. Kajoli shivered in her dust-grey tatters and crossed her arms upon her breast, shrinking into herself. Each hand clutched the thick, shapeless roots of some unknown plant—all that the earth of Bengal had yielded her after hours of toil, for the earth had been plucked clean by ten thousand other hands, all its hidden roots seized, boiled, eaten away.

Her six days on the high-road were six dragging chains of agony on her feet. The last two days were the worst of all—there had been nothing to eat save the stems of water-lilies and the red seed-berries of banyan, food for birds. And as though hunger was not enough to bear, this day there was heavy rain. Mother could not walk; the dew of autumn nights had seeped into her bones, and she had to hobble and drag herself with pain, and now she lay down utterly exhausted under a tree that gave little protection from the driving torrent. When the rain ceased, Kajoli had gone far down the meadow in search of roots, and then, while she walked back, out of the bulging bank of cloud night had descended. But Kajoli was now back on the high-road. She had only to go a little way to the tree shelter where Mother rested.

And what good were the roots she had gathered with such toil if the rain-soaked twigs failed to make a fire?—she mused wretchedly as she walked slow-foot, wobbling on her thin legs, her belly distended.

The rumble of a hundred wheels tore through the night like far thunder, and in a minute the great fire-wagon was passing by, a big angry light on its snout. How lucky the folk inside! thought Kajoli, with a deep sigh. Seated on benches in light and warmth. No loads to carry. No night fears. No loneliness. Moving thunder-fast—four hours to the city. Four hours! Kajoli, hungry and footsore, could see the fire-wagon even when it was gone and all was darkness and silence.

Telegraph wires ran overhead. She paused, weary, leaning her back against a tall steel pole. Wind strummed the wires and spoke: zmmm! as her ear pressed against cold steel, a hurrying stream of sound. The sound of word passing, she knew. What word? No word, ever, of the great hunger of the peasants and their helpless trek through devastation?

Zmmm! she attuned her heart to far messages passing, eyelids closed, lips parted a little in wonder. Zmmm!

A heavy tread of boots, *shup shup*, up the road. Her startled eyes looked, and saw a khaki-clad man striding up with measured steps. Her body clenched, but there was no fear in her heart. She had seen many soldiers on the high-road, passing by in swift motor-trucks. One day they had thrown her some bread—it had been a festive day with soft, thick bread and boiled jackfruit. The soldiers were all kindness—before the recruitment they, too, had been peasants.

The sepoy drew level and stopped, peering at the figure by the telegraph pole. He edged up, looking close. His tall, thick-set body towered over the girl.

"I am hungry," said the girl in the voice of prayer. "I am hungry."

The sepoy clacked his tongue with pity. He thought of his wife and children at home, a thousand miles away in the Punjab, and deep relief came upon him that he had never failed to send them his month's pay—the dear ones at home would not ache from hunger, and the girl, Chand, having grown of marriageable age, had been given in wedlock to a youth who too had joined the Army and was safe from want. Yes, his kith and kin were shielded from hunger. This war was good, this mobilization. In peace-time he had never had enough to eat—with the landlord and the moneylender sated, little was left to him of his harvest. But now he had bread in abundance, enough to fill two hungry stomachs, and even at this moment he carried in his uniform pocket some of his rations, flat wheaten pancakes wrapped in paper, lest he came upon some famished folk as he strolled a little way from his camp with the air clear at last from rain. For the sepoy had feeling in his heart. He had known hunger in his body, and he could feel hunger in the bodies of others.

He unwrapped the bread, watching the girl's face, his keen eyes peering in the dark. He saw the eagerness, the passionate ecstasy that filled the face with a brightening. It was a flood of comeliness on the lean, pinched face. His hands held back, he stared in amaze until her voice like a prayer broke the spell: "I am hungry."

He was her god of destiny! He held all of her in his mighty fist, a moth to be released or crushed. And the wonder of his terrible power and the wonder of her drugged ecstasy made him withhold the hand of charity until the

126

voice of prayer sounded once more, a faint rustle: "I am hungry."

He gave her bread. Instantly she dug her teeth into the lump, swallowing swiftly, not chewing, not lingering for the feel of bread on her tongue, swallowing hard. And the soldier clacked his tongue with pity, for his heart was warm. He watched her and reached out a hand to the *sari* drawn over her head, the white, red-bordered *sari* that Kishore had spun because of some fondness in his heart—now all grey with road dust. And the big hand fumbled to her cheek and to her throat, traced the soft hollow. As it crept down to her breast she shrank a little, unaware, still drugged with eating. In a minute the bread was all gone, and then the realization burst upon her that she had eaten all; nothing was left for her brother, her mother—nothing. Tears broke in her eyes, pouring down her cheeks.

"Still hungry?" the god of destiny spoke soothingly. "Do not cry. Look. I have plenty more. There! You shall have all. And more." He groped in his tunic. "*Rupees*." He held out two shiny ones. "You can buy a *sari*—what rags you have on your body!"

The silver had no meaning for her, but the bread, so much bread; it would mean life for her dying mother and her brother. Her answer came like a groan of anguish. "We be hungry. A little bread. God will give you abundance. Hunger eats us——"

He clutched her arm. She shrank a step, her eyes opening wide on his face—a face that had shed its kindliness, a hard face, copper-like. She knew that face. She had seen that face peering from the Army trucks that roared past. But she did not cry out, cower. All feeling was dead in her save one dull ache: remorse that she had eaten all the bread, all.

The soldier's grip tightened round her thin upper arm. He pulled and led her away from the road down the wet, sloping grass to the meadow. A night bird croaked harshly from some tree-top. A stooping bough stung the girl's face like a whiplash, and she nearly fell, but the soldier held her in his firm clasp. She walked on as in heavy sleep, led by the other's will, barely aware, for her body was a bit of rag to cover her soul, and the rag was of no account, a mere encumbrance, and she had fled her body, fled to her mother and her brother, who needed bread to eat.

The soldier was a man of feeling. But he desperately needed

a woman. It was over a year since he had seen his wife. And in this instant he was back home with his wife. He could barely see Kajoli's face in the dark, but he knew the smell that was ever with her—the clean woman smell, like rain-wet earth that was part of her. He spoke words of caress, words lain buried in his feelings. The soldier was lost in a twilight, half dream, half reality. . . .

A piercing shriek, a deep, heavy groan. The soldier felt blood against his skin and jerked up frightened, panting, looking hard.

She lay inert, lifeless. She bled.

The soldier crouched, peering, and felt her nostrils for her breath. He leaned his ear against her heart and listened. She had only fainted. The roots she had dug from the meadow hung loose from her tiny fists. The soldier saw how young she was—more a girl than a woman—and he saw, too, that she was bearing a child. Then she groaned again, deep and long, and at that sign of life the soldier heaved a sigh of immense relief. He pushed all his bread into her fist. He took out the money he had—three large silver pieces and some smaller bits—and tied them to her *sari* corner. There was a rustle near by. In a panic the soldier sprang to his feet and fled.

The girl stirred, weak, and groaned on with her pain. She heard a familiar shrill: Hukkahuahua! That cry shook her from her stupor. She lifted her eyelids and struggled to sit up, but her hips had deadened and her spine, and now the vile cry drew closer, closer, till it was blowing upon her face like scorching wind. It was a long, exultant note: Hua-hua-a-a! The jackal was gazing down on her, tongue lolling. Cold sweat bathed her body. She felt the snout of the animal and shuddered and screamed in mad terror, and her voice was a faint gurgle in her throat. Mad, she screamed over and over again, and all her shrinking body screamed. . . .

A blasting pain shrieked out of her womb, rending the flesh with claws of steel, tearing with ten knives together, till for an eternity of moments she grew rigid from head to toe, then fell to pieces, smashed, voiceless, as though lifeless.

The jackal tilted its head skyward and shrilled a long-drawn wail of a cry. It hung on, watching, the smell of fresh blood hot in its nostrils, and it shrilled with excited glee.

The girl seized her ebbing strength and screamed again, as she felt the animal crouch across her thigh. She felt its teeth

128

tear the blossom of her womb. In a twilight of life and lifeless-
ness, unable even to pray for death, with the jackal astride her
thigh and the eternity of time crawling and crawling. . . .

Onu was not far from his sister. He, too, had found a few
edible roots. When they lost each other in the darkness, he
called her name twice, and, hearing no response, he thought
she had gone home—home!—and he sat down awhile, resting
his weary feet, then walked on. He saw a soldier rush by and,
eager to draw his mind, he called out his sister's name: "*Didi*,
where have you gone?"

The soldier stopped and turned back. He was breathing
hard. "What is wrong, youngster?" he cried.

"I am hungered," gulped Onu.

The soldier stepped back and gripped his arm.

"There is someone you are looking for?"

"My sister. She is hungered. I am hungered. Mother's
hungered." And he swallowed once or twice and begged with
a pathetic face: "Give us a little bread, mighty soldier——"

"She is young? She is pregnant?" The voice came strained.

Onu nodded his head. "Hunger eats us——"

The soldier's voice carried a tremor. "Run this way, childling, run down the road. She is sick, badly sick. She lies in the
meadow all alone. Twenty, thirty strides from the road—
there." He pointed with his hand.

The boy grew pallid. He begged no more, walking off at
once. He tried to run, but his legs were leaden. Oh, if only he
could lay down his head and sleep!

Then he heard the jackal's cry and a faint scream. How eerie
were the two cries in the dead silence of night. Onu felt his
heart kick against his ribs, but he turned to the sloping wayside
grass and followed the direction. He had a dread of jackals.
Ghosts wore the bodies of jackals, he knew. And he had a
dread of ghosts. His eyes bulged because of his dread, a chill-
ness ran down his spine. But Kajoli lay in the meadow, sick
and helpless, and a jackal hua-huaed near about. Kajoli, too,
had a dread of jackals. Onu pressed on. "Rama! Rama!" he
cried the name of a god, for ghosts feared that name.

He saw first the shape of the crouching beast and, close by,
the prostrate body of his sister, silent and still, as if asleep. He
paused, but only for a moment, and in that desperate moment
he, a timid boy, grew into a man, strong and unafraid. He
walked on step by step. "*Didi*, do not fear," he cried. He
yelled at the beast: "Go! go! Shoo!"

The beast growled in answer. It was in no mood to go. With a challenging shrill the jackal was ready for battle. Its eyeballs glittered.

Onu still came on. He saw the baleful beast ready to spring on him. For an instant he had a sinking feeling in his knees. He stepped back, farther back. The jackal watched his movements. "Hua—a—a——" the vile throat triumphantly barked.

Onu was making a strategic retreat. He knew he had not a moment to lose, with the beast crouching near his sister, but he could not fight it with his bare hands. Backing away, he found the tree he wanted and seized a thin bough and snapped it quickly. Then, with sudden enormous power, he took a deep breath, brandished his leafy stick and yelling "Go! go!" he dashed forward, charging blindly.

The beast cowered and fled.

The spirit had won. Onu dropped to his knees and bent over his sister's face. "Speak, *didi*," he moaned, "look at me, *didi reh*——"

Her eyes, black pools of pain, rested upon her brother. Her tortured, twisted lips moved to form words, but no sound came from her throat. Onu burst into a loud wail. "Oh, *didi, didi reh*——"

He saw the blood-soaked mess between her legs, and in the violent shock of it his wail ceased. He became a man again. Kajoli was dying. Only Mother could save her life. He must rush and tell Mother. And Kajoli, as if she knew his thought, breathed at this moment, a far whisper: "Ma——"

The beast might return while she lay alone. But there was no other choice. "Do not fear, *didi*." Onu spoke fast. "I'll run hard. Mother will be here in no time." He let the stick lean against her body; the sight of it might keep off the animal.

As he rushed down the highway he heard a motor vehicle chugging far behind. More soldiers, he thought, and recalled the man who had told him of Kajoli's sickness. If only the soldier, with such kindness in his heart, had not gone away!

The soldier, having spoken to the young boy on the road, had rushed to his camp on the newly-built aerodrome. Remorse stabbed him. What had he done? The soldier was God-fearing, honest with himself. At home he had been a devoted husband and a loving father. Left alone, the girl might die of bleeding. Pregnant. What devil had seized his soul? The soldier was wretched.

At the edge of the airfield the ambulance truck stood ready

130

to set off—Captain Bannerji of the Indian Medical Service was proceeding to Calcutta on duty. The soldier spoke with quick decision.

"*Sa'b*. I was coming across the meadow. I saw a woman lying stretched on the ground. A mere girl. Helpless in the meadow."

"A destitute," said the other. "Nothing I can do."

"A pool of blood, *huzoor*. Foul work. Some murderous fellow is about." The soldier had to create an impression.

"Not my duty," snapped the officer as the truck moved.

"*Sa'b*, the jackals will eat her alive," the soldier cried, his voice breaking. "It is right on your way——"

"Jump in," the Captain snapped again.

The soldier bounded into the truck, relieved. He knew his officer.

The soldier's trained mind had retained a landmark—a broken palmyra, its bushy top clipped off by hurricane. The truck drew up.

A minute later the Captain flashed his torch upon Kajoli. He gave a start. "Run," he ordered. "Get the stretcher."

They carried the girl into the ambulance. She had lost much blood. She was in danger of sepsis, hanging on to life by a thread. The Captain set himself to his task.

The truck-driver handed a cigarette to the soldier as they stood a little way from the van.

"No new sight—bodies dead and dying on the meadow. Man and woman, old and young——" The truck-driver clacked his tongue thrice. "A curse has come." And he clacked again. "I saw a battle such as few have seen. Three or four vultures fighting a jackal over a corpse. The fury of it! That was two months back. Now there are no such fights—vultures and jackals all have enough and to spare. And the sky is full of vultures as if by magic, and if you walk a bare hundred yards a jackal's face grins at you."

The soldier had no taste in his heart for this talk. He walked some paces, his eyes searching, gazing down the meadow. Where had he gone—that youngster, the girl's brother? So small and hungry and helpless. Why were these innocent people doomed to hunger and death while the Army had rice and wheat to squander? Who but the peasants had created the food-grains—not the Colonel, not the Brigadier, not the *Jungi Lat*, the C.-in-C. With the peasants wiped out from the land none would get a mouthful to eat. When you came to think of it, the peasants were as much in the war as the makers of shots and shells and those firing the missiles—who could fight with no food in the stomach? And he, himself a peasant, had made use of the undeserved bread he possessed to do wrong to a famished peasant girl, pregnant. The curse of his *kismet*!

Then he saw the boy come out of darkness not twenty yards away, accompanied by a woman. The mother? The soldier could at last breathe with ease. He advanced to meet them, speaking quickly: "Mother, she is hurt, but there is no fear. She is in the best of hands. Our *Kaptaan Sa'b* is tending her. Come this way." And he strode to the ambulance and cried, "*Sa'b*, the girl's mother has come."

Captain Bannerji appeared at the door, relieved, yet alarmed at the prospect of the mournful scene he must witness. "Make no noise," he said in a low voice. "I have given her the needle and put her to sleep. She needs sleep."

Tucked in an Army blanket, she slept like a tired child, her cheeks more wan than ever, the blackness under her eyes blacker. The mother sat beside the girl, gazing in silence. She did not speak a word. She shed no tears. She sat very still—a languishing earthen image over which the sculptor, forced into economy, had spared his clay.

The Captain gave her a surprised glance. Shock? Apathy due to long suffering? Or was it a mother's true inherent strength? He felt relief. "There is no worry," he said gently. "But she will have to be in hospital for some weeks. I am taking her to Calcutta. An hour's drive, but we must go slowly—she can't bear any jolting. You will come?"

There was no answer for a while, and then the mother's eyes brimmed over with tears. Kindness seemed to have gone from the face of the earth, and now it poured on her so unexpectedly. "Live long, my son," her voice husky. "Live long."

The Captain sat beside the driver. The engine roared. "Do not deny us your blessing, Mother," the soldier called out miserably.

"Blessings upon you, my son," the mother answered, and in her heart she said, "God's blessings upon all of you who are kind."

Onu clutched Mother's arm excitedly. It was the first time he had ridden in a motor vehicle. Which moved faster, the *wind van* or the wind itself?—so he puzzled as he laid himself down, his head on Mother's lap, and in a minute he sank into weary sleep.

132

The mother sat rigid, her pain too deep for expression, and her eyes were upon her daughter and beyond her, for she saw, too, the faces of her husband and her son in prison, the three faces together. And, strangely, her worry at this moment was not so much for Kanu's sentence of imprisonment as for his aching ear—did it ache still, and no one to give him relief with a hot fomentation? And her husband—struck mute by prison rules. Song was his breath of life—how live without song? Mixed with those sorrows was the terrible immediate sorrow. How could Kajoli bear the pain of her lost child? And if Kajoli died? The mother's eyes clung to her girl's face. She herself, thought the mother, had not long to live; she could feel death in her bones. When she died, what would happen to Onu? The mother's gaze turned and brooded on the face of her boy as he slept.

Then the misery spilled out of her eyes without restraint. A stranger's kindness had stirred her to tears. The cruelties of a heartless world made the tears rush down her cheeks in a flood. Deep, broken sighs quivered from her bosom.

The truck slowed down, lumbering across the great bridge over the Ganges. Strand Road. . . . Dalhousie Square. . . . The city lay in blackness, cars and vans rushing about like fire-eyed animals. Bowbazar Street. . . . The truck passed into the hospital gates.

"They won't let you in except in the set hours for visitors," said the officer as the girl was being carried away on a stretcher. "I'll speak to the surgeon." And he fumbled for words, a five-*rupee* note in his hand. "If you will keep this—you have no-where to go——"

The mother shook her head. "Your kindness is all I need, my son. We are peasants, not beggars. We have come upon hard times."

The officer walked off into the hospital. The driver moved the truck out and parked it at the street kerb.

"Now you have to get down, Mother——"

"Onu," the mother called, "this is Calcutta city. Get up, my son."

The boy slept on.

A motor-cycle sounded up the street. The truck-driver spoke with concern: "Civilians are not permitted the use of a military truck, or else I would let you wait in it till Kaptaan Sa'b returns. There are M.P.s about, military *policewala*. Kaptaan Sa'b acted against the rules in helping you."

133

Policewala! The frightened mother strained to lift the boy in her arms and gasped with the effort. The truck-driver came to her help.

Onu, ejected from the van, lay now on the pavement, still fast asleep. The mother stood looking about. Buildings rose steeply everywhere, enormously tall and broad, each one big enough to swallow all the men and women of Baruni village! She and her son would surely find a roof for their heads—they could not bear any more the wet of autumn nights. They would work hard and earn their keep, for they were no beggars, she and her son. The hospital to which Kajoli had been taken had the grand look of a king's mansion. Yes, the poor and needy were cared for in the wonder city. And why not? The city had money to spare and jingle. The people had great kindness in their hearts, like that young khaki-clad military doctor. There would be food. Onu would go to school—city folk were all set on book-learning. Before many days passed Kajoli would be back from sick-bed, some flesh on her wasted body, some colour in her faded cheeks, for she would have eaten well.

And the secret, ever-throbbing hope: Somewhere in the city wilderness was he, Devata's grandson. He would surely know them. He could not have forgotten them. How could he? Had she not seen kindness in his face? Was he not Devata's grandson?

In the hour of midnight the lone mother stood on the pavement of a strange city and saw bright silver streaking the edges of a massive pitch-black cloud.

CHAPTER XIV

As the first early-morning bus from Lakeside drew up at the front yard of Howrah station, Rahoul stepped out, a dread in his heart. What if the rice had not arrived? The goods office would not open for an hour yet, but it was better to walk about here, waiting for the hour of business, than to sit at home and brood. Half the night he had been sleepless, brooding. A wagon of rice was due to arrive overnight, a gift from the people of Bombay. Gifts of money had been pouring from all over India. Yes, all India was rushing to save Bengal from destruction. But money alone could not solve the problem. You had to find food-grain and wagons to carry grain. A hundred obstacles lay in your way. Wagons were scarce for civilian use—many were being used for military traffic. Wagons from India had gone to the Middle East along with hundreds of miles of rail lifted from the tracks. India's communications were sore-pressed and tired. Guns, not grain, moved into Bengal.

Grain moved out of Bengal, though, even out of deficit areas! While ten million peasants groaned in hunger, the rice they had raised with their toil moved according to plan out of Bengal.

What if this wagon-load had not come? The relief Centre would be doling out its last stock to-day. And to-morrow, and all the to-morrows? The five hundred destitutes whose thread of life lay twisted around this Centre would have to die.

Die they must, in any case, so it seemed. If not they, their brethren. Public charity ran many free kitchens, but how feed a hundred-thousand every day with your slender means? And destitutes were still streaming in, wave after wave.

Wave after wave of hunger-stricken masses surging from the countryside. A great many were in no fit state to consume solid food. They ate and died. To give them rice was to kill them. They needed a special diet. And glucose. Rahoul felt a bitter laugh in his heart. Glucose indeed!

It was anyhow better to die in a flicker with food inside you than to shrivel day after day for three weeks, for a month, until the end. Strange how much a human body could go through before life left it at last. The first few days the man suffered most. He was mad with hunger. Then he grew listless. He laid himself down. His mouth was too tired for food, and he only wanted to be left alone. His eyes died. He wasted to a skeleton, using up whatever shreds of flesh he had anywhere on his body. Rahoul recalled a shape; the man had no flesh on his buttocks—it was as though the curving flesh had been sheared off clean and the skin stitched up over the bare thigh-bones. He could not even absorb water, let alone food. But he was not yet dead. Someone had placed before him a pot of rice. The rice lay untouched.

Rahoul recalled another shape. A shrivelled caricature of a man came toddling at the heels of others, struggling to keep pace with them, gasping. He kept to his feet by sheer force of will. He saw Rahoul at the gates of the kitchen. "Father, it is true? You will give us rice to eat?"

"You will have rice, it is true."

In the dull yellow eyes a gleam of life had come. "I have

walked a long way. I have just crossed Mother Ganges. For five days I have not eaten. Five days, Father." And he toddled in, muttering to himself, "Fool, you will have rice to eat, rice, O fool of a hungry one——" Tears of joy coursed down the hollowed cheeks.

Fate, ironic, denied him his last mouthful of rice. As food came into sight, ready to be served, the man shuddered with an excitement that he could not hold. Food was being handed out. His turn soon. . . . As he sat watching, the bleary eyes bulged with fearsome desire, a groan of agony broke from the thin throat, and the man slumped on his side, dead.

Rahoul walked the platform faster, his breath deepening, his hand waving once or twice before his eyes as though to ward off a swarm of insects—or a vision.

A knot of people had formed at the far end of the platform. Sharp words, sharp gestures of anger. A row? Rahoul walked on to the crowd.

The centre of the commotion was a man who sat on a large packing-case, a pencil in his hand, stooping over a writing-pad. Some yards away on the platform, half concealed by another packing-case, a destitute woman lay on her side, her legs drawn up, eyes closed, a baby at her breast. The woman lay still, but the baby moved its lips faintly as it suckled.

The mother was dead.

A ticket-collector had seen, as he strolled by, the man on the packing-case and the famished woman, motionless on the ground. He had drawn close, curious, peering down at the paper tablet. An artist making a pencil sketch of the woeful little group. Destitutes were not allowed on platforms, but this woman seemed to have slipped in somehow under the cover of night, and lay fast asleep. She would have to be turned out, miserable one. The unhappy ticket-collector cleared his throat and gave the order. No response. He lifted his voice and repeated his order. Nothing happened. The collector stepped close and cried out in horror. She was dead!

"She is dead," the railwayman said to the artist, his voice toneless.

"*Hoon*," said the other, deep in his work.

"You knew?" Eyes amazed, brows drawn.

Yes, he knew. He knew that the child was suckling the breast of its dead mother.

"This is very odd. You didn't consider it your duty to report to us? The mother dead, the child alive, suckling——"

The artist shook his head, hardly listening. All his being was fixed at this moment on his wretched model.

"You simply didn't bother?"

The other shook his head again, slightly.

"You have no pity, then, no human feeling?"

The artist lifted his eyes for a quick instant. "Let me work in peace." And he drew the lines.

The collector glanced at the baby. It had no strength left to cry, but it had the security of its mother's breast. The woman must have been dead for hours.

"If you had any sense of decency, any human feeling, you would have reported. You've been standing here, gaping in your vulgar way, making a picture!" The railwayman had a clouded, scornful face. His heart was swelling with emotion—you could see that under the polished buttons of his white, spotless uniform.

"Do not distract me, I beg of you," pleaded the other, and a swift bitterness hit his tone. "What am I doing but trying to make a report? Not to the railway people. I have to report to India."

The collector lost his temper then. "You brute!" People came rushing to the scene, drawn by the magnetism of a row, and they glared at the man, while the indignant collector cited his facts. Yes, the fellow was a brute, the listeners agreed, glaring harder. He had no feeling at all. It was men like him who had brought upon Bengal the darkest misery in her history.

They stood by, the bunch of people, jeering at the artist, but he spoke no word in self-defence; he seemed withdrawn from his accusers, unaware of their presence. His face grew tense. He was lost altogether in his work, now looking at the destitute group, now drawing a line, a curve.

A stout, well-fed man advanced to the artist. A large black moustache bristled on his plump face as he worked up a fierce rage. He snatched the pencil from the artist's hand and flung it far on the rail-track. When his hand returned to the assault, the artist, wakened from his absorption, concealed the pad in his tunic. "What madness!" he cried. He looked about, at this face, at that face, in utter bewilderment.

The crowd went crazy. It rushed upon him, beating him with cruel fists, snatching at the pad, while the victim, felled to the ground, desperately shielded his possession with his body.

The unequal struggle lasted a minute or two, and the sketch

was captured and torn to pieces and the block of paper flung away.

Then the artist sat up, bruised, panting hard. He was a pathetic sight, buttons ripped from his tunic, undervest revealed, but there was fire in his eyes.

"Fools!" he cried, and the voice was shrill between sharp-drawn breaths. "Fools! You think you have destroyed my picture? It lives on in my fancy. You can't destroy my fancy. I shall yet make my report. India will see that dead mother nursing her child."

A policeman came into view. The group of men, pleased with their work, moved, melted away. It was not every day that you had a chance to bring to book a born criminal, one who had no human feeling.

Rahoul slipped down to the rail-track, collected pencil and pad, handed them to their owner.

"Good writing-paper is scarce these days," he said, "unless you pay black-market rates."

The artist gazed at him in a distraught way.

"Bad luck," Rahoul went on. "Those fellows didn't know what they were doing. They hit you? No, they hit the mother lying dead. You have the picture within you. Let India see the picture."

No response wakened in the other. His eyes rested on Rahoul's face, unseeing, filled with the vision of the dead mother and the child at her breast who needed to be created.

"I have a caption for your picture. 'A situation over-dramatized.' With those honest angry fellows sketched in. What do you think of it?"

In that instant they turned to look at the mother and child, and the next moment they turned their eyes away. Neither spoke for a time. The artist seemed to be struggling with some inward pain. His face brooded. When he spoke, his voice was heavy with emotion.

"What will happen to the child? I have neglected my duty, it is true. So much time thrown away. The child needs immediate care."

"The mother has had the rare luck of dying on the platform," Rahoul pointed out. "The railway people will take charge. The child will be sent to a foundlings' home. The body will be taken away by the Corpse Disposal Squad, and by noon it will be burning on the Ganges bank. Why not do your work in peace a short while till the good people return?"

138

The artist turned his eyes again to the corpse, but only for an instant. There was revulsion in his heart.

"I can't bear the sight. Sickening. You think I am a brute?"

Rahoul stared at him. The artist had lost his detachment, and, with detachment, vision. He seethed with human feeling.

Rahoul heaved an unhappy sigh. It seemed to him as though the dead mother on the platform nursing her tiny one now died for the second time.

.   .   .   .   .   .

The heavy sound of traffic wakened the peasant mother at daybreak. Her startled eyes opened and saw no canopy of leaves overhead, but a jutting balcony of sinister aspect, and then she remembered—remembered that she had left the high-way far behind and lay on the hard stone ground of the wonder city. It was a dream suddenly realized.

Out on the high-road bird songs had proclaimed the break of dawn. Here it was the rumble of a thousand trucks like the one in which she had ridden. The unfamiliar scene made the mother's heart beat fast. Anxiety mingled with bright expectation. Onu would have to be protected from murderous wheels—how be sure that they would not dash upon you if you were too near? She turned her face to gaze at the tall building where Kajoli had been taken. She was safe there, Kajoli, the mother felt sure. If only the girl was bearing her child still and he could be born in that great mansion where expectant mothers were cared for in the city way!

Onu was awake. He sat up, looked about and moaned, "Mother, I die of hunger."

Her fingers smoothed his unkempt locks of hair, and parted them in the centre, for in the city you should look neat and tidy even if, perforce, you had to wear tatters.

"We shall have food, plenty," she consoled him, and then she wondered who would give them the food. Scores of people had passed by, and no one had taken any notice. She saw a man approach a squat iron pillar five yards away, and as he pressed a handle water poured out of its mouth in a stream. The wonder of it—you had at your door all the water you might need! The man rinsed his mouth and scrubbed his teeth with a tree twig. Mother and son watched him, and when he was gone the mother said, "Come, Onu, we'll wash at the water-machine before we feed."

While she washed Onu walked a little way to the lamp-post

at the mouth of the alley. All at once his face grew excited. He hurried back to his mother.

"I saw folk in that lane, scores of them, Mother, some awake, some lying asleep."

"What folk?"

"Our folk. Folk same as us. Hungry. Rags and all."

The mother walked up, perplexed. Perhaps those were new-comers like herself. The city had not yet had time to take care of them. Then she saw a familiar figure emerge from the alley —she did not know the man, but she knew the face stripped of flesh, the jutting framework of bones, the hunger-swollen belly and wobbling walk. The man stopped by a garbage can and bent on his haunches. His skeleton fingers dug into the pile and returned with a banana skin. He drew back, he bit into the yellow skin, eating.

"Why, my son, they do not give you food?" stepping up with pity and concern. She had no hesitation in speaking to a stranger who clearly had been a peasant.

The man lifted his watery eyes a moment and nodded his narrow head. "They give us food." His skinny throat worked as he ate.

The face of the mother brightened. What a dread had come upon her for an instant!

"We arrived deep in the night, my son and myself," she mur-mured, as she drew Onu against her bosom with a sudden ache of warmth. "He is hungry. Is it too early for a mouthful?"

The man shook his head. "Never too early for a mouthful."

The mother felt impatience. If only he could see the ques-tions crowding in her heart, if he would tell her all even unasked!

The man held out the fruit skin. "Take this, then. Children must be fed." And he dug his gnarled hands into refuse, seek-ing more peel.

"Do not slight us so, my son. We are not beggars, nor scavengers. We left the village because of the bad times."

Then the man turned and looked her full in the face. He paused for a little and said, "Mother, I too had land—two fair strips. I had children. They died on the high-road, all four. We had to walk a very long way. The mother of my children, she too died. I live on—Fate knows no mercy, and the spark lingers undying in my dead bones. Here in the city we are less well off than pariah dogs." And his head bent, and his peasant face was dry and wrinkled as tobacco leaf.

140

The mother began to tremble so that she could not keep to her feet—she had to sit on the pavement. She struggled for words and spoke hoarsely.

"Calcutta has no pity for us starving ones?"

"There is pity. They have set up free kitchens to give you rice gruel. Not enough. Not all can get it every day. Too little grain, too many mouths. You must come with me, Mother; we'll manage."

"At what hour, my son?" The mother felt heartened.

"High noon. Many hours yet. The childling is hungry. Let him eat peel. It is filling."

Onu ate peel, having washed it first at the tap. The mother could not bear the sight. She turned her face, looked away.

Other destitutes were approaching the garbage can to hunt for food. The mother moved off. She was faint from weakness, but—to feed on polluted leavings! Rather would she starve.

"Put up with us in the lane-way," advised the friendly destitute. "They won't let you stay on this street. They do not like to see our faces—we are no gay sight! Scores of us live in the back lane-way; it opens on to unbuilt wasteland enclosed by tall house walls. Why, it is as though the village has come together to hear a song!"

A picture flashed in the mother's mind. Her husband sat under the thick-leaved banyan, his legs crossed, singing a devotional *bhajan*. All the village sat by and listened. Even the children forgot to play and quarrel and cry, listening in rapt silence.

"Only there is no song," the destitute added.

"There is no song," echoed the mother.

They went into the alley. A sickly stench of stale sweat and filth made the mother close her nostrils with her palm. A man was groaning intermittently.

"Dysentery," the friendly destitute explained. "It is good for him. They will take him to sick-hospital." He made a brooding face. "Will they? Will he have luck?"

The mother thought of her girl in the big mansion and shuddered at the vision of her lying in this alley in child-pain. Her inner grief at her daughter's miscarriage was then softened. *She* would not have to live in this hell—not for many weeks, anyhow. A great tenderness came upon her for the child Kajoli had held long in her womb. *He* knew all; he, the unborn son, as he lay enclosed in the womb-flower, could see the shape of all life to come. And he had perished of his own will so that the mother could be taken to the city and sheltered in sick-hospital. The godling boy! Mother felt her heart choke with emotion. She wiped her eyes with her palm.

They stood still at the street corner watching strange city sights. Motor-wagons of five hundred shapes and sizes. Tram-cars. A short, stout motor-cycle darting off like an arrow with a fierce roar loud enough to burst one's eardrums. The cease-less rumble of traffic oppressed their nerves. They came back to the death-like stillness of the alley—their shell and their shelter for months to come.

A blue motor-wagon with one thick red stripe down and an-other across paused at the alley-mouth. Men with a stretcher picked up the destitute who had dysentery and put him in the wagon. Lucky one! For some time he would live like a king!

The day moved slowly, and an hour before noon the colony gave signs of new life. Faces grew excited. Dim, deep-sunk eyes showed secret sparks. Presently the colony moved—men, women, children. It was meal-time.

"Hasten, Mother," said the friendly destitute. "Four hun-dred meals, no more, served in the compound of the newspaper *Hindusthan*. That is the free kitchen for our area. You fail to cross the massive iron gates and there is nothing for you, nothing to eat."

Other colonies were tottering to the kitchen. Alarmed at the fast-swelling numbers, the mother took her mind to the god Shiva, in his old temple near the village banyan, praying fer-vently : "Father of all three Earths, take mercy, Father, do not deny us. See us, Father, through the massive iron gates."

"To-day you rested because of your weariness from long walking," the destitute spoke; "to-morrow, Mother, you must go about in the morn with your son, searching and picking in the rubbish cans."

"Fruit skins?" The voice toneless.

The man nodded. "Much else. Peels of vegetables. Leav-ings. You'll soon know what to pick. This gruel has not much power—you will feel empty by sunset. Then you must eat peels and stalks and rotten vegetables, all steamed together on a fire." He paused, then continued : "There are big black rats in the alley—dozens. Some of us catch and eat rats."

The mother's face sickened. She cleared her throat as though to speak, but she said no word.

"Those garbage cans—they are our food-bowls, Mother. We pick out of them before the city's scavenger folk come with their
142

vans. Sometimes we pick at night—less competition. I saw two women fighting like animals over a dust-bin—it happened yesterday."

And the mother spoke no word, only crying in her heart, "Father of all three Earths, do not deny us. See us, Father, through the massive iron gates."

The joyous fragrance of hot rice gruel at last! The destitutes had earthen pans or half-shells of coconut in which to receive the dole—three cigarette-tinfuls. The mother had no such receptacle—her few belongings lay discarded on the highway. She spread out a corner of her *sari* for the portions offered to her and her son—the *sari* was not of ample length, so that her bosom was a little bared, but the destitute mother had begun to shed her shame.

She made each mouthful last long. Her son was hungry, and he could eat up both the portions. The mother ate sparingly.

When each grain of rice had been eaten and the earthen pans licked clean, the destitutes blessed the rich ones of the city who had given them free food. "Live long, Father. Be richer still. The wealth-goddess will bestow tenfold more on thee."

No thought came upon them that they had a right to be fed. It was an act of mercy to let them stay on the city pavements, the more so to give them free gruel. The rich ones of the city had no need to care for the famished. If they did so, it was because of an inner wealth, a richness of the spirit. "Live long, Father. Be richer still."

When the destitutes were back in the alley, the sick man who had been carried away in an ambulance was lying stretched out again in his old place.

The friendly destitute who seemed to know all about the city's affairs answered the mother's query:

"They had to bring him back. Sick-hospitals are full to the throat. They took him round. No place anywhere. Bad luck!"

Then the mother thought again of her Kajoli, and felt consoled. And she rehearsed in her mind for the tenth time the words she would speak to her when they went and saw her in hospital in the afternoon hour set for visitors.

"You have found a good place, Mother? And food?"

"We have a good place, girl. We have food. They have given me work—decent work and a fair wage. The city cares for us as it cares for you."

"Onu, Mother? He is happy?"

"He is happy. Onu has picked up city ways. A smart city boy with a new *dhoti* round his waist."

"You? You have no new *sari*, Mother——"

That was the question she dreaded, for she had not made up a fit answer yet. While she mused, a violent screaming tore from the city's bowels, flooding the streets. Onu clung to his Mother.

"There is no harm," the friendly destitute explained, with a shake of his narrow head. "It is the *sireen* [siren]. A warning that Japanee air-ships are coming over the skyway with bomb-loads. People must rush into a slit trench."

No one in the colony moved. Some eyes looked up skyward. The destitute went on: "The Japanee have no quarrel with poor folk like us. Why should we fret? And what if we are hit? What is our life? What is our death?"

Japanee? Up there on the sky path? They were not to come by the sea path, then, landing some way near Baruni village, at a spot three days' cart ride from the village banyan? False, all that talk, dust in the eyes of peasant folk, talk made up to panic them and rob them of their grain?

The mother's face hardened with anger and scorn. Her eyes were haunted by lucent grain.

The mother feared for her son. She longed to hide him in the thing called slit trench. Where to find it? The destitute made no move. He laid himself down to sleep.

"How make that fierce scream of battle?" Onu in wonder asked.

"Why," the all-knowing man answered promptly, "out there in the Fort they have a bugle as tall as a palmyra and with a hundred throats. A white soldier, posted at each throat, pours down air into it with a blowpipe. That makes the big song, the air poured into a hundred-throat bugle gasping out of the huge mouth yawning at the top end."

No enemy planes were approaching the city that day. The siren was only a test. It sounded for ten minutes, then broke off abruptly.

And life roared again in the city. And the restaurants bulged with food. And the cinemas overflowed. And enormous tank-carriers trundled on the streets with their caterpillar loads.

At night, as the alley slept, the man with dysentery groaned with his gnawing pain and lay awake in filth. Big black rats scurried and skipped. A swarm of lice scented newcomers and crawled out of old habitations, migrating to the heads of the

144

mother and son. With stench in their nostrils and lice in their hair, the destitutes of the high-road acquired the new status of city destitutes.

CHAPTER XV

Monju awoke with a start and listened, straining her ears, her hands clutched over her breast. The awful moaning as of some animal in fierce pain. It ceased for a moment, then began again—a long, humming groan. Monju could not bear it. She leaned over her husband as he lay asleep. "Waken. Hear me? Waken."

He opened his eyes and stretched his limbs, and then he, too, heard the cry.

"Some hungry wretch," he said, slipping out of bed.

"My heart is chilled. Crying like that at our house-door so late in the night!"

"One house-door is as good as another." He turned on the light. "Hunger bites more at night, perhaps. Who knows?"

He leaned from the window facing the street. The hooded lamp revealed a figure. He looked long and hard.

"A woman." He turned and walked to the door. "It can't be hunger. When hunger is so bad, there is no cry—only silence."

Monju sat up in a sweat. The electric fan spinning overhead from a rod in the ceiling made the heavy heat of the breathless night roll about in ponderous waves. Monju drew her forearm across her moistened upper lip. What was happening out on the street? If only she had the courage to look through the window! Dead bodies terrified her. And the dying ones—she dreaded them, too. Her husband seemed gone a long time. In his hurry he had not closed the door behind him. Dark shadows lay thick in the corridor. Monju feared darkness as though it cloaked hideous death. Hideous death lurked everywhere, pressing the city in its skeleton grip. Monju had longed to get away, but her husband would not go from the hunger victims whom he served. He had offered to send her to her parents at Simla. How could she go, leaving him amid the devastation? It was not as though she alone had need to escape. Rahoul needed it more, far more. He had lost all mind for research. So restless, so unhappy. The way he sometimes gazed at his food and ate a morsel, and suddenly his face was sick and he rose and walked away. The look of intense sadness that often filled his eyes, and that, when caught off guard, he tried to cover with a smile. When she saw that glance and that smile, Monju felt like weeping. Yes, she must find a way to break her husband's will. She would fall ill, and the doctor would advise a trip to the seaside, and Rahoul would have to take her. No time to lose. The black tide over Calcutta swelled ever higher——

The ceaseless, whining wail, the long, hollow wail threshing out of depths beyond the throat, out of the belly's deep despair: "*Ma! Ma-go-ma!* A sip of rice-water, pray, *ma, ma-go-o!*" You heard it and you heard it, and sickness rose to your throat, and the food you ate stuck like glue. You heard it day in, day out, every hour, every minute, at your own house-door and your neighbours', till the surfeit of the cry stunned the pain and pity it had first started, till it pierced no longer, and was no more hurtful than the death-rattle of stricken animals. You hated the hideous monotony of the wail. You hardened yourself against the wail. The destitutes became a race apart, insensitive, sub-human. You had no need to feel for such creatures. Were they grateful for help? A destitute woman had been given a bowl of rice-water for the child in her arms. Suddenly she had burst into wailing: "*Ma-go-o!* What is this you gave us? My child is dead. Look. *Ma-go-o*, what have I done to you that you killed my tiny one?" The shamed, bewildered folk of the house had to pay two *rupees* to quieten the broken-hearted woman. They had not known that the woman had been carrying a dead child from door to door, blackmailing charity. They were like that, the befouled ones.

Monju and many of her kind had shielded their hearts this way from the great misery of the time, lest that misery broke through and pulled their hearts to pieces.

Rahoul was back in the room. He hastened to the telephone at his bedside and gave a number. As he waited for the reply he looked at Monju and said, "A woman giving birth. *Trying* to give birth." His voice low, grim.

She stared, hardly believing her ears, murmuring, "Giving birth?" But he was remote, speaking into the mouth-piece. He grew annoyed, and presently he banged down the 'phone. He picked it up, gave a number again, his eyes on a page of the Directory. His anger grew as he spoke, and Monju heard him shout: "Hang your rules. Why can't she lie on the floor,

146

if there's no empty bed? It means nothing to you, a doctor, that a woman gives birth on the streets?" He jammed down the receiver again and gave a third number.

His face burned as he rang off at last.

"Monju, you will help me? We can't let her lie helpless on the street. The hospitals say they're all full. They won't have her." The blood rose heatedly to his head. "The swine! The crooks!"

"Shall I ask Mother down?" breathed Monju, her eyes very wide, but Rahoul snapped in impatience, "Later. We must bring the woman in first." He snatched at a sheet, rolled it up and rushed away.

Monju followed him, in her heart alarm, excitement. She paused at the house-door, looking out furtively. The woman moaned no more. She lay upon her back, her legs apart, her eyelids closed. Over the worn, flattened frame covered with a yard of rag lay in sudden contrast the curved mound of her body. Rahoul picked her up gently, laid her upon the stretched sheet. Her eyes, now opening, were brimmed with agony. Faintly her lips moaned, and an answering voice gave comfort: "Do not fear, Mother." As he spoke, Rahoul glanced at Monju, signing to her, and she came quickly from the doorstep. They lifted the woman, carried her into the sitting-room and laid her on a divan, her hair spreading dustily over the brocade cushion.

"I'll ring up for a doctor," said Rahoul as he watched the woman close her eyes and lie still, quietened, as if rid of pain and shame, sunk in a daze. "Stay with her, Monju, while I send Mother down."

Monju stood by the divan, gazing at the limp figure. The wasted peasant face was grooved at the temples and cheeks and overlaid with the stuff of pain—pain so palpable that you could touch it, feel it, with a moving finger. But the pain carried no revulsion, balanced as it was by the tenderness of an expectant mother, a grace that came from within, so that you felt no shrinking pity, only sighing compassion. You had to soothe her with a whispered word. You looked into the depths of eyes where dream hid under helpless alarm, so, anyway, you fancied.

You soften to suffering most when you can imagine yourself placed in like suffering. That is the law. Unconsciously Monju recalled in her heart the pains of motherhood, now remote and dim, while she looked down at the worn frame, the hips narrow

147

for want of succour. How would such a feeble one fight the last stage of her desperate battle? She was having pains in the dust of the street through half the night, away from her husband, from her kin, no one to deliver her baby, not a soul near her. Monju was aghast at the reflection. Tears welled to her eyes. She held her breath as the woman stirred and faintly moaned, and then her limbs were restless in a writhe. Monju listened anxiously for footfalls on the stair—if only Mother would hurry down!—and then the destitute woman opened wide eyes at her, at Monju, and let a half-scream pierce the sheath of her silent endurance. Desperate struggle grew in her body. The thin, drooping arms stiffened and the fingers clutched at the divan cover, while she bit her tongue so that blood flowed, streaking from her twisted mouth.

Monju rushed to the door. Alarm roughened her voice as she cried, "*Ma! Ma,* hurry!" and she turned and darted back to the woman and saw the trickle of blood reddening the mouth and the sunken gazing eyes flickerless. "*Ma!*" she shrilled from the door.

Then they were hastening down the stair, Mother and Rahoul.

Rahoul stood still. Mother, too. Then—it seemed a long time—Mother bent over and gently closed the eyes fixed in a wide, unending stare.

"Dead," said Rahoul, looking away.

Dead? So swift and easy? Like dropping asleep? Monju could not move her eyes from the face. Monju grew in that moment, for she was absolved from the obsession of a dread.

That was the way it happened. The oppressive autumn night brought Monju a new realization of life. She had been remote from the grimness of life, fearing it, hating it as uncouth and vile; but suddenly that life had come upon her in a flood of warmth! First she had lent her strength to aid the stricken one, and the glory of service was a strange new experience, an unknown exaltation. Then the destitute woman was revealed in her human context. Not a pauper ever whining for morsels, hanging on hard to a battered existence, a deathly life without meaning. Not an unwashed, unclean shape with matted locks in which lice bred. A young expectant mother about to make new life and denied, cast out on the street, till at last she could not bear the struggle, and with her unborn one she was but refuse for the corpse-disposal squad.

Out of the flame of travail that had consumed one woman a

148

glow quickened in another, an understanding, a humanizing tenderness, so that the creatures of misery were no longer a race apart, soulless and dead—men and women all.

"Excellencies and Hon'bles," said Rahoul later when the night had ended and the corpse-disposal squad had come and gone, "they have killed one more of our womenfolk. They shall pay—pay hard for everything."

Monju stared. Behind the livid, excited face she saw a beauty she had missed all these years. She saw her husband's true spirit, his hunger for a happier life for the common man. And she knew then that amid the harsh realities of the world pattern, the dominating animalities, the spirit in him doomed him ever to wasteful unrest and unhappiness.

Her glance deepened warmly upon his face, and the wrench of tender emotions in her heart made it beat so fast that she panted a little.

.   .   .   .

At a crowded corner of Chowringhee Road a street gamin plied on the pavement with others of his tribe the busy trade of a boot-black. Onu stood by, leaning his four-foot figure against a lamp-post, watching intently.

So had he watched scores of time, and the whole process lay clear in his mind. Right foot: brush off dust, brush hard; smear cream. Left foot: brush, smear. Right again: rub with a rag, let the shine come out like glass. Finish off with a piece of cotton-wool dipped in a red dye and passed over the rim of the soles. You earned a two-*anna* piece. Onu held his breath because of the vastness of the amount. Two *annas* for such slight labour. Others, even adults, tried hard to take away your trade. Still you could perhaps win four customers and earn a half-*rupee* a day.

A half-*rupee*! Onu could see the silver piece in his vision. If he had the capital he would buy brush and shoe-rest and two tins of smearing cream, one brown, one black, and set up business. Then he would work hard, shining the shoes of rich folk, and make a living and buy food for himself and his mother, so that they would not be destitutes begging and eating at a free kitchen. Kajoli due out of hospital this afternoon. Joy for Mother to have her back after a month almost, yet more pain than joy, for Kajoli, too, would now become a destitute, eating from a free kitchen and sleeping on the street with a hundred others and getting lice in her long, thick hair.

149

And Mother had told her they were so well off in Calcutta city! How would Kajoli bear the shock of the truth? That worry lay heavy in Mother's heart.

Oh, if only he could get the capital on loan to set himself up on the pavement as a shoeblack! Onu felt his heart burn from his craving that had no chance to be fulfilled. And his head grew dizzy from hunger—it was a long time since he had eaten, and the ration of gruel was less filling, these days. A garbage-can was close at hand. The boy dragged himself to his accustomed task of feeling about in the pile for scraps of food.

A bright lovely print in colours, clean and undamaged save for a fold at one corner. Onu picked it up eagerly and wiped the smooth face with his palm. A giant ship bristling with long fingers of guns and a fleet of skyplanes like the ones you saw over Calcutta city—seven, eight, nine! Flame and smoke rushed from the guns at the ship's snout. Kajoli would like the picture; her eyes would be amazed at the sight. She did not seem to care for pictures any more, though. In the days gone by, how she thrilled when she could get one! Pictures often lay buried in refuse-heaps, and Onu had collected many for his sister—a score and more. Two or three he had taken to Kajoli at the hospital; the rest were to be a surprise on the day of her return. Kajoli had hardly looked at them, seeming not to care, and she had said, "Onu *bhai*, why worry so for your sister?" Onu could read her heart. What good were the lovely prints if you had no walls to hang them on? But, then, they wouldn't always be destitutes? They would be back home some day and reap the new grain in the fields. Back home, Kajoli would have pictures enough to brighten the walls of mud.

Odd! mused Onu, with a sad twist of his mouth. When you had need of pictures, you could not get them. When you had no need, they flew upon you. Odd!

He gave a little sigh and dug his hands deeper into rubbish. A jam-tin showed itself. His heart jumped. Some thick sweet syrup would be left on the sides and, with luck, a little solid material at the bottom. But as he picked up the tin a dog came snarling, claiming possession. Onu dropped it in alarm and stepped back. He had no strength in his starved body to fight the dog.

A bigger boy, passing that way, took things in at a glance. He came dashing, kicked at the dog, snatched the jam-tin from its teeth and stood ready for counter-attack.

And the dog attacked. It was mangy and famished; all the

hair had fallen from its skin, so that it looked curiously naked, hardly like a dog. But it fought well because of its hunger, and bit the foe. Then Onu picked up a stone and bashed the animal between the ears.

The dog hung its head, yelping, slinking away.

The big boy was panting hard because of his weakness and excitement. He had blood on his arm, but he had also the spoil of victory. On the brink of his enjoyment of it he became aware of the youngster who stood with eyes wistful and strained.

The big boy hesitated for a time, clutching the jam-tin tight, gazing down at it, then with a sigh he looked up, he held out the treasure. "Lick this side; the other side belongs to my mouth. Lick."

It was truly an act of self-sacrifice. And it was, truly, a second victory.

Onu licked.

Destitutes and dogs in those days often fought for possession of the rich city's ten-thousand rubbish-heaps, in which scraps of rotting food lay buried. It was not every time that the destitutes won, routing the dogs on the streets and the dog within themselves.

CHAPTER XVI

"*Chalo, chalo,* lazy pony!" cried little Khuku, riding on the back of her grandfather, who crouched on all fours and moved across the carpeted floor. "Gallop!" Her legs prodded his ribs.

He had gout in one knee, but he made a gallant effort, hauling his bulk to the end of the room and back again.

"Good pony!" shouted Khuku excitedly, and the pony neighed with pleasure. At that moment the mother, Monju, appeared in the doorway.

"Father, no chemist in this city has any Adexelin to sell——"

She broke off short as she saw the figure crouched on the carpet.

Samarendra tried with one arm to set his rider down, but she held herself firm. "*Chalo!*" she ordered again, prodding harder. "*Chalo,* lazy pony."

"Khuku, get down quickly, bad girl. Four years old, and behaving as though you were half that age. Hurry!"

"Show Mother how well you neigh, good pony," begged Khuku, but the mother stepped forward, dragged her down and gave her a slap.

Khuku stood rigid, face clouded. It was often her way to pause on the edge of crying—a delayed-action effect, the crisis seeming to pass off and then the sudden outburst. Samarendra knew the signs, and took preventive action. He drew the child in to his arms. "That Mother, she is the naughty one, not my Khuku-ma. Now close your eyes—both——"

Khuku closed her eyes, first one, then both, knowing what would come, her chubby cheeks dimpling with pleasure. In a moment she opened one eye, then both, and there was the usual slab of chocolate held out in his palm. Khuku snatched it and ran off with a gay shout.

"Father, you are spoiling her."

He smiled. "This little girl is over-clever for her age. Have you noticed? I have been teaching her to count up to thirty. There's one stumbling-block: fifteen. Every time it is thirteen, fourteen, sixteen——" The face wrinkled with affection.

"She needs Adexelin, so the doctor says, but we can't get it at any chemist's because of the new price control. It's all gone to the black market."

"Leave it to me." Samarendra moved to his writing-desk. "If Khuku-ma needs Adexelin she shall have it."

"And, Father, the cheque?"

"Oh, that? What damage do I have to pay this time?" He picked up the cheque-book with a sigh.

"You see, Father, the wagon has failed again, and our stocks are low—very low. So we have to buy rice once more from the black market." She watched him fill in the form. "Father, make it big," she pleaded.

She was in the thick of relief work these days. Helping her husband to run the free kitchen. Helping, too, at a milk canteen that doled out milk to under-fours—a bowlful a day for each hungry mouth. Then there was the home for foundlings about to open.

"There! Is it big enough?"

Her eyes shone. "It is big enough, Father."

He basked in her radiance. His secret mind might have taken note that some of this amount would return to him *via* the black market and its intermediaries working up to *Cheap Rice*,

152

Ltd., but he was not aware of such an ungenerous thought. It pleased his heart that his act of charity would save a few hundred lives. That heart was in the right place.

Monju hurried off with the cheque, as excited as her little daughter who had been given chocolate.

Adexelin, pondered Samarendra, sitting back in his chair, a smile broadening on his face. Yes, it would be best to speak to Sir Abalabandhu, prince of the black market.

A curious character, Sir Abalabandhu. Samarendra admired and envied the man, and yet he held him in sore contempt. The senior Director of *Cheap Rice, Ltd.*, and its moving spirit, it was this man's hand that had spread well the grease of corruption to win the Company great privileges; more, it was his organizing genius that had solved the intricate problem of storing the vast accumulated food-grains—secret dumps that lay in the heart of famine areas. (Samarendra blacked out in his mind that unhappy side of the picture. He was like the Right Honourable at Whitehall who called the famine an act of God and cast a blind eye on the clear process of cause and effect. Besides, if he would not trade in rice because of some scruples, were there not scores of others to rush and take his place?) Abalabandhu had come from another province and amassed great wealth in Bengal. Authority had rewarded his services. Wealth and honour—Abalabandhu had won in full measure the twofold blessings for which Samarendra still struggled. The man had a curious complex, however. He took an odd pleasure in relating the sex adventures of a person he called *my friend*; under the thin disguise of *my friend*, so Samarendra and others felt sure, even if they had no evidence in support of their belief, he expressed his own shameless perversion, an innate morbid streak.

"As I was saying, that agent chap had to gag the destitute girl"—the talk had flowed at the end of a Board meeting—"you see, while my friend waited outside at the bedroom door, that agent chap gagged her and then whacked her—my friend could hear the rough fist meet her body—he whacked her, mind, taking care not to mark the face—you wouldn't spoil a statue you have to sell, would you? When she had had enough, the agent chap came out and said, 'It's all right, sir; she is a fool who had to learn a lesson, and it is her first time with a man.' My friend stepped in, somewhat cynical about that 'first time', and at sight of him the girl burst into tears—she had drawn features and sunken cheeks—the girl knocked her head, wailing, on my friend's boots, and she called him father, and begged of him to save her; and he, being the sentimental sort, patted her head and made her sit on his lap on the bed and soothed her with tender words, and the girl cried more because of his kindness of heart, and then he had his will, and, believe me, my dear brother, it was truly her first time!"

Samarendra had been aghast, angry, sickened. Mild-natured as he was, even he, even Samarendra Basu, could have struck the shameless creature across the mouth. He controlled his feelings. He sat in dumb silence, looking down and snapping his finger-joints.

Sir Abalabandhu carried his fifty years lightly, always careful to look young. A Chinese barber dressed his black hair. An English tailor cut his silk suits. Neatness encased him. Well-mannered, genial, he exuded warmth for his friends, very keen to help them in every way. You needed extra petrol for your car and had no coupons? Cigars long off the market? English wool for your daughter's knitting? Sleeping-tablets of enemy make? Sir Abalabandhu would get them all for you—a word to him was enough. "My dear brother," he would say reproachfully, "why haven't you told me all this time? You must have suffered much inconvenience. I am so sorry."

No wonder, then, that his fellow-directors on the Board put up with his talk, which gave him such obvious pleasure. He seemed unaware that his frank, smooth brutality shocked his friends. But he knew. And he loved it. That, too, was his perversion.

"Was it fair on your friend's part to take advantage of the helpless woman?" a fellow-director had ventured to remark.

Sir Abalabandhu had stared in honest amazement.

"Don't you understand, my dear brother? That girl would have starved otherwise. Starved, thinned into a skeleton, then died. My friend treated her with great kindness and consideration. He paid her very generously, I can tell you—much more than she had the right to claim." He had paused for a little to slip cake into his mouth, then, resuming: "He saved her from a horrible death. Haven't you ever looked at the pavements of our city as you drive by? The filthy bodies of both men and women, old and young, strewn all about? Ugly sight. Fancy, not to have one grain of rice to eat for days on end. Just try it for half a day. Skip your lunch." And he had paused again, munching cake, while the laughter gathered inside him and burst out presently in big whoops. That laugh was a splash from the well of his perversion. It was the sort of laugh that has thick bodily substance. Between two whoops he cried, "Put nothing in your mouth, brother, just for one day, and then you will know."

He was entirely free of social conscience. Yet he was known as a man of charity. Who had not heard of his princely donations to the War funds? His picture, cigar in mouth, appeared in the illustrated papers. He was seen strutting in a news reel, lifting plump fingers in the victory sign. His Excellency granted him interviews. Her Excellency asked him to luncheon. He pulled the strings of publicity with deftness and ease.

"Brothels have become big business," he had continued his talk that day. "Conditions have never before been so favourable. There is a fine balance between demand and supply in the line—both have gained greatly from this War. You see, the fact is, a lot of moneyed people have a liking for these skinny girls new from the countryside. Skinny, mind"—he lifted a neat forefinger to emphasize the fine distinction—"not skin-and-bone. The famished ones must feed well before they go into business—feed on rice and ghee and milk so that their bones may put on meat. Hair to be rid of lice, smoothed. A hundred other details. It pays. No better investment in the whole money market." The laugh was gathering deep in the well. "You know nothing of your own good city, my dear brother. And nothing, if I may say so, of human nature." The puffy eyelids had flickered amusedly.

True that he knew nothing of human nature, Samarendra had felt sure then. What could he make of this one? A family man with wife and children. Had he none of the normal feelings? Not even shame? It seemed incredible.

"We have a Controller for almost everything these days." The fellow-director who had spoken before spoke again with forced airiness. "Why don't they create a new post—Controller of Brothels?"

"Brilliant idea!" said the filthy mouth, pursing with keen delight. "Only he'd have to be politely named Controller of Social Sickness."

"Your friend would be highly eligible for the post, wouldn't he?"

"He would. None better." The whoop had burst.

Sir Abalabandhu had enjoyed the hour immensely.

His talk was filth, his company was agony, yet his friendship

155

a precious gift not to be thrown away. A Director of many big concerns, a timely hint from him on their workings before the Reports came out could bring you a fortune on the Stock Market. And had he not breathed life and ruthless energy into *Cheap Rice, Ltd.*? Samarendra soothed his inner revulsion. Rich, he hungered to be still richer. He had great need of this depraved one.

The depraved one could see this reaction in the heart of piety. The picture added one more whoop to his laugh!

Samarendra put his cheque-book aside. The money he had given for the destitutes had yielded an instant return. A strain somewhere on his conscience was eased.

Adexelin? Yes, Sir Abalabandhu with his whooping laugh and *my dear brother* would get Khuku-ma all the Adexelin she needed.

.   .   .   .   .

When Kajoli came out of the hospital gates she saw with a start that there was no joy in the face of Mother, only sorrow. The eyes were swollen as if with much weeping, the voice was low and hoarse. They walked mutely to the alley's mouth, and then the mother stood still and hung her head, sudden tears trickling down hollowed, withered cheeks. And Kajoli cried in alarm, "What is it, Mother?"

She answered after a time: "I have told you nothing but lies, girl, lest you fret yourself on our account. We are homeless destitutes. We have no work. We sleep on the street. We have nothing to hope for—nothing."

An awful dread came upon the girl, but only for a moment. She said, "Mother, I knew." Kajoli lied. With her swift understanding she saw the great need to soothe Mother, to take away her shame and sorrow.

"You knew all?" The mother lifted her hand to her face in a gesture of bewilderment.

She made a small sound of assent. "I knew all."

Then the mother felt a suffocating load lift off her chest.

"There is our home!" She pointed to the alley. "It is much worse than the high-road. We live worse than cattle. The rich men of the city look upon us as pests, as vermin."

Kajoli stepped into the alley. Her black pupils widened with horror, filling her eyes. Her knees weakened, sinking, but she kept to her feet with the force of her will. Mother and Onu had lived in that festering hell for a month while she lay in comfort in hospital. How the two had suffered! Kajoli felt shamed that she had not shared their misery and pain.

A fat, middle-aged woman sold betel-leaf from a stall at the corner, a few yards off. She had watched the girl with interest, listened to the talk. A young girl with a good face and figure, and a new *sari* on. Attractive. She seemed to have eaten well. How, then, could she be a destitute's daughter unless—— At that moment the girl went walking ahead, and the woman hurried to seize her chance.

"Mother, a betel-leaf for you," she hailed, her large teeth smiling.

The mother walked up eagerly. It was ages since she had held a betel-leaf in her mouth. And in the old days a lifetime away she had been addicted to it—ten leaves a day.

The woman drew the facts out of her. The girl had been in hospital. She had been cared for, and her face had filled out a little. The kind-hearted doctor had given her a new *sari*—the old one had been cast off. That explained the strangeness. The woman watched the girl with sharp interest, a harsh glint in her narrow eyes.

"Take two betel leaves from me every day, Mother. You do not have to pay. Why, you can pay me tenfold when the old times return, as they must. You have a house, you have land, I know."

Kajoli came back, a pallid smile on her face. "Come, Mother," she cried softly. Her lips pressed together as though swallowing sickness.

"Such a golden image!" said the betel-woman with a sigh. *Bhagwan!* "Have a betel, child." She handed her a well-folded one fat with spices and turned to the mother. "Take some fried rice, Mother. I have plenty. And some treacle to sweeten it—fresh treacle thickened from the juice of date-palm."

What kindness! The mother felt overwhelmed. Fried rice with treacle. It was countless time since Kajoli and Onu had had anything good to eat.

There was a date-palm on her land, on the eastern strip—a friendly, fruitful tree. The juice had surpassing fragrance. How the children loved the treacle from that juice! And her husband and Devata, too. That tree had a spirit of goodness to make such fragrance, so Devata had said. Some trees were evil-hearted and bitter, some had the sweet spirit of goodness.

157

"There he comes," said Kajoli, gazing up the street pavement, and she called "Onu!"

The boy was walking fast on his spindly legs. He carried a paper bundle tied with a string.

"Pictures," he said, his bony face joyous. "Pictures for every wall. Even for the shed where our Mangala lived. Look, *didi*. Tell me if you have seen such pictures, ever."

So Kajoli started her new life as a destitute of the city.

The betel-woman, honey-tongued one, hailed Kajoli in the evening as she came out of the alley. Kajoli feared her, though. She was somehow like the city woman who had come to the village with an evil proposal, the jackal emissary. That was how Kajoli, mixing up images in her mind, felt about such creatures—jackal emissaries.

The jackal lay crouched upon her mind, a hideous, ever-present shape. All the repulsions of life resolved themselves into the jackal shape. Her terrible experience had built in her a strange contradiction: she had become stone-like within, yet highly sensitized. She was as dead as darkness and as living as a flame.

The betel-woman knew human nature. She took her time. She offered the girl a seat in the stall.

There was a sort of improvised booth at the other corner, a canvas structure, with rows of photographs exhibited at its entrance. Every photo showed a group of two—a grinning alien soldier with a gay-faced wench on his knees. Soldiers went inside the booth and came out after a while, smiling with pleasure and holding a picture. What was the show about? wondered Kajoli, and the woman told her. A fellow could step into the cloth room and have his likeness taken with a girl—the paper image would be ready for him in a quarter of an hour. It was a memento of India, and good fun, so the soldiers thought. The girls belonged to the place. They earned two *rupees* a day, just for sitting gaily on the knees of an alien in khaki uniform for the brief pose.

The betel-woman gave Kajoli a quick, keen glance. "Not that they will have you. They engage only half-caste girls with neat English frocks on." And she chuckled and leaned her head against the plastered wall of her booth, and the wall sucked a little sticky oil from the shining bun of her hair.

"Paper! *Hindusthan!*" cried a newsboy as he dashed by. "Japanee skyplane downed near Calcutta city. Paper! *Hindusthan!*"

The girl listened, looking at the young newsboy, and an odd jumble of images lay for an instant in her heart. The hungry mass stooping over gruel-bowls at the *Hindusthan* Centre. . . . Skyplane zooming across Baruni village, darting towards her. . . . A woman and her little girl child feeding from the same bowl, each swallowing fast, so that they could dig into the other's share. . . .

Two coloured U.S.A. soldiers were coming up the street. Kajoli held her breath as she saw a bold street urchin run to them and speak in broken English: "Hey, Jim. Want me show you virgin?" The aliens looked down at the four-foot height and shook their heads with a broad grin. The brave boy then lifted his arm and slapped one of the soldiers on the back. "You no good, Johnny. No come? Why no come?" And as they passed on he remembered some more of his sales talk and yelled, "Small cash, good fair virgin; too small cash."

The betel-woman laughed with all her teeth and explained the words to the ignorant peasant girl. There was a brothel round the corner, a new one—all destitute women from the countryside. They lived well, those once-famished creatures; they enjoyed every comfort. They made good money. Agents went about the city streets picking good-lookers, paying them sixty *rupees* in advance; why, even seventy. In the house the women kept half their takings, and the other half went to the proprietor. Both parties made money. The women wore gold on their rounded arms. And not one of them could boast half the looks Kajoli had. What fate! *Bhagwan!* A golden lotus wasting in mud and filth. The heart grew sick at such utter injustice.

Then Kajoli knew that the woman was truly a jackal emissary. And she shuddered and kept away from her. The persistent woman pursued her into the alley. The agent fellow had seen her; he was all eyes for her. Seventy *rupees* in advance—a fortune! That carcase of a fellow might even part with ten more if properly squeezed between the jaws of a No and a Yes! Why rot in this hell from which there was no other way of escape? Why put up with this living death? And must you think only of yourself? Your mother, your little starved brother? What wrecks they are! Sad! Have a heart. Yes, have a heart. Eighty *rupees*—a fortune. It would mean life to them. Else they would surely die——

Kajoli shunned the brute shadow of the jackal emissary.

CHAPTER XVII

It could not have been by design that the two messages with the same date-line appeared on the news page almost side by side. A correspondent had wired from Midnapore: A destitute mother who could not feed her three children tried to drown them in the Ganges. Reuters had cabled from Australia: Miners had gone on strike against insufficient ration of butter.

One world. One commonwealth, in all truth, Rahoul reminded himself. Topping the news page was a cartoon of the Right Honourable at Whitehall washing his hands of the famine in water poured from a jug by his chief, the Prime Minister.

Lips scornful, Rahoul flipped the pages. Pictures of destitutes. . . . A woman sat on the pavement eating from a bowl while her famished child sat by and gazed.

The camera had done its work well. The child, a skeleton with unwinking eyes, perhaps too feeble to cry, gazed on while the hunger-mad mother ate with ravenous gulps.

The cruel picture seemed to deepen a dread that came upon Rahoul often these days as he tried to assess the deeper implications of the famine, the over-all effect. It had a physical aspect and a moral one. Death would claim two millions, perhaps three. Millions more would escape by the skin of their teeth, but they would never be strong again, especially the children and the rickety babies who had had so little succour, who had been exposed much to sun and rain. A physically shattered race would grow up in the ninety thousand villages of Bengal, a sapped, half-living stock that would pass on its bitter heritage and perpetuate itself unless a more civilized Government made a great effort to avert the dread fate. That was the physical aspect of the story.

Then the inner degradation. At the outset the famished parents gave what food they could collect to the children—there was not enough for all to share—but as hunger bit harder the finer feelings began to be stilled, deadened. Men and women slid in spirit to the level of animals. Rahoul recalled a story in the papers. A starving mother with a child at her breast was given food at a kitchen. While she ate, the child died in her lap. But the mother ate on. She finished her meal, and then left with her dead child. There was another story. A destitute woman with three children, after a day's hard effort, collected some handfuls of rice. At sunset, as she lighted a fire, a hungry man snatched away the grain and fled.

Rahoul, as he sat at his table in the Relief Centre, feared the emotional hardening, the dehumanizing. And this grim picture in the paper strengthened his dread.

A passing phase? When times grew normal again the innate humanity of the masses of Bengal would soon be re-lit? Rahoul was far from sure. It was too much to hope that the burning experience would leave no scars on the spirit, would not twist the spirit beyond repair for a generation, for an age.

But this mother? Would she not again be her warm, loving self? Rahoul gazed intently at her, and felt tenderness fill his heart. Fancy took him a year ahead. The famine had blown off. The mother had survived. She was back in her village home.

It is nearly dusk. The mother walks the village path, a small package in her hand, a *pice*-worth of salt from the grocer. This day there were red sweet potatoes to eat with the rice, and they would need a little salt for seasoning.

Back home, she unwraps the package and pours the salt into an earthen jar, and she is about to cast the news sheet into the oven as kindling, but there is a picture in it, and she thinks: What picture is this? She smooths it, and a cry goes forth from her lips like a gasp. She has recognized her dead child—for the image of him ever fills her eyes—and though she cannot see herself in the evil shape in the picture, she knows it is none other. There she is, a mother filling her hunger-swollen belly while her skeleton child looks on beggingly. He died. Maybe those mouthfuls would have saved him. A monster, not a mother. A monster that ate its birth child.

Dusk deepens into night, and the night grows, but she does not rise to light the kitchen fire and boil the rice: she sits with the picture in her lap, crazy with her shame and her anguish.

Rahoul thrust the paper aside.

One other mother haunted his thoughts often these days— the peasant mother at Baruni. She and her daughter Kajoli. Kishore. Onu—Rahoul could hear the happy mush mush of his shoes! If only he could see a way to find out where they were. What if they had been borne off in the flood of hunger? The horrible dream he had had one night! The peasant mother and her young son lay dead on the high-road, not far from Calcutta. A vulture swooped down to peck their flesh, and Kishore caught it in a snare. He roasted the carrion-eater on a fire and offered the bitter meat to Kajoli, who lay dying: "Kajoli, eat. Eat this meat and live, Kajoli." Then Rahoul cried out in his sleep: "Wait. Here is rice—all the rice you need. Wait——" In that instant Monju pushed at him and he awoke, wretched, drenched all over with sweat.

What if they were in this city among the homeless hundred thousand? Not likely, though. Kishore knew the city, and he knew Rahoul's address—he would have come over. So Rahoul reasoned over and over again, and yet, looking out from bus and tram, walking by the street corners where destitutes lay huddled, he scanned the faces, intently, with hope and with fear. Against all reason, Rahoul searched, ever searched.

And one day he passed by a garbage can over which scarecrow slips of boys stooped, Onu among them, picking. He saw the dismal group, unseeing, withdrawn, wrapped in thought. He passed on. . . .

And one day as he walked one side of the street the peasant mother walked the other, a few yards away. And each, unseeing, passed on. . . .

"The gruel is ready, sir." Ohin, a relief worker, spoke from the office doorway. Ohin was an undergraduate at college. He had fainted from hunger in the classroom before he was taken on at the Centre and earned a daily meal. Many students of the poor-middle class knew the pangs of hunger in those days. Inflation had done its ruthless work, and they had edged very close to the pauper's level.

Rahoul walked to the kitchen. Men were busy steaming three kinds of grain in large cauldrons. When ready, the grains, poor grades all (and a goodly lot of grit to add to the weight—traders knew their job so well!), would be mixed together. Rahoul looked on with distaste. The "standard gruel" was hard to digest. Its calories were less than a third of what the human body needed. He who lived on the gruel would not die, but he would be starved slowly. The kitchen was helpless.

The emotional deadening—that thought persisted in his mind as Rahoul went through with his routine inspection. But there was a streak of light in his inward gloom. A strange happening: the strangest experience in his life! Heard from others, he would have laughed it away as romance. Could you dismiss the evidence of your own eyes?

It was after nightfall. Street lamps were dim under hoods.

Rahoul was walking past Red Road towards the Chowringhee tramway. Near the military encampment white soldiers stood grouped around a young destitute girl who sat on the roadside under a lamp-post, her head bent low. Rahoul felt his heart miss a beat. Kajoli! Then, as he looked, his face paled with dismay. Not Kajoli, though she was somewhat like Kajoli. The girl wore a ragged garment, but she was not altogether famished. Grace lingered yet on her face with the scarlet marriage-mark on her brow. The soldiers stood in silence, as though tense with some expectation. Rahoul, too, stood by, wondering.

A soldier moved from the group and dropped a *rupee* into the begging-bowl, which showed a few other silver coins.

She said no word, only rose to her feet, languid, slender of limb, no taller than Kajoli. Arms drawn folded over her bosom, she stood erect and lifted her face starward, the moulding of her neck revealed. Her lips curled with a smile that was somehow no smile. Then the arms unfolded, stripping the ragged garment from her breast. So she stood bare, the hooded street light full upon her, a bronze image with eyes reaching starward. . . . The crowd gaped, but no word was spoken, no titters came. Moments went by, and the girl dropped her face and drew the *sari* back to her bosom and sank on her knees. She hung her head. She looked shamed.

Another *rupee* clinked into the bowl. The girl stared at it for a long moment, then rose once more and bared herself to the flooding light, arms up-flung, bronze, again, a different mould. And the ravages of hunger showed on her flesh. And as she sat down and her face lowered, she looked more shamed. When a third *rupee* had clinked into the bowl and she stood again, the lips that curled with the smile trembled, and at the corner of each eye a big tear glistened.

The cruel clink in the bowl once more. . . .

An M.P. chanced on the scene. He gave a swift look and briefly ordered the men, "Get along." One who had come late hung on with a *rupee* in his fist, but before he could drop it into the bowl the M.P. took him by the back of his neck, made him turn round. "Get along."

The soldiers would have something luscious to talk about when they went home to America and England.

The destitute girl picked up her bowl. She wiped her eyes, gazing at the coins, lips twitching with some thought, and she rose and started to walk towards the Strand. An irresistible impulse made Rahoul follow her down the blacked-out streets, past Council House, a good way, and he had to walk slowly behind her, halting once or twice, for she dragged her feet. Something about her troubled and perplexed Rahoul. The pain-marred look on her face, the struggle, that the aliens had missed, or perhaps accepted as part of the show. There was nothing brazen about her, Rahoul felt sure, his eyes haunted by the glisten of big tears. Aware, sensitive, she debased herself this way because of desperate need. Would she not keep away now that she had earned enough to last her many weeks? That would be her true test.

Rahoul waited as he saw her stop at a cheap eating-shed and heard her order six *rupees'* worth of flat coarse bread. Why so much bread? Rahoul in wonder waited in the dark.

"Trade is good, young woman?" said the shopman, with a suggestive leer.

The package of bread in her arms, she walked on, turning at last into a mean alleyway. The place was choked with desti- tutes, like a hundred others Rahoul knew. And again he stepped after the girl.

Life stirred in the dim, dismal lane in the instant of her com- ing. The destitutes sat up, faces eager and joyous, and they cried thinly, "The mother!" "She is back, the mother," the words tossed about. "Our own mother, she is back." It was strange how their lips loved to call the young girl mother.

She held the basket in the crook of one arm and started to give away the bread, and Rahoul, watching, suppressed a whistle. He watched her as she spoke gentle words. "No, Uncle; you must not eat heavily on a sick stomach. "Haru, you must not gulp down your bread before you chew it well. Chew well, my golden one." "Sister, will you eat two pieces? No? One is enough?"

She had the bearing of a princess! Rahoul stood by, en- chanted. Having served all, the girl sat down among the people and ate her portion of bread.

She had shed her extraordinariness. A simple village maid, like others of her kind. You would not see in her the drama- tized figure on Red Road. Among her people she was herself.

But she had risen to a tremendous crisis. She had overcome her shame and her fear of strangers—alien soldiers—and de- vised her broken-hearted way to earn good money—on her, a destitute girl, so many lives hung!

She had sold her shame, the convention-bound moron would
164

so decry her, she had abased the body's sanctity. But Rahoul, walking out of the lane, felt as though he had glimpsed the sanctity of the human spirit, and was dazzled by too much richness and beauty.

That was the streak of light to illuminate the gloom of his heart.

Yet the destitute girl made him unhappy, too. Somehow she kept on reminding him of Kajoli. There was no real likeness between them, only both were peasant girls, just ordinary peasant girls. Did he then see all peasant girls of Bengal in the Kajoli image? But where was Kajoli? In what horror of destitution was she lost?

As he left the kitchen, Ohin, his young assistant, drew near and said, "An old man wants to see you, sir. He is waiting at the gate."

"A destitute? You know we can't issue any more tickets——"

"This man has a ticket. He wants to surrender his ticket. It's very strange."

Rahoul looked puzzled as he walked to the gate.

"Father," said the old man as he held out his card, "I have eaten for two weeks. Now I can live without food for a time. I can move about and beg and find food-scraps and keep the bones together. Give my place to one whose need is more than mine. Hundreds of such folk are about, helpless ones."

"No, no," said Rahoul. "You are worn and weak. You need feeding. Keep the card. The gruel will be served in a minute."

But the skeleton dropped to its knees, and the skull bent itself slowly to the dust of the roadside.

"Father, there is no end to your kindness of heart. I owe you my life. I can give you no service in return. I can do no good to my brethren save this much: I can give my place to a more needy person unfed at a kitchen. Do not deny me this one joy, I beg." He gasped through his teeth with the strain of speech and slowly picked himself up and walked away.

The richness of the human spirit! Rahoul could have laughed at the oppressive dread he had felt. He gazed at the bent, half-naked figure receding down the street, and it filled him with wistful pride and joy, standing out in his mind as a signal of hope and deliverance for the hunger-stricken masses of Bengal.

.   .   .   .   .   .

"Very hungry, *sa'b*. One *pice*, eat rice. Very, very hungry, *sa'b*——" moaned the boy in rags in the familiar destitutes' singsong, plodding at the heels of a tall white soldier in dust-colour garb as he came out of the doors of Metro Cinema House.

The soldier stopped, looking down. His blue eyes grew deep with compassion. He smiled and spoke words of which the boy could make nothing, and he passed a gentle hand over the little beggar's dusty mop of hair. Then he gave him a half-*rupee* piece.

The soldier passed on. Onu stood dazed. No one had ever given him so much money. And no stranger had touched him with fondness—ever. He was a thing to be hated, shunned, feared. Onu lifted his hand to his mop of hair as though it still retained that wondrous touch. His eyes blinked. Onu felt like weeping.

The silver gripped in his fist, he trudged the street in the direction of a cheap cookshop where he could buy rice—two big platefuls with lentils or potato, for the money he owned. Onu was elated. He could see the rice—his for the asking! Eyes closed, Onu enjoyed the feel of hot cooked rice in his mouth. Presently the imagined feel would be reality.

The cookshop was far off in Bentinck Street. Onu, tramping slow-foot, laid a thin baby hand on his empty stomach—how it had swelled, as though bulging over-full with food! Odd, mused Onu, his hand on his stomach, his mouth twisting in pained wonder. You eat over-much for months and years, and your belly sticks out fatly—look at the rich folk. You starve for months; your arms, legs, face, chest, are bone, just bone, and again your stomach bloats roundly like a balloon. Odd!

In a while his thoughts took a new turn, and he was re-living the experience of the past night. The siren had been screaming for an hour, flooding the city streets with its fear. Onu could see the tall body of the siren, tall as a palmyra, with a hundred throats and a white soldier posted at each throat and pouring air into it with a blowpipe—that air, streaming out of the big mouth at the top end, made the big song. Then, in a while, the other fierce noise—enormous wings crashing through the sky, tearing the sky to pieces. Onu had often wondered what sky-pieces would be like—why, the blue, beautiful sky was stuff like thick silk, and if a big thread chanced to fall in the desti-tutes' lane they would no more have to be naked, they would have good wear a-plenty. But no sky piece fell, only a Japanee bomb, and it snatched off the back of the big building flanking the laneway. At daybreak the lane was full of people : soldiers and A.R.P. officers came visiting in shiny cars, and they walked boldly right into the lane's stink and filth amid the stretches of unwashed, sprawling bodies like patches of earthworms, all because two or three destitutes had been hurt by a Japanee bomb, and yet the big folk had never stepped on to the spot before when the destitutes had laid hurt by hunger and many had died, too weak to walk to the free kitchen and with nothing to eat for days.

They had put the bomb-hurt ones in a motor wagon with one red stripe down and another across. Taken them to sick-hospital.

Before, too, men from the alley, ailing inside them because of the rotten garbage food they ate, rode that lovely wagon. Back home in an hour! Not room enough in sick-hospitals. But there was room enough, room reserved, for men hurt by a Japanee bomb: so the big officers said, lest the destitutes grew to fear a Japanee bomb.

An idea knocked then on Onu's mind. He turned it over, and his face lit. He was now a few steps from the cook shop in Bentinck Street, but he did not stop; he passed on. He walked a good way farther till he reached a back-street temple. He went to the temple yard, where flowers were on sale.

Onu gripped his silver bit a long time, staring at the flowers, as though musing in his heart, then at last he loosened his clasp. "Blossoms of the jasmine," he spoke to the flower-woman and held out his coin. His mouth was parched, and there was great hunger in his stomach.

The woman eyed him with keen amazement. Match-thin legs, you could see the knee-joints, and even the bones looked worn thin. A destitute boy who had not long to live. The goddess in the stone image had no pity for such guileless ones who had done no wrong, harmed nobody?

"What fairer flowers than the flowers of devotion?" she said with tenderness. "Stand before the goddess, my son, let her see you, let her see whatever you have in the bowl of your heart."

Onu shook his head. "The goddess loves the white flowers of the jasmine." He rubbed his grimy fingers carefully on his rags before he reached out for his purchase.

"Keep your money, then. Take all you need." The woman held out a big lotus-leaf cup full of jasmine.

"If I do not pay, Mother, where is merit in the offering?"

That was true. The unhappy flower-woman took his money and returned him some small change. Onu mused for a

167

moment and put down the small change before her. "Maybe," he said, "this is enough for a butter lamp?"

The flower-woman heaved a sigh. What had come upon the famished boy that he was so very extravagant?

The lotus-leaf cup in one hand, lamp in the other, Onu passed on to the temple sanctum, where the goddess sat on a high pedestal. He rose on his toes to place his offering at her feet. He held his *prodeep's* wick to the flickering flame of another on the pedestal, and, crouching down, knocked his forehead thrice on the ground.

"Mother," the prayer flowed fervent out of his depths, "I ask naught else from thee. Mother, I only ask this much: let a Japanee bomb hurt me, Mother. Then the motor-wagon with one red stripe down and another across will come and pick me up and take me to sick-hospital. They will give me an iron bed to lie on, Mother, and a clean piece of cloth to put on, and, maybe, a blanket to wrap myself in against cold, and food—all the rice I can eat, Mother. And I can sleep my fill, Mother, and even if it rains hard I'll not get wet, because of the roof over my head, and there will be no need to walk and walk and pick from muck-heaps and fight the angry dogs, but I can lie down, being hurt by a Japanee bomb, with a doctor to care for me, a doctor to wash my blood with medicine and put a fever-stick in my armpit to know the heat. And let the wound take long to heal, Mother; for then I can stay long in sick-hospital, a bed under me and a blanket over me and rice for my mouth, as if I am a king. Mother, I ask naught else of thee, Mother, only let a Japanee bomb drop from the sky and hurt me, Mother."

Onu had moved far away from the eager-hearted boy who had lived for his kin, strong, protective, for their sake. The problem of his own survival now absorbed him. His defeated spirit pulled his emotions to itself. And his introvert emotions weakened his fighting power. It was a vicious circle.

CHAPTER XVIII

KAJOLI HAD made her grim decision. She would sell the last thing she owned—herself. Mother was dying. She ailed, and could not eat the poor fare her son and daughter provided, begging on the streets and picking in the garbage. She needed shelter, too, because of the severe winter cold that had affected her chest. All this could be had for the money the agent offered. Eighty rupees. This body of hers was worth so much? thought Kajoli with grim wonderment. This body had been defiled on the high-road. Let it be defiled over and over again, then, if Mother's life could be saved at that price. Mother had suffered enough; she had not the strength to bear it any more. How she had shrunk and aged! Even her speech was almost gone, and she breathed with heavy pain. Kajoli could not look at her without a burning in her eyes, a weeping in her heart. Yes, she would give herself to the claws of the jackal. He, the jackal, had torn up her child. What matter, then, if he tore her, too? The money would see Mother through for a year; then perhaps the times would brighten and Mother and Onu would be able to go back to the village. There was the land. Some day Father would return from prison. But not Kanu *bhai*, and not *he*, her husband, for (the feeling was a perpetual fever in her blood) they would be hanged. Perhaps by this time they had been hanged —many had been hanged, so the betel-woman said, knowing from the talk of her customers and the cry of news-hawkers. And she, Kajoli, would never return home—the very shadow of her would be defilement. She would give herself to the jackal dark after dark, till the end of all dark. Kajoli, attuned to self-murder, jerked her chin in the old way of decision.

She brooded over the vision of her husband, as she brooded over that vision every now and again. A stranger had descended from the blue sky and claimed her as his bride and shared with her the sky-blueness that was in his soul. Then he was gone. Hanged—the certainty had grown in her—they, men of the jackal world, could not bear so much sky-blueness in the soul of a man. He had made an attempt to rescue the doomed one, Kanu, and they, men of the jackal world, had seized him and put him in chains and hanged him. Else he would not have failed to return, he would have walked back from the earth's end. Hanged—it happened on the day she heard his voice in sleep in the hospital, and the voice said in a murmur, "Kajoli!" and the voice had so much tenderness that she wept in her sleep, and later the nurse asked her, "You moaned all night— you were in pain?"

One prayer she had in her heart: that she could have him for her husband in the lives to come. She had no need of Heaven; only let her be born again on Earth and again, that she could have him for her husband. That was her prayer.

G 2

169

So Kajoli spoke her decision to the betel-woman, and the woman, triumphant and beaming, showed her the roll of notes, eight ten-*rupee* ones, and Kajoli said, "Give it to me in advance."

"Not all?" said the woman, screwing shrewd eyes in suspicion.

"All," said Kajoli.

"What if you don't come?"

Her glance lay steady on the woman and she said, "I will come."

Under her cool gaze even that shameless woman felt shamed and she hurriedly answered, "I know. You will come."

Kajoli took the money. She would come at midnight, when Mother slept.

She tied the wad of notes to the corner of a piece of old sacking that they used as washcloth, and placed it folded under Mother's head. She wrapped a slim arm around Mother and nestled and pressed her face against Mother's breast, like a child who was tired, desperately tired. And as tears spilled from the closed eyelids and she bit her lip hard to hold them back, Mother fondled her and passed a caressing hand through the unkempt mass of hair and murmured fond words, blessings. And it was as though Mother had received a sign, as though she knew. But she could not know.

The mother was taking leave of Kajoli for a reason of her own. She was going away. Early that morning she had seen an old man swinging in the air from a tree on the Ganges bank with a tattered cloth tight round his throat. He had hanged himself. The mother watched the corpse. That man had proved with his dying gasp that he was a man still, undefeated. In a while it would have been too late. He would have become mindless as an animal, without the power to die at will—did you ever hear of a starving animal drowning itself? And the mother had envied him and made her own decision. She had become a heavy burden to her children. It was hard enough to feed oneself; what misery to have to provide for a decrepit mother who ailed without cease and could not walk down to the free kitchen? She must act before it was too late, before she lost her power to think and feel. She must act at once.

Mother Ganges hailed her!

In silence she blessed her son and daughter, committing them to the care of all the gods. "Let bright days come upon them. If they are guilty of wrongs in past lives, let the punishment be mine alone, let me alone work it off, let me drag suffering from life to life." And as she blessed, she passed her fingers over the girl's head, caressing, grieving that there would be none to do the hair, so thick in the comb, and none to pick the lice. Her eyelids weighed down with her feebleness, and she sank into sleep with this ache in her heart, and her daughter's face, tender and warm, tucked against her bosom. . . . When she awoke, the lane was dusky with the nearness of dawn. She sat up anxiously. Where was Kajoli? Gone, to ease herself at some street corner before the cover of darkness was lost. Onu lay fast asleep. The mother passed her hand all over his face and blessed him again and again. She grieved that she could not have one last look at her Kajoli, and she wept quietly a minute. There was no time, and she set off, her feet heavy as lead.

Then she mused: "Why shall I let this *sari* of mine be lost? Worn, ripped, it would yet be much use to my daughter." And she turned back and took off her *sari*, wrapping her slight figure with the old sacking. The thick roll of notes touched her skin. Some useless scrap, the mother thought, hobbling away.

In the pre-dawn glimmer the half-naked mother dragged herself down the blacked-out streets of the great city till she reached the bridge. Her legs trembled with fatigue as she walked to the middle of the span to be clear of the jetty and the mass of anchored water-craft—a steamer was smoking even at this early hour. Faces haunted her, all assembled together— her husband, her three children, her son-in-law. There was a song, a *bhajan* song, and her husband had sung it always for her ears alone. There had been much happiness in her life before the heavy woes came. She looked down at the dark water, and sudden fear chilled her heart. Her sunken eyes lay fixed and tears blinded them. Her breath came gasping and choking in her throat. She clutched the white breast-high rail, clutched hard. Then she heard a motor-van coming over the bridge, and turned, saw the glancing lights. Swiftly she lifted her foot to the rail and hauled herself with desperate strength. . . .

. . . . . .

Kajoli hung her head. Her feet dragged, shuffling, on the street. The betel-woman had taken her first into the shop for an hour. Rinse your mouth, girl, and clean your teeth with English paste, that they may look young and white. Scrub your face with the lather of soap. Take scented oil in your cupped palm and rub it on your hair, so rough and dust-grey, the nest of sparrow! Look your best, girl, before you cross the doorstep of your gay new life. Kajoli, in a daze, followed her bidding. And at early daybreak, as she walked the street, she was still in a daze, with no power to think or feel, frozen within. A tram-car rumbled by. The city was stirring awake. At a corner of the street a newsboy dashed up with his bundle, shouting to the few passers: "Paper! *Hindusthan!* Dehra Dun prisoners start hunger strike."

She half-listened, passing on, accustomed to news-vendors' talk. Ten paces had she gone when the cry rushed again, close at her heels: "Dehra Dun prisoners start hunger strike." The words stood out in the smooth stillness of dawn.

It was strange how all at once a bell of memory somewhere in her rang suddenly. *Dadu*, a prisoner in Dehra Dun jail-house. Hunger strike. *Dadu* going hungry. Her face twitched as though she was straining to grasp those words. Hunger strike. *Dadu*. Her eyes widened a little.

And she passed on.

"Hunger strike!" scoffed the betel-woman. "Hunger enough in our Calcutta city. To give up your food when you may eat! In every jail-house, look east, look west, look north, look south, there is a hunger strike—the vendors of news pour it into your two ears every day, every hour. *Bhagwan!* Why not take the useless sons of owls out of the cool comfort of jail-house and put them in a beggar's lane here? Good for them." And she grinned with all her teeth.

Another newsboy went rushing by. "Paper! *Bharat!* Congress leader fasting unto death."

"That one!" said the betel-woman, proud of her knowledge of public affairs. "Man of seventy and more. Fasting at his ripe age. Not much juice to spare in his old blackened bones. Madness!"

"What name?" asked Kajoli in an under-breath. Suddenly her heart was beating hard.

"Man with a goodly beard. I saw a picture of him. Devash. Yes, Devash Basu; that's the name."

Then, in a flash, Kajoli saw him.

He stands there, the tall, white-clad figure, with uplifted handcuffed arms, and the pale silver of his hair and the pale silver of his flowing beard are touched with a light that is not of the sun alone.

"Friends and comrades, do not betray the flag. Do not be-
172

tray yourselves. The supreme test has come. Be strong. Be true. Be deathless. *Bande mataram!*"

. . . She saw him in jail-house in the garb of a convict, wielding his body's hunger like a sword, strong as ever, and true and deathless.

And she, *dadu's* grand-daughter? Hunger-trapped, she had sold herself. What if *dadu* knew?

What if *dadu* knew one day? This, the final gesture of her life, would hurt him more than all the oppressions he suffered in jail-house and all the pangs of his hunger battle——

And her heart was beating harder, harder, knocking against her ribs, so that she had to press her hands to her breast.

"Kajoli, you made your *pronam* to the flag, you are a fighter," so Father had said as the *Red Turbans* handcuffed him and took him away. And no one had cried—not she, not Mother, not Kanu, nor even Onu, all having made their *pronam* to the flag; fighters all.

As her numbed senses broke out of stupor, dead images lived again, the past that had lain quenched in ash-heap showed new sparks. Her father, her Kanu *bhai*; they had fought for the national movement. Her husband; he had fought for the workers. Undefeated, all. No jail-house could ever break their spirit. And she? Lost, utterly lost, selling all of herself.

What else could she do? Mother dying, needing succour, needing shelter. Mother could hold on no more. Onu, too. They would live at the price of her doom.

And the full meaning of her doom came upon her like a sudden blow that made her gasp for breath. Tears rushed to her eyes—it was ages since she had cried; tears flowed down her cheeks, and she wiped them off with her fingers and walked a pace ahead lest the betel-woman saw.

So she tramped the street, and the voice companioned her: "Kajoli, you are a fighter!" The voice grew. The voice beat in her blood-stream, rang in her ears.

A fighter? Had she not yielded to her fate without a struggle? Become one with the mass of mindless destitutes? Feeding at the free kitchen. Picking from muck-heaps. No grit. A mere beggar-woman. And soon to die—die a thousand deaths.

Dadu, uncrushed by the might of an Empire, would be broken by her at last.

Dadu, cast among destitutes, would have been strong and true.

And this horror, the betel-woman! Released from the

deadening shock that had snared her into easy surrender, sensitive and self-aware as of old, Kajoli felt a great tide of shame overwhelm her, so that her skin tingled and a hot sweat broke out on her palms. And the hundred words of the woman, as she recalled them, crawled upon her flesh like a hundred scorpions.

Escape, some way of escape—her chin jerked in decision. Her fists clenched and unclenched.

Then the vile betel-woman, who had done no good ever to anybody, did one good turn to her helpless prey. Unawares, she threw the girl an idea.

"Such hot news is god-sent bliss for the vendor folk—they get the best out of it. The papers sell like peanuts at a fair. If you sell twelve copies you get two *annas* as your commission."

"And many times twelve copies I could sell every day?" The girl spoke as though to herself, vaguely, and her lips parted wondering.

The betel-woman laughed, happy, with a big fee due to her because of Kajoli.

"Why, girl, gentle-folk would love to buy their paper from you, if you also gave them a pretty smile free!"

Kajoli fell silent. A line of thought struck her, and her face tensed. There was a gleam in her eyes.

"Not that way," said the betel-woman at a street crossing, ten minutes later. "We go straight on."

"This way," said Kajoli, and her feet hurried.

"Which way?" The woman scowled.

"*Hindusthan*," said the girl briefly.

The woman's face recaptured its grin. She knew the feeding centre run by the *Hindusthan*.

"Why, you will have one last look at the place that's fed you? What fancy! *Bhagwan!*" She shook her head at the strange ways these down-and-outs had. They were like animals. "Slow! slow!" she cried, out of breath, for the girl was trotting along like a mare. "There is no hurry."

But she walked faster, with new strength in her feet and power in her spirit. And she saw herself darting about at a street corner with a big pile of the *Hindusthan*, selling the paper like peanuts at a fair. And she heard the high tones of her voice: "*Great Congress leader starts hunger strike!*" And why, there was Onu *bhai*, and he, too, was rushing about, crying: "*Paper! Hindusthan!*"

She paused at the massive iron gates.

"You will have your money back, every *rupee*—though,

Bhagwan knows, woman, you don't deserve such mercy." And an afterthought : "Less a loan—deposit for the paper."

The betel-woman was speechless for a moment. Her eyes bulged. "What mad talk is this?" she cried hoarsely.

The girl looked at her. A sudden lovely smile gave the thin moulding of her face an exquisite grace.

"Look. Under my arm—the *Hindusthan*, three score copies. Can you see? '*Paper! Big news! Great Congress leader starts hunger battle!* That's the talk."

"Mad! mad!" The betel-woman's voice tore from her throat in a shout.

The girl as she stepped to the gateway turned round, the hundred dishonours of her battered life vivid in the rush of blood to her face.

"Jackal-woman!" she breathed with fierce contempt, and lifted her hand, and the plump cheek of the evil one resounded with a smack.

.   .   .   .   .

This is All-India Radio. Here is the news.

Samarendra hated the smooth voice as it trailed on, but he had no strength to move down from his bed and silence the machine. The servant had come as usual and turned it on for the morning news—Samarendra was a late riser, and he liked to hear the news in bed—and before he spoke a word the man was gone.

With a helpless sigh Samarendra bowed himself to the torment. He was on edge. The night had added years to his life. It had smashed him like a shell-burst.

Deep in the night the first blow had fallen. A telegram. Business telegrams came at all hours, and Samarendra had sleepily opened the yellow cover. Then he had gasped. His face was deathly pale.

A message from the Defence Department, intimating with regret that Captain Kunal Basu, Indian Artillery, had been listed as missing.

"What is it? What is it?" cried his wife, who had come rushing from her room. Her face was alarmed, her voice mournful.

He shook his head and cleared his throat. She must not know the truth. It would kill her. It was a boon that she could not read English.

"Nothing. Business matter."

"Then why do you make such a face?"

· "What face? No good news. Don't you see? A bad turn in business."

"Business?" She watched his face intently, eager to be re-assured. Let business be ruined. She had no need of riches. She had been content with the old simple way of life. Only—she touched her forehead with folded palms—"Keep my sons from harm's way, oh Mother."

When she was gone he slipped into bed, and in a moment the blankets over him heaved. He was sobbing violently, like a child, but in a smothered way, in utter silence.

All night he lay wide awake with memories of his son. He saw him grow up from childhood, go to school, win prizes. Then college and the silver cups won in tournaments—Mother kept them arranged on a glass shelf. A soldier at last. What a figure in his smart uniform! The sad day when he came home on leave to say he had been ordered overseas. The woeful hour of parting. The mother broken-hearted. Two years went by. . . . Missing. Missing.

Missing. What did it mean? In enemy hands? Then he would be in discomfort, but out of danger anyhow. He would no longer have to face gunfire. Samarendra, an optimist ever, clung to this desperate hope. Dread shadows lurked behind the hope, but he would not look at them, he would keep his mind averted. He longed to speak to Rahoul for reassurance, strength. Rahoul was not in the house; sleeping, perhaps, in his office at the relief centre; sometimes, when work delayed him and he missed the last bus and tram to Lakeside, he slept in a camp cot at his office in mid-town.

Missing . . . missing. . . . He saw the Captain of Artillery hurl shell after shell into an enemy position. The enemy answered with heavy fire. The Captain fought on till the last shell was spent. Cut off from his line, he had no way to fall back and escape. Calm, collected, he waited for the enemy as though he were on a playing-field. He put up his hands at last and spoke the Italian word for surrender.

Even in the depth of his woe the father's heart knew a throb of pride for his heroic son.

The historic break-through at El Alamein. The thousand-mile dash to Tripoli. Onward with the Eighth Army into the hills of Tunisia. Kunal always in the thick of battle. Twice had he acted as Company Commander. . . . Sicily. . . . The landing at Salerno. The last letter Kunal had written was from Naples. Samarendra had a sudden longing for that

176

letter, a hunger for its words, but Mother had kept the precious letter locked up in her jewellery box——

The dread shadow pushing forward, grimacing ghost faces——

A second blow had come three hours after. As the phone on a bedside table started ringing his heart seemed to stand still with intense expectation. Another message, again from New Delhi; Captain Kunal Basu, Indian Artillery, previously reported missing, had returned safely to his line. The hand that picked up the phone trembled.

Rahoul speaking from the other end.

"Father, this is to say good-bye. I am under arrest."

Once more, when the receiver was back in its place, Samarendra began to sob like a child.

He had achieved astounding success in business. He had made a fortune. It was all for his two sons. In his younger days, he recalled, he had known want and felt humbled and shamed, as though he were part of an inferior threadbare pattern of life, a denizen of some drab, stricken world. How he had hated this poverty! Then the dream had grown in him that his sons would have to endure no such misery. They would have the best things of life. They would have the dignity, the superior air, that wealth gave. But they for whom he had planned and toiled so hard never understood his sentiments. And he never understood theirs. It was as though they were aliens speaking a language that he did not know. What need had Kunal to join the Army? And Rahoul—could he not serve his country best as a scientist, when he seemed already on the brink of great things? Those questions were big in his heart. His old father had, strangely, understood the grandsons, while he himself had failed—utterly. Those three, each so different, had yet belonged somehow to one world. It was as though the old father could see his spirit reproduce itself in his grandsons. Those two had given him happiness in his old age in the tribulation of prison (and now the self-imposed suffering of a hunger strike for the rights of political prisoners) —Samarendra had read the prisoner's heart, gazing at him through the iron bars for a brief hour at Dehra Dun.

The smooth voice of All-India Radio trailing on, jarring on his nerves. . . .

The first day of the new year had dawned. What a new year for him! His Majesty had conferred the season's Honours as usual, and All India Radio was naming the recipients.

K.C.I.E.; . . . C.S.I. Familiar names rushed on. Another big plum for Sir Abalabandhu, as though he had not had enough. Knights. C.I.E. Samarendra gave a start. His name! He had been awarded a C.I.E.!

Companion of the Indian Empire. The Empire that had claimed both his sons. Samarenda rose, staggered out of bed and silenced the radio with a snap. *"Hai hai hai!"* A sobbing breath tore out of his throat. *"Hai hai hai!"*

When the bliss for which he had hungered for years came to him at last, it hit him like a curse, an evil thing!

The telephone rang again, chill, piercing. It rang unattended for half a minute, then Samarendra touched it with a lifeless hand. What more blows were to come?

It was the manager of *Cheap Rice, Ltd.* The big, eagerly-expected deal was about to come off, and he wanted immediate advice. Sir Abalabandhu was not in town——

Life surged back to the hand that held the receiver. Life drew a gleam from the eyes dulled by too many tears. It looked as though Samarendra would slip back from his tormented individual self and become once more a submerged will, a tiny piston-ring of the massive social engine of his class.

But it was a momentary spark. The weary eyes closed. The receiver dropped from a limp hand. It lay over the bed while the metallic voice came rapid and anxious: "Hello! Are you there? Hello! Hello!"

.   .   .   .   .

The black police van drew up at the relief centre and claimed its Secretary in the grey hour of dawn.

He was far from surprised. Long had he been protected by his scientific research, but he had now broken his own shield. Heedless, the last two months he had done no work in the laboratory, no pretence of work. And with bitter smouldering rage he had been speaking to the students, a widening circle. He had addressed them the day before. This War, he had said, was a repetition of other wars in history. The high-sounding slogans of die-hard politicians seemed as empty as the slogans of fascist make. The Four Freedoms did not include the freedom to be free—not, anyhow, for Asiatics. Bengal was in the grip of a vast terror surpassing all horrors of the past. This famine, this brutal doom, was the fulfilment of alien rule. The final commentary. The Excellencies and puppet Honourables had first denied there was a famine. They had blacked out the
178

famine. When at last the news broke through into the world, they issued false statements. . . . Imagine two million Englishmen dying of hunger that was preventable, and the Government unaffected, uncensored, unrepentant, smug as ever. Imagine women committing suicide because of their shame of nakedness—Indian mill cloth was denied to the people that the Army could be provided. In this grave hour the patriots, the people's trusted leaders, who felt deeply for them and would have moved the heavens to avert the doom, were held rotting behind bars. "Quit India!" so cried the two million dead of Bengal, smugly and non-violently murdered by the Excellencies and Honourables. The anger was warm in his voice, and he had paused till his speech was cool again. "Quit!" cried all India. "We shall not argue with you any more," said India. "You have done us some good along with much evil. For the good you've done you have been paid in full. The accounts have been settled. Now, for God's sake, quit!"

Freedom from subjection was not an end in itself, he had continued. It was the instrument of a new struggle and of a new life—the struggle to avert the post-famine doom that would linger for decades in the backwash of devastation. And the new life, free from hunger and fear and exploitation. Release from the crushing weight of the colossus would be the starting-point for a vast striving to make a saner order of life for all the people, to secure for one-fifth of humanity a human destiny.

That was the way he had spoken to the students for an hour. It was natural enough that India had to be defended against him.

They allowed him a few minutes to speak to his people on the phone. He hated to waken them. Monju would be sleeping soundly, with little Khuku pressed against her, and she would have to be awakened. How could he leave without listening once more to her voice—the voice that would be denied him long? First he would speak to Father. There was a separate line to his room.

Father had been awake, it seemed, for he answered as soon as the bell rang.

"Father, this is just to say good-bye. I am under arrest."

Father spoke as though his throat was clogged.

"You, too, Rahoul?" Some moments' pause. "Rahoul, I must speak in English, lest Mother overhear from her room. There's bad news. Kunal has been listed missing. I have re-

ceived a telegram from New Delhi." Then, as though praying:
"Rahoul, you do not think Kunal——" The voice halted,
choking.

Rahoul stiffened at the telephone. But he spoke in a calm
voice. "Father, so many officers and men are listed missing,
then they turn up. Don't worry. Kunal has been taken
prisoner—at the worst."

"Is there no chance that he may turn up in his line——"

"Of course. It happens often. Father, I have not much
time. If you will ask Monju to the phone——"

And the voice from the clogged throat, brokenly: "God will
protect you, my son."

Monju spoke with knowledge of his arrest—Father had told
her in advance, to avert shock. She was calm, strong with some
hidden strength.

"So you begin your new journey?"

"Monju," he called, "you knew it was only a question of
time? Not that I wanted this to happen; but, then, Monju,
I had to be true to myself."

"Darling"—the softness of her voice caressed him—"I, too,
shall go your way soon——"

"You, Monju?" The voice ached.

A pause, and then: "I am not the silly thing I used to be,
you know that."

Yes, he knew. She had grown fast. Once the process
started, women grew faster than men. Renewed in spirit,
Monju was free from misgivings, completely fearless. Rahoul
was proud of her.

"Khuku will miss you so—she'll cry her heart out for
Father——"

The police officer spoke a word, and Rahoul tore himself
from the receiver, and he heard Khuku sob and saw her face
tear-sick, and his arms yearned.

The black wagon sped away in the gloaming of dawn. It
carried ten other passengers. In anger and challenge the
prisoners flung the battle-cry of the subject people: *Bande
mataram!* And men who heard it on the street echoed the challenge as the wagon rushed by: *Bande mataram!*

He, Rahoul, was completely self-possessed. Somewhere on
the long, winding path of the years he had shed his fear of
suffering and loneliness. What happened to him as an individual did not matter. It only mattered what happened to his
people. He was indifferent, too, towards his captors, and his
180

mind was without hate, without anger, in a *nirvane* of passion-lessness.

As the wagon went over the Ganges Bridge he turned and pressed his forehead to the grille for a glimpse of the river.

He gave a violent start. He saw, caught in the car-light, a woman struggling to climb the rail. "Stop! look!" he shouted to the guards, and saw metallic faces and empty, metallic eyes. Helpless, he turned back to the river, and in that instant the ten voices boomed : "*Bande mataram!*"

He saw her pause, flop to her feet. He saw her hand lift to her face and her face turn about on the stem of her neck as though seekingly. Pulled from her frenzied desperation? Saved? His anxious eyes clung to the figure till the lorry swung out off the bridge.

Another prisoner trying to escape from hungerland, he brooded with a deep sigh, not knowing that it was the mother for whom his eyes had been ever awake—the peasant mother.

He laughed in his tight-lipped way as he recalled the third freedom. There it was, the freedom from want, even if the four of them, the charter of rights of a hunger-tossed century, did not include the freedom to be free.

The bitter mockery left him, and sadness dimmed his eyes, haunted by the endless vision of misery. The millions who had died gasping for food. The millions who had yet to die of disease. The uprooted millions who would live on without a living, broken in body and spirit, shreds of humanity. The prisons packed with men and women who had dared claim a larger life for all. No enemy occupation could have effected a fiercer devastation.

The prison walls loomed ahead.

Another black wagon had drawn up at the gates. Out of that hearse a song came. It was the prisoners who sang as they waited for the gates to swallow them. There was no defeat in the voices, but a secret, excited triumph.

"The more their eyes redden with rage,
   the more our eyes open;
   the more they tighten the chains,
   the more the chains loosen!"

The familiar words of Tagore, who had known the pulse of the people. Listening, Rahoul began to lose his sadness, for in that instant he saw past the clouds of pain—he saw the horizon of the east illumined by a new dawn. Freedom could not drop from the skies, nor be asked from lands beyond the seas; but there, in the vast swamp of suffering and struggle, would it break into bloom, growing out of the seeds of the spirit. It was the four-petalled lotus of the people.

He was alone and in enemy hands. Yet he was far from alone. He was a ripple in the risen tide of millions for whom prisons enough could never be devised, nor shackles forged. And strong exultation burned in his eyes and a strange intense look of conquest kindled in his face as he gave his voice to the united voices:

> "The more they tighten the chains,
> the more the chains loosen!"